"You had me investigated?" she demanded furiously

"You've got a lot of nerve, prying into my personal life.... Was it interesting?"

"Jo," Mike said. He looked into her eyes, nearly drowning in the hurt he saw there. "I had to do it. There were some things I needed to find out."

She drew a deep breath and looked down at the floor. "So you've heard the rumors...." Turning to him, she shrugged. "Well, there's not much I can do about them. They're not true."

"Aren't you forgetting something?" he teased.

She frowned, puzzled. "No...what?"

His voice was low. "There's a very strong possibility the rumors may be true now."

She reached for his hand and smiled. "Maybe so," she said. "In that case, let them talk all they want."

ABOUT THE AUTHOR

Beth Stanley has set her first Superromance novel in her home state of Illinois. Raised in Baltimore, Maryland, and Washington, D.C., Beth now lives in Lansing with her husband, two cats, a parrot and a large assortment of stuffed animals and porcelain dolls. She frequently lectures on writing at Chicago area libraries and colleges. *Count on Me* is her third published novel.

Count on Me

BETH STANLEY

Harlequin Books

TORONTO • NEW YORK • LONDON
AMSTERDAM • PARIS • SYDNEY • HAMBURG
STOCKHOLM • ATHENS • TOKYO • MILAN
MADRID • WARSAW • BUDAPEST • AUCKLAND

Published February 1992

ISBN 0-373-70486-0

COUNT ON ME

To my mother,
Dolores B. Velde,
who, by her example, taught me so much
about compassion, integrity
and independence

CHAPTER ONE

FIVE O'CLOCK—quitting time.

Joellyn Keene watched the rapid exodus, amazed at how little time it took for two hundred people to get through one exit. And the door on the other side of the plant would be even more congested, she knew. There were three hundred people going out of that one, while a hundred and fifty more were coming in for the second shift. Without looking, she was sure the ones going out were moving faster than the ones coming in.

She decided that for once she would just put on her coat and leave on time, too. She was exhausted. Being accounting manager hadn't turned out to be the plum position she'd expected when they first offered it to her. The long hours, which had even included Saturdays for the past few weeks, were taking their toll. She hadn't been able to keep her standing appointment at her hairdresser's for three weeks now. It probably wasn't standing anymore, but things had been going that way lately. One frustration after another.

She ran her fingers over the bottom edge of her blunt-cut blond hair, wincing when she found quite a few straggly ends, and lifted the phone to dial her hairdresser. She'd better keep this appointment, if she could even get one. Philippe was a busy man.

She loved going to the hairdresser. It was the one place nobody could get at her, the one place she could relax. Philippe's expert fingers would snip and arrange and soothe her cares away while he told her how wonderful she was and how beautiful she looked, never expecting anything more complicated from her than an occasional yes or no.

She hung up a couple of minutes later, vastly relieved that Philippe had assured her she was *still* his favorite customer and, of course, of *course,* she could come in this evening, right away, in fact, and why hadn't she been in for weeks, she must look a *mess!*

Yes, she looked a mess. But she couldn't begin to explain why to Philippe. After all, he'd never been up to his silver-tipped feather cut in a major corporate theft investigation. If it *was* really theft, and the jury was still out on that as far as she was concerned.

There was no way a million dollars' worth of tubing could have vanished into thin air. It was impossible. She didn't believe it. She didn't *want* to believe it, because if it was true…she shook her head, trying once again to force back the surge of panic that arose every time she thought about it. If it was true, then the red finger of suspicion was pointing straight at her Uncle John, and she loved him too much to believe he could be involved in a theft.

Not another one, after all this time…

This private agony was tearing her apart, and she felt totally alone. She *was* totally alone; none of her staff was aware of the true extent of the ongoing investigation, but they could all feel the pressure. It had filtered into the office atmosphere like a gas leak spreading over quiet countryside, unfamiliar and insidious, causing frayed nerves and a lot of major accounting mistakes. Mistakes she was spending far too many hours trying to unravel.

All that in addition to trying to track down a million dollars' worth of apparently missing aluminum tubing.

It was *too much*.

She closed her black notebook full of penciled sheets covered with numbers that all seemed to blur together. She couldn't sit here staring at the figures any longer; Philippe was waiting. Maybe she could look at them again tonight when she got home, maybe then something would jump up off the pages. But she had the sinking feeling that her effort would be for nothing. There was nothing to see. The answer simply wasn't there.

She was reaching for her coat when she heard a quiet cough behind her. She turned, and a surge of pleasure rushed through her when she saw her uncle leaning against the doorway, watching her.

"Uncle John!" She dropped the coat back onto its hanger and rushed over to give him a quick hug. "How wonderful to see you! How come you're still here? It's past quitting time."

She glanced at her watch. Five-fifteen. Her appointment was at six, but still... this was her family, the only family she had close by. She'd have to make time for him. It was bad enough she hadn't been to his house in months, but she'd been so busy...a few more minutes couldn't make that much difference. Philippe would understand.

She leaned against the edge of her desk, watching the way John's shoulders drooped as he settled down in her chair and gave her his familiar, lopsided smile.

But smile or not, John didn't look good. The past few months had taken their toll on him, too. His sparse light brown hair was showing unmistakable streaks of gray, much more so now than before. His skin was sallow and hung in folds under his neck, folds that had once seemed so endearing she used to tweak them and tease him about losing weight. But now he obviously *had* lost weight, and the folds weren't endearing at all—they only made him look ill. And the lines around his eyes weren't laugh lines anymore.

"Just dropped by, Jo, to see if you were still here." He smiled. "You usually are. You work too hard. But then I always told you that, didn't I? Even when you were a little kid."

She reached over and patted his hand. "Right on target as usual. We're all working too hard right now."

"Yeah. That's why I'm here. I wondered if you'd found anything yet."

She shook her head, dismayed by the look in his eyes. He looked almost...pleading. "Nothing, Uncle John. Nobody's found anything. It's almost as if that tubing just got up and walked out all by itself. *If* it's gone," she added.

"Oh, it's gone, all right, Jo. No use fooling ourselves about that. Question is, where?"

"The real question is, how?" Randy Wagner's voice preceded him as he strode toward Joellyn's office and appeared in the doorway. "John, I thought that was your voice. What brings you up here? Things too boring out on the shipping dock?"

John gave him a rueful smile. "I wish I could say they were. It's anything but boring out there even when things are quiet. Now it's just plain awful. I'll tell you, Randy, I'm so worried I can't see straight."

"We all are, John. We all are." Randy pulled his pipe out and proceeded to light it.

Joellyn watched with growing impatience. She was forever waiting while he tried to light the damn thing. Hadn't he ever heard of a pipe lighter? The one he used was for cigars—Lanagan used one just like it all the time. Come to think of it, it probably was Lanagan's. Randy was forever walking off with her pens; why not the controller's lighter?

She closed her eyes, silently counting. One . . . two . . . three . . .

She heard him take several short puffs and then exhale. She opened her eyes, relieved to see the pipe was finally lit.

John glanced at Joellyn, then back at her boss. "To tell you the truth, Randy, I came up here to see if you'd found anything yet. Jo tells me you haven't."

Randy puffed on his pipe and stared curiously at John. "She told you the truth. We haven't. Getting you down, huh?"

"Goes without saying," John admitted. "It'd get you down, too, if you were the shipping dock manager, wouldn't you say so?"

Randy nodded. "Yes. It's hard to say who's in the most hot water around here. Me, the assistant controller who's supposed to be keeping track of things, or Joellyn, who's supposed to see to it that I keep track of things, or you. But then they're looking at everyone right now."

John looked down at the floor and shook his head. "It isn't so hard to see who they're taking the closest look at. I know they suspect me."

"Uncle John!" Joellyn protested. "They don't. No one's said a word against you. Don't say that. Don't even think it!"

He snorted. "Honey, *you* might not think it, but it's a sure bet *they* do. After all, who's the most logical one?" He tapped his chest. "Me, that's who. They always go after the shipping manager when something like this happens. And don't think I don't know it. Those detectives have been bird-dogging me for weeks now. I can't hardly move without one of 'em breathing down my neck." He sighed. "Can't say as I blame 'em, but it sure makes it hard for a man to do his job."

"I can understand that," Randy murmured. "Look, I'm going out with a couple of the guys over to the Watering Hole. Either of you want to come along? It might do us all good." He glanced at Joellyn. "Unless you have a date or something?"

Joellyn gave Randy a deliberately mysterious smile, irritated by his constant curiosity concerning her love life. "As a matter of fact, Randy, I do have plans." She watched his searching expression but kept her eyes blank. She'd never admit her only plans were the hairdresser. She had no love life. She hadn't had a love life for so long that she'd almost forgotten what it was like. Suddenly eager to change the subject, she asked, "Where were you all afternoon? We were looking all over for you."

Randy's unruly brown eyebrows arched above his metal-rimmed glasses, giving his gray eyes an elfish look. "Upstairs in the Inner Sanctum," he said, giving John a conspiratorial wink. "Big meeting. Come on to the Hole with me. Tell you all about it then."

Joellyn shook her head. She'd been working with him for three years now. She knew him as well as anyone at United Tubing did, but she would never understand how he could drink martinis every night of his life and still show up for work the next morning. But that was his business. Besides, Randy was very good at his job. He was a real pro.

"Randy," she asked, "doesn't your wife get mad at you for stopping for drinks before you go home?"

He shrugged. "Why should she get mad? Most of the important business in this country is conducted over a couple of drinks."

"But is what you do at the Hole really 'important business'?" she asked. She riffled through a stack of papers on her desk, wishing he'd leave so she could.

"What could be more important than chewing the fat with your buddies after a hard day at good old United?" he protested. "Come on, Joellyn, unwind a little. Do you good. You, too, John," he added.

John pulled himself up out of the chair and gave Randy a tired smile. "No thanks, Randy. I got a lot of things to take care of tonight. Jo..." he turned to face her. "Before I go, how's your mom? Have you talked to her lately?"

"A couple of days ago," she said. "She's taking cha-cha lessons now. Can you believe it?"

He chuckled. "I can't believe she moved to Florida after all those years in the first place. But then after your dad died...well, I can understand wanting a change, I guess."

He stared down at the floor for a moment, bleak memories washing over him. He should understand it. He'd been a widower for five years now himself, and it wasn't getting any easier, even though people had told him it would. He still missed Joy every night and day of his life. His house, once so full of warmth, seemed like a cavern now, cold and dark and empty. But still he hung on. Maybe it was the job...although lately he'd found himself wishing he'd made a clean break like Joellyn's mother had. But then she always had been the smart one....

He leaned over and gave Joellyn a brief kiss on her cheek and murmured, "I'll talk to you later, hon." Then he gave Randy a short salute and left. Joellyn watched him with concern as he turned into the hall and disappeared from sight.

"Don't you want to know what went on upstairs?" Randy asked a moment later. "I think you should." His gray eyes danced. "Come on, Joellyn. Come with us."

She cringed inside. *Oh, sure. And have the women in the office convinced their gossip was true, after all? No way.* She remembered only too well the words she'd overheard the day she'd gotten her last promotion.

She'd walked into the ladies' room and stood in front of the mirror, checking her contact lenses.

"Did you see the notice on the bulletin board?" The voice floated over the top of one of the stalls.

"I sure did," a second voice answered. "Joellyn does it again."

"Yeah, but what does she do? She's the only one around here who ever gets promoted."

"Well, I only know what I heard."

"Yeah? What did you hear?"

"I heard she was sleeping with Barlowe in Corporate Finance—you know, the tall one with the blond hair."

"No kidding! Are you sure? He's married and has a couple of kids!"

"He said it himself at the office party. He was bragging all over the place. He swore up and down it was true. I heard him!"

"She must really be desperate," the first voice drawled. "Nobody needs to get ahead that way."

"Well, she's done pretty good so far, hasn't she? Don't worry about her. She'll just fling that gorgeous little size nine body of hers around and bat those ol' blue eyes. She'll get ahead, no problem."

Joellyn's first impulse was to slip out the door and pretend she'd never heard those words. She stared at her face in the mirror, shocked to see she'd lost all her color except for two bright pink spots on her cheeks.

The pulse at the base of her throat throbbed unevenly. She was furious, and determined to see who the voices belonged to. She stood at the door, blocking the way as Marilyn Norris, the billing supervisor, and Dianne Patrick, the controller's secretary, tried to walk past, avoiding her eyes.

"How *dare* you!" Joellyn said, so angry her voice quavered.

Dianne's eyes flashed. "How dare I what? Speak to your boyfriend. He's the one who said it!"

Joellyn stood her ground. "That's a lie. The whole thing is a lie. I'm sorry if you're unhappy about my promotion, but I got it because of my work, and that's the only reason! Do you have any idea how much overtime I've put in here—unpaid overtime, I might add?"

"If you were *working,*" Dianne asked, "why didn't you make them pay you?"

"Listen to me!" Joellyn insisted. "I never had anything to do with John Barlowe or anyone else here!"

"Sure, Joellyn," Dianne said. "Sure. Now would you mind letting us by, please? Some of us have to get back to our desks."

Joellyn had moved aside, tight-lipped, while Marilyn and Dianne had swept past her and out the door. Since that day she'd gone out of her way to avoid causing gossip, but more and more lately she'd been thinking about leaving United, maybe even the Chicago area.

In spite of her recent promotion her career was now at a total standstill. She could not, even in her wildest dreams, imagine ever being given the assistant controller's job, even if Randy left. She deserved it, but she knew how the company worked. If Randy left, management would bring in a man from the outside or the corporate office without giving her a second thought. The Neanderthals!

And there was no one keeping her here, either. She'd been on the verge of heading for Florida to be near her mother when the inventory started disappearing. And there was the gossip—it still persisted, and she knew it. She couldn't bring herself to walk away and leave them wondering. And then there was the fresh, crisp air after a snowfall, and kids painting winter scenes on the store windows, and in early spring the smell of the first lilacs . . .

She pulled herself back to the present and reached for her coat. "Randy," she said firmly, "either tell me what the meeting was about or don't, but either way, I have to leave. I'm late!"

"Now hold on a minute," he said, frowning. "Good Lord, Joellyn! I've never seen you so irritable."

"You've never seen me working ten hours a day six days a week," she retorted. "I'm tired, and worried."

"I guess you are at that," he agreed. He peered closely at her eyes. "Awfully dark shadows you've got there, lady. You'd better lighten up a bit and stop working so hard."

Stop working so hard? Who was he kidding? She felt the quick adrenaline rush she always got whenever he annoyed her. It had been happening a lot lately; he was getting to her much faster than he used to. How could he be so blasé? Nothing seemed to bother him.

"Look," she snapped, "you're the assistant controller. I'm surprised *your* eyes don't have dark shadows under them. Doesn't it bother you when the auditors snoop around asking questions? They're driving me *crazy!*"

"Hold on—wait a minute." He touched her arm. "Yes, of course I'm bothered. After all, everyone in the place is under suspicion. But there's no point getting into a sweat over it. *We* didn't do anything wrong."

He smiled. "At the very least, Joellyn, you and I should be on the same side. I want to know what happened to the tubing and I'm sure you do, too. Let's not fight between ourselves, okay?"

She buttoned her coat. He was right. They had to maintain a united front. "Okay," she agreed. "We won't fight." She picked up her purse and headed for the door.

"Hey!" Randy protested. "Don't you want to hear what I found out upstairs today?"

She stopped and glanced pointedly at her watch. Five forty-five. Philippe would be upset if she was much later, and it would take her at least twenty-five minutes to get there. "All right," she said wearily. "Tell me what you found out, but *please* make it fast."

"Oh," he said, "only that we're getting a new vice president tomorrow."

Her mouth opened in astonishment. "Vice president of what? We already have six. How many VPs do we need around here?"

"Don't ask me, but now we have seven. This one's vice president of manufacturing."

She raised her eyebrows. "Are you kidding?"

He lifted both hands toward the ceiling. "That's what they tell me." He laughed. "And, hey, you should have seen Lanagan's face. He didn't even know about it until today."

"They didn't tell *Lanagan?*" She was incredulous. "How can they hire a vice president and not tell the controller?"

"I don't know, but they did. Just goes to show you they can make major decisions without consulting him. He's really ticked off, too."

Joellyn was struck with a sudden thought. "You know, I wonder—" She stopped in midsentence.

"Wonder what?"

"Do you suppose..." She shrugged. "Never mind. It's a silly thought."

"What's a silly thought?" He drew slowly on his pipe, emitting small puffs of blue-white smoke out of the side of his mouth.

"Well, I was just wondering ... you know, we had talked about bringing the FBI in. I wonder if he's really a VP. Maybe he's an undercover man."

Randy hooted. "Oh, boy! Your imagination really *is* working overtime." He laughed again. "Are you sure you don't want that drink?"

Joellyn flushed with embarrassment. How could he be so sure of himself? Did he know more than he was telling her? He probably did—after all, she was only middle management. Upper management never told their middle managers everything. They had to keep some things to themselves. Otherwise, what was the point of being upper management?

"Randy," she said, "it's been a long day, and I'm very late. See you tomorrow." She headed for the door and walked into the icy March twilight, breathing deeply. Ah, yes. It was great to be outside and away from the stifling office atmosphere, even if it was beginning to mist up outside.

She reached her car and slid in, trying to ignore hands on her dashboard clock that every day lately seemed to be moving faster and faster. She gunned the engine and swung out of the parking lot, watching the clock out of the corner of her eyes.

A new VP. That was a surprise. Well, at least when she met him her hair would look decent for the first time in weeks.

If Philippe didn't give up and go home ...

JOELLYN WAS WORKING at her desk the next morning when she spotted Randy and another man she'd never seen before heading her way.

He wasn't bad-looking. In fact, he was downright good-looking in a craggy sort of way. But that was okay. She supposed manufacturing vice presidents should look craggy. The people in the plant wouldn't pay attention to him if he was too smooth.

She held up a paper, pretending to read but actually sneaking quick looks while he made polite conversation with one of the supervisors. It wouldn't do to seem too interested. She'd just sit here and wait. They'd get to her eventually.

Curious, she took another peek. Smooth, this man was not. His sandy red curls had successfully resisted his barber's attempts to contain them. Strong jawline . . . a little too strong, actually; it jutted forward, defying anyone to argue with him. But that was okay, too. He had a tough job on his hands, *if* he was what they said he was.

He appeared, from this distance, to have a crescent-shaped scar just to the left of his mouth. His thick red-blond eyebrows jumped when he laughed, a deep, full-throated rumble that reached all the way to her desk.

Score ten points for him. At least he laughed.

Long, athletic legs with well-fitted dark blue slacks, legs that seemed to ripple with movement, ready to spring any second even though he was standing still— not too surprising, considering what was going on in the plant. He had to be tense if he had any idea what he was getting into.

She ducked her head to at least give the appearance of concentrating on the latest report compiled by her subordinates and made a quick red circle around a number she knew had to be wrong. Then two dark shadows fell across her desk.

"And this is our accounting manager, Joellyn Keene," Randy announced. "Joellyn, this is Mike Walker, the new vice president of manufacturing."

Randy smiled as Joellyn reached up to shake Mike's hand. "Joellyn heads up the whole department," he said. "Keeps it going for me. Does a very nice job of it, too. I never have to touch a thing. Joellyn does it all."

"Well, not quite all," she said, smiling. "Just most of it. I'm very glad to meet you, Mike."

Mike struggled to conceal the surprise he felt. She didn't look like any accounting manager he'd ever met before. Blond hair fell over her forehead, partially covering her face until she reached up and swept it back. Then he saw the green-flecked eyes, and the dark circles under them.

He could understand the dark circles, from what he'd been told in the preliminary briefing. He just hoped she didn't have anything to do with the missing inventory, or what seemed to be the missing inventory.

But unfortunately she might. That was one of the first things he was supposed to check out. Too bad— she was a terrific-looking woman. Small. Light blue business suit, obviously expensive ... He made a mental note to check that out. White high-necked silk blouse that draped across her throat. Barely any makeup at all—that was nice. Different. He remembered the hours his ex-wife had spent in front of the mirror.

Mike forced his eyes away. He wasn't interested in women, particularly this one. His divorce was still too fresh in his mind. A year hadn't been long enough. *Ten* years wouldn't be long enough.

"I guess you're one of the first people I'll have to talk to, Joellyn," he said. "From what I've been told, it appears we have a real problem here." He looked around, not sure how much he should be saying, but she had an enclosed office, and no one else was within hearing distance as long as he kept the conversation low.

"We certainly have," Randy said. "I've been assistant controller here for close to three years, and as far as I know, this is the first time anything like this has ever happened. Right, Joellyn?"

"That's right," she agreed. "Nobody can figure it out. I don't know how much you've been told..." She looked questioningly at Mike.

"I think I probably have the full scoop. Or at least as much as anyone else knows," he said. "But why don't you run through it again for me? I'd like to hear it from your viewpoint."

It was a little hard to keep his mind on the business at hand. He was still astonished to find a manager with eyes and hair like hers. He'd never seen hair quite that color before. Perfectly styled, it looked like melted sunshine. Stunning... absolutely stunning.

"I'm not sure how much I can add," Joellyn said. "What it boils down to is that over the past four months a million dollars' worth of aluminum tubing seems to have disappeared. Nobody has any idea how it could have happened."

"We've gone over everything time and time again," Randy said. "I've double-checked the work myself."

"He's right." Joellyn looked at Mike. "We've gone through all the records. All we know is that it looks like it's gone, and nobody knows where."

"I'm sure there's a reasonable explanation," Mike said.

"I'd like to hear it," Joellyn said, eyeing him.

Mike cleared his throat. "I'll come back a little later and go through your books with you. From what I've seen out there—" he indicated the factory "—and been told, it sounds to me like they need a thorough going-over."

Joellyn's eyebrows shot up at this unexpected remark. Her cheeks flushed an angry pink. "Are you seriously saying you think a simple error on my books could have caused all this?" she demanded. "Didn't they tell you they've been gone over several times?"

"Well, it's probably not a simple error," Mike answered, painfully aware that his bluntness had done it again. "What I meant was, maybe someone new could spot something not quite right, something that's compounded itself over the past few months. Something you might miss because you're too close to it."

"Oh, I know what you meant, all right," she said. "And you're welcome to come back anytime you want and go through my books. Nice meeting you." She dismissed him with a curt nod and turned back to her computer run.

"Nice meeting *you*, Joellyn," he said to the top of her head. "I'll be back." He followed Randy out of the office.

MIKE FELT right at home in the factory, his ears finely tuned to the shrill whistling and clanging of the production lines. He winced and dodged, frowning as a towmotor driver careened around a corner, defying the federal safety codes. It looked as if control in the plant was pretty loose—something else to check into.

He thought back over the quick exchange in Joellyn's office. "What's she like?" he asked Randy after a minute.

"Joellyn?" Randy scratched his head, his brow furrowed in deep concentration. "Oh," he answered, "Joellyn's all right. She's been here a long time. Matter of fact, she came here as a junior accountant right out of college. She's pretty sharp—at least there've been no problems as far as her work goes."

"Oh?" Mike glanced at him curiously. "What kind of problems *have* there been?"

"Oh, none, really, except—well, she doesn't have many friends here." He laughed uneasily. "She works all the time—all business, know what I mean? Kind of keeps to herself. Then a while back I heard a nasty rumor about her from one of the women. I don't think it's true, though."

"What rumor?" Mike persisted.

"Oh, I probably shouldn't have mentioned it. Just some stuff about—well, she started out here as a junior accountant. Then she got promoted to staff accountant, then supervisor, all before I came on the scene. I was around when she was promoted to accounting manager. As a matter of fact, I recommended it. But the women in the office think..."

"The women in the office think what?" Mike pressed.

Randy glanced around uncomfortably. "Oh, evidently one of the men at the corporate office got a little drunk at the company office party and did some bragging about her." He colored. "You know the kind of stuff I'm talking about."

Mike nodded, his face impassive.

"I don't believe it," Randy said. "Never did, but the women were jealous of her promotion and they turned on her. It's a shame, though. Joellyn's a nice person." He looked as though he wanted to end the whole conversation.

For crying out loud! Mike glanced over at Randy. Disappearing inventory and a gorgeous accounting manager who was rumored to be sleeping with someone at the top? He didn't believe it. He didn't *want* to believe it. But it wasn't impossible. He'd seen it happen before.

"Well, never mind all that," he said shortly. "Let's get this grand tour over with. We have a lot of work to do."

He'd left Philadelphia for this? He snorted with disgust. At least Philadelphia had the Liberty Bell and the Phillies.

And his son.

JOELLYN SLIPPED her key into her apartment door lock at ten-thirty that night and flicked on the light in her entranceway, still seething, even though her Wednesday evenings with the special kids at the home usually had a cleansing effect. They were so dependent and loving and needing that whenever she was with them, reading to them, talking, or sometimes just holding their hands, trying to understand whatever they were trying to communicate, they almost always made her forget her own problems.

But not tonight. She was still simmering. He had his nerve! Another one, thinking he could blast in and save the company from whatever this poor, hapless woman had done to foul up the works.

She'd been through it already with the auditors, and then the detectives, and she was thoroughly sick of it. The questioning looks, the insinuations, the immediate assumption that she had done something wrong for no reason other than that she was a woman.

ERA or not, it looked as though it was going to take another century before men changed their way of thinking. At least at United. She shook her head, disgusted. They were hopeless there.

She kicked off her shoes, glad to be home and inside, out of the raw dampness that pervaded the Illinois air. Her apartment, always warm and cozy, looked especially inviting tonight.

Loosely woven lined bouclé drapes were pulled tightly against the blasting Midwestern wind. She was dying to open them so that during the day the sun could filter through the peach sheers underneath, if only the sun would come out again. *Damn* springtime in Chicago, anyhow! The rain never seemed to stop.

She sank down wearily onto her Japanese silk sofa and closed her eyes, but only for an instant; her sheepdog lumbered sleepily out of the bedroom, spotted Joellyn, reared back and projected herself through the air like an MX missile headed for an enemy target and landed with dead-on accuracy in Joellyn's lap.

Joellyn laughed and extricated herself from the sheepdog's clutches, dodging wet kisses while she slid the patio door open and hooked Penny's collar to a line running the length of the apartment.

She slid the door shut against the wind and hummed contentedly to herself on her way to the kitchen. A cup of tea was just what she needed. As usual, in her rush to get home, feed Penny, then rush to the kids' home, she'd skipped dinner again. And at lunchtime she'd been too angry to eat.

She passed one of her plants and idly dipped her finger into the terra-cotta pot, testing the soil. It was completely dry. She thought back, mentally ticking the days off on her calendar and winced when she realized she'd been so preoccupied she'd forgotten to water her plants for over two weeks now.

But who had time even to think of it? She'd been running here and there, working late; even a simple thing like finding the time to pick up her cleaning was a major project these days.

She headed for the kitchen sink and her watering can, grumbling to herself.

Lucky plants.

All *they* needed was a little water.

CHAPTER TWO

MIKE MUNCHED on an Italian beef sandwich he'd picked up on his way to his apartment. He winced at the lukewarm cardboard taste, missing the Wednesday night spaghetti dinners he'd always had in Philadelphia. Everybody there knew Wednesday was spaghetti night; why the heck didn't they know it in Chicago?

Annoyed at the sandwich, himself and the world in general, he lifted the phone and dialed his old number in Philadelphia. He'd never been good at remembering phone numbers, but this one was embedded deep inside. Engraved in his soul. This was the number he'd shared with Dani, and then David, before things had gotten out of hand. Now the only reason he had to call at all was to talk to his son.

He'd phoned David the day he'd moved into this apartment, and he still flinched whenever he thought about that conversation.

"Daddy!" David's excited voice shot over the wires and straight into Mike's heart. "When are you coming to see me?"

"Soon, David, soon. I'm in Chicago now. Remember, I showed you on the map? It's not far. You can come visit me soon."

David had hesitated, his voice growing small. "I'll have to ask Mama and my new...my—" He stopped, and Mike's stomach lurched.

"That's okay, David. Of course you'll have to ask your mama and your new . . . her—" He stopped, too. How could he expect a six-year-old to know how to handle this situation when he, himself didn't know?

"Well, what do you call him, David?" he asked gently. "It's okay. You can say it." He was praying inside, *Don't let it be Daddy. Please, God, don't let him call another man Daddy....* "You should call him whatever your mama says, son."

David's voice had sounded very small over the phone. "He's real nice to me, Daddy. Sometimes I call him Daddy Joe."

It had been a year since he'd moved out at his wife's request. A year in which he'd laboriously found and furnished a two-bedroom apartment in Philadelphia, which he'd subleased to a honeymooning couple right before he'd left for Chicago.

He probably wouldn't be going back. He wasn't planning on it, anyhow. What was the point? He'd see David as much now as he had living there. Dani had seen to that.

Oh, he could have stayed in Philadelphia. And he could have insisted upon keeping the house after the divorce. It had been *his* family's house. But then his wife—he corrected himself, ex-wife—would have moved David out of the only home he'd ever known, and he couldn't bear to do that to his son. Six years old was too young to be uprooted unless it was absolutely necessary. And it wasn't really necessary. He put his sandwich down, half-eaten. Suddenly he wasn't hungry anymore.

No, it wasn't really necessary to move David out of his home. They'd only gotten a divorce.

He stared at his hands, appalled at the empty feeling that coursed through him, refusing to subside even now, a year later.

Only a divorce?

The end of his world was more like it.

Hurt? It had hurt plenty. Anyone who thought men weren't hurt by divorce was crazy. The feelings of defeat and insecurity and inadequacy when a marriage ended were exactly the same, man or woman. Gender had nothing to do with it.

It had been his own fault. All of it. He was the one who had spent too many nights and weekends away from home, building a minor empire that was destined to fall apart for lack of the most necessary ingredient.

Love.

Where had it gone, that blistering, scorching passion he'd once felt for Dani when they were both twenty-four? Had marriage and a child changed it all that much? He didn't think so. It wasn't the marriage. And it certainly wasn't David. It was his own ambition.

Amazing, what a degree from the Harvard School of Business could do for you. He had business contacts all over the world. It had been one of them who had lead him here to a cramped efficiency apartment just south of Chicago and to a position that both intrigued and worried him.

Maybe this time he'd made a major career mistake. Maybe he should have taken a regular nine-to-five job. He didn't really have to do this.

He listened to the phone ring in Philadelphia. What a lonely sound it made when nobody answered. He checked his watch—where were they now? Eight o'clock...nine in Philadelphia...past David's bedtime, unless it was a special occasion. Then he remembered what the special occasion was.

It was David's stepfather's birthday. Daddy Joe's birthday. He and Dani had taken David to Disney World to celebrate.

Disney World. He'd always intended to take David to Disney World, but he'd never had the time...and now someone else had taken the time and done it. Daddy Joe. Daddy Joe was real good to him. Daddy Joe took him to Disney World, no problem.

He missed his son. God, how he missed his son.

He flipped on the television, running the events of the day through his mind while a prime-time movie flashed onto the screen. Damn! He'd already seen it. Wasn't that just his luck—new town, no friends yet, lousy weather, and the summer reruns were beginning in March.

But he had a brand-new job. A new start. Certainly the best job he'd ever had as far as money and position went. And it *was* interesting, no doubt about it. The board of directors at United expected him to figure out what auditors and private detectives hadn't been able to. He was the last resort before they called in the FBI. But he could do it. They knew he could do it.

That was the reason for the large salary and bonus they'd promised him. During the past few years, he'd established a reputation for himself as the best manufacturing troubleshooter in the business.

Vice president was only a title.

Oh, he was qualified for the title, no problem there. He knew all about factories and production from the inside out, but his specialty was corporate crime.

Don't worry about production, they'd told him. The plant manager will take care of that for now. Just find the missing tubing.

All one million dollars' worth of it.

IT HAD BEEN a terrible morning. Everything that could go wrong had gone wrong. The internal auditors were back again, setting up shop in an empty cubicle outside Joellyn's office, digging into everything they could think of.

No one could find the computer runs they'd requested. The auditors seemed possessed with some sort of eerie sixth sense that unerringly caused them to ask for files and records that had been buried in the upstairs storage room. And everyone knew what it was like up there. It was dusty, creepy, and it took forever to find anything stored there.

Joellyn had her good heels on, and the floorboards were split. She did *not* want to go up there, but it looked as though she would have to. Randy was off somewhere, probably in the coffee shop. But he was here; you had to give him that.

It was more than she could say for the rest of the accounting staff. Two of them had called in sick this morning and the third was making definite flu noises.

Joellyn slammed the computerized general ledger shut and leaned back, sighing with resignation. She needed another couple of minutes before she could make herself go upstairs.

They'd never told her about attic archives in college. If they had, she might have changed her major.

She'd been thinking about a nursing career, anyhow, right up to the last minute when she made the decision to go into accounting. And once she made a decision, she rarely changed her mind. So accounting it was, and now she was reaping the benefits of it—a trip to the attic.

She was standing, preparing to leave, when she saw Mike Walker striding toward her office.

"Hi!" he said, smiling warmly. "Going somewhere? I was going to sit and chat with you for a few minutes."

"Well, how nice," she said, not feeling it was nice at all. "You got here just in time. I was on my way upstairs to the storage room. I bet they didn't show you that on your little walk yesterday."

He looked startled. "I was upstairs yesterday—in the president's office."

She grinned briefly. "Not *this* upstairs you weren't. Not too many people have been up there. Want to come along? It might be interesting." It wouldn't be interesting, but she didn't have to tell him that. "Besides, I hate to eat dust alone."

"And I was going to buy you a cup of coffee and a doughnut," he said. "Well, dust it is, I guess."

Joellyn led the way. "Follow me." She motioned toward the stairs. "This is one United experience you'll never forget."

"I have a feeling that's going to be true of most of my United experiences," he retorted, climbing the stairs two at a time. He got to the top before she did and reached back to help her maneuver the last step, which curved toward the door.

She was out of breath, but he didn't seem fazed at all by the long climb. "You're in pretty good condition," she remarked. "Where did you come from, Colorado?"

He laughed, the same easy, deep laugh she'd heard yesterday. "Philadelphia." He smiled at her curious look.

She opened the storage room with her key. "Well, that lets the air out of my theory. I could have sworn you trained with the mountain goats the way you took those stairs."

She stepped carefully over the third floorboard, the one with a creak that always reminded her of the shrieking noise in *Psycho*. She didn't need to hear that today. Her nerves were already shot.

"No mountain goats. Just clean living," he teased, following her exact footsteps. He'd noticed how she'd avoided the one board—it was probably loose. She must have been up here quite a few times. Hiding things? Or removing them before anyone else could find them?

"And a membership in the best health club I could find," he added. "I need to find one around here pretty soon or my pecs'll be down around my ankles."

She was puzzled. "Pecs?"

"Pectorals. Muscles. You know, those things that bulge when Clark Kent rips off his shirt in the phone booth." He looked around. So...she had her own key to the storage room. He'd seen her take it out of her purse. Why didn't she keep it in her desk?

"Well!" He made a wry face. "This certainly is interesting. Boxes. And mustard-green filing cabinets. What *will* they think of next? What are you looking for? Can I help?"

"The auditors want all the subledgers pertaining to last year's inventory. They have to be in one of those boxes. Maintenance brought them up in January." Her eyes swept over the room. Dusty dark brown boxes were stacked waist-high in some places, chest-high in others. "I have no idea which stack they're in," she said. "Just start looking."

She searched around for a few minutes, pulling boxes open and peering inside. She knelt on the floor, trying to keep her nylons from getting torn on the rough wood, looking into boxes and watching Mike at the same time.

His pecs appeared to be in perfect working order. Yesterday she hadn't noticed, but he *did* have muscles. His jacket didn't hang that way because of shoulder pads. Those shoulders were real. But then an FBI man would be in good condition. She was sure of that, although the only FBI men she'd ever seen had been on TV. They probably hung out at health clubs, too...

Mike slid one of the heavier cabinets around and peered behind a stack of half-hidden boxes. Out of the corner of his eye he couldn't help noticing the precise way Joellyn knelt, with her ankles bent under her knees just so.

He was sure she was totally unaware of the effect the curve of her knee was having on him. Her skirt hiked up just a tiny bit, and she reached over and yanked at it without looking his way... Sure enough, she was ignoring him. Randy was right. She did keep to herself.

He sighed heavily. It was just as well. No point gumming up the works with a wild case of physical attraction. Not with this woman, anyway. He had too much on his mind to be getting involved. He took another quick look. Just the same, she sure did have nice knees. . . .

He reached for another box, opened it and his eyes lit up. "Ah, here they are, I think. Right where I thought they'd be. Under just about everything else in the room."

"Good thinking," she agreed, nodding. "You're going to fit right in here."

He pulled the computer runs out and helped her up. "Does this entitle me to coffee?" he asked hopefully.

She consulted her watch. "Maybe another time. I have to get these downstairs. Then I have a staff meeting."

"Lunch?" he asked.

"Can't," she said. "No time."

"You don't eat lunch?" he asked, surprised. He couldn't believe it. Nobody skipped lunch.

"Not lately," she answered. She locked the door behind them and headed down the stairs. Mike followed close behind her with the ledgers. "I'm too busy," she called back over her shoulder. "But thanks for finding the books for me."

He handed her the books and watched her disappear through the office door. She was going to be a hard one to pin down, he could see that. But he had to talk to her. And he couldn't waste a whole lot of time about it, either.

JOHN SAT HUNCHED over his desk, doodling on a shipping form, waiting for the next truck to arrive. The gooseneck lamp on his desk made a circle of blinding yellow on the scratched metal desktop, spotlighting the shaky circles and stick figures he was drawing.

It was impossible to concentrate. It had been that way for weeks, ever since the commotion had started here. Not his fault, none of it, but they all thought it was. The way they looked at him when they asked the same questions over and over and over—he knew that look. He'd seen it before.

He'd seen it the first time when he was in his early teens. Cars were a big-time thing for him, even back then. He knew every nut and bolt in every automobile made. If John Terrell couldn't fix it, it couldn't be fixed.

But somewhere along the line he'd lost his direction. He'd started listening more to his friends and less to his parents. Then one night his friends convinced him to help them steal radios out of parked automobiles, just for the hell of it, just to see if they could get away with it.

They didn't get away with it. It had taken the police in their tiny town exactly three hours to figure out who was responsible, and his reputation was gone from that day on.

Funny, he'd always wondered what would have happened if they had prosecuted him right there. But they all said no, that he was just a kid. They didn't want to do that to him. But just the same, they all had that look.

That look bothered him. It didn't do any good to try to get away from it—it was always there. No matter where he was or what he was doing, it was always there. He'd committed a theft once, the look said. They expected he'd do it again.

So he did, and he got pretty good at it, too. No use laughing about it now, passing it off as a young boy's prank. He hadn't been *that* young. He'd known what he was doing. But the thrill of it was what got him. Just like the thrill of gambling and winning, of driving in a stock car race and winning—why lie about it? He'd been looking for excitement and he'd gotten it.

But thinking back on it now, he wished he'd stopped after the first time in jail and ignored the looks. Things were bad enough—the family was dirt-poor, father out of a job most of the time—no, he couldn't blame it on that, either. No use making excuses. His sister stayed straight, went to college, became a teacher—thank God she did, too. She was the only one who saved him in the long run. She and her husband and the kid— Joellyn.

The look was what finally did it for him. That chief of police drove him *crazy* with that look. Every time he drove through the town. Every time they hauled him in for questioning, no matter who had committed the crime. Every chance the chief had, it was always that look...until one night when he was out drinking and the chief pulled him over and didn't say a word, just gave him that look, and the next thing either of them knew the chief was in the hospital with fifteen stitches in his head and John Terrell was in jail to stay.

Ah, well. That was a long time ago...a *long* time ago. That kid didn't exist anymore. Not since he'd met Joy. And then look what happened...

The phone rang, jolting John out of his reverie. He picked up the receiver and spoke softly for a few minutes, deeply engrossed in the conversation. He didn't see Mike Walker come up behind him until it was too late.

He'd already said into the phone, "Yeah, we'll send it out later on this week. We'll use the same truck as always. Sure. You collect the money, then transfer half into my account, just like you always do."

JOELLYN HAD SPENT the day with the auditors, going over the prior year-end closing, her mind periodically jumping back to the few minutes in the attic with Mike.

After yesterday, she hadn't been sure she wanted to talk to him at all, but he had seemed nice this morning. Maybe she'd jumped to the wrong conclusion—after all, he probably hadn't meant to sound suspicious of her. He probably did have to take a look at everything. But still, if he looked too much, found too much... What if Uncle John *was* involved? How could she possibly manage to help Mike and at the same time help her uncle if he needed it?

It was a horrible decision to have to make. When Uncle John sat in her office, she had absolutely believed he was innocent of any wrongdoing. But still, if the tubing was stolen, she had to admit even she might believe him involved in spite of her deep love for him. How could she not? She knew too much about him. And yet... Memories of her childhood flashed through her mind, of losing her father... Uncle John had been there to help her and get her through the worst of it.

The blood ties between herself and John Terrell were thicker than water. Much thicker. He had been there for her. And she would be there for him, no matter what. It was as simple as that.

She bent over her desk with her eyes closed, resting her head on her arms for a minute before she left for the day, just for a minute. She was so *tired*. Then she heard a voice directly in front of her desk. Startled, she looked up and saw Mike.

"Tired?" he asked, smiling down at her.

"Of course not," she said sarcastically. "I always look like this."

"Good! Then you aren't too tired to have dinner with me." He searched her eyes. The shadows were even more pronounced than before.

"What makes you think I want to have dinner with you?" She didn't want to have dinner with him or anyone else she worked with. Especially him. He was the enemy.

"Well, for one thing," he pointed out, "it's dinnertime. Do you always work this late?" he asked abruptly.

"Late? What time is it?" She glanced at her watch. "Oh. Six forty-five." She exhaled softly, disgusted with herself. One of her major problems all her life had been her utter inability to keep track of time. It just seemed to slip away from her no matter what she was doing; there never seemed to be enough of it. "I had no idea it was that late. I have to get home."

"Oh? Someone there waiting for you?" He waited for her answer. He knew she wasn't married. But maybe she had a—what was it his mother always said?—a "friend." Maybe she *was* involved with someone . . . someone here, or at the corporate office, as he'd heard.

"Not really," she said, reaching for her coat. "Just my dog. I have to feed her and let her out before I can think of doing anything else, and to tell you the truth, I'm too tired to go out."

"Is there any reason why you can't, besides that?"

"I can think of several reasons why I shouldn't," she said.

"Name thirty-five," he challenged, smiling.

"I don't think that's necessary," she answered. "I just don't think it's a good idea."

"Dinner," he said, "is always a good idea at dinnertime. Especially when you haven't had any lunch."

She laughed in spite of herself. "You're used to having your way, aren't you?"

"Most of the time, yes," he admitted. He reached into his shirt pocket for a package of lemon drops. "Want one?" he offered, holding the box toward her.

"No thanks," she said.

He slipped the box back into his pocket. "Well, then, how about dinner? Remember, I'm new in town. I need someone to show me around. And a woman of your impeccable taste is bound to know some class A restaurants. Am I right?"

He was pretty sure he was. His sharp glance took in her outfit—a two-piece black linen suit, still crisp after the day she'd put in. To stay that way it had to have been constructed exactly right. He knew that much about women's clothing from observing Dani at close range for so many years.

Joellyn felt herself weakening. There was some sort of attraction here. The current definitely flowed between them. She wasn't sure why, but she found herself beginning to like him in spite of herself, even though she felt threatened by him.

But still, there was her self-imposed rule. No dating the men at work. Up to now she'd held fast to it with no trouble, but then, up to now, Mike Walker hadn't been on the scene.

"About dinner," he reminded her, glancing at his watch. "If we hold out much longer, senility's going to set in. Your blood sugar's getting lower by the minute, and so is mine."

She hesitated. She shouldn't...she knew she shouldn't. But a voice inside whispered, *Why not? Who made up this rule, anyhow? Nobody else follows it.*

"Just one question," she said, "before I answer yes or no."

"Ask me quickly," he teased. "I'm getting faint."

She smiled at the absurdity of that statement. She couldn't imagine anything ever making him faint. "Is there a *Mrs.* Walker?"

He turned his head and reached for her coat, but she saw the quick flash of pain. "There is an *ex* Mrs. Walker," he said quietly.

"Oh." Joellyn stood, slipping her arms into the coat Mike held for her. "Well, in that case, I guess we'll have dinner."

She stood in front of him, and he was surprised to find himself buttoning her coat, his large fingers fumbling with the small buttonholes. He reached for the matching scarf, turned it around in confusion and finally wrapped it around her neck, smiling down at her as he tucked the ends under her collar. How did she get him to do that? he wondered. All of a sudden it just seemed like the most natural thing in the world.

And all of a sudden his fingertips were warm from the brief, fleeting touch of her skin.

"Where are you taking me?" he asked as they walked out the door.

The wind whipped around them as they stepped over the puddles in United's parking lot. "There's a place not far from here called the Cottage," she replied. "Want to try it?"

"Sounds homey," he said.

"It's French," she said, trying not to smile. "You pick the entrée from a blackboard and they do the rest. The food's fabulous. All you have to do is choose the wine, but the wine steward will do it for you if you'd rather not."

"Ah. They have a wine steward, do they? I knew you'd come up with something out of the ordinary." He gave her an amused, secretive smile. "As for the wine, I'll try my humble best not to disgrace you."

"There's only one thing..." Joellyn began, looking flustered. "My car's here and I have to go home first. I really do have to feed my dog and let her out. Then we'll go for dinner."

"Right," Mike said. "Where's your car?"

"It's parked right there. The red one."

Mike looked, then whistled under his breath. A Porsche! She must be making *some* salary to have bought a Porsche. Either that or... but he'd find out over dinner. A couple of glasses of wine and she'd tell him a lot. Most people loosened up after a couple of drinks... unless she was used to it. But she didn't really look like a drinker.

"When did you get that baby?" he asked, nodding toward the Porsche.

"A few months ago," she answered. "Like it?"

"Of course! Sure I like it. What made you decide on a Porsche?"

What had made her decide on a Porsche? She'd asked herself that question many times. She wasn't totally sure why she'd bought it. All her cars before had been conservative four-door sedans, usually brown or beige.

But she had celebrated her thirtieth birthday six months ago, and that day something had happened inside.

Panic? No, not exactly. More like a feeling that time was running out on her. Her old nemesis, time.

All of a sudden she'd begun wondering where her life was going. It seemed to be going nowhere for her. Oh, her job was coming along pretty well, but almost everyone she knew her age had been married at least once. And they all seemed to have kids; or, anyway, the ones who wanted them had them.

True, she had the kids at the home. They were wonderful, and she loved them all. But they weren't *her* kids.

She'd taken a long look at herself on this particular birthday. She'd spent the day alone, just window-shopping in the city and thinking.

Here she was, thirty years old. The thought of it made her shudder. Thirty seemed so, so *old*. She didn't actually feel any different that day, but there was definitely something missing. This was the first time she'd ever looked at her life in quite that way.

Six hours of soul-searching and window-shopping all by herself. Some birthday.

On the way home she'd gone past a Porsche dealer, made a U-turn right in the middle of traffic and swung her tan Chevy into the dealership parking lot. When she left two hours later, she was still alone, but she was driving a red Porsche.

A few drops of rain whipped across her face, bringing her back to the present. She shook them away. "The Porsche?" she said. "Oh, I don't know. I just felt like getting a new car and I saw this one. It was red. I like red. Why?"

Her reason didn't ring true to him, but he said only, "Let's get going. My car's over there."

"Just follow me," Joellyn said. "I don't live far from here, but you might get lost."

"I know what you mean," he agreed. "I got lost three times trying to find this place. Now, no showing off how fast that Porsche will go, okay?"

"Gotcha," Joellyn answered absently, searching in her purse for her key. She slipped into her car, warmed up the engine for a minute, then roared off, leaving Mike struggling to close the gap between them.

Fifteen minutes later Joellyn pulled into the parking space at her apartment. She was just climbing out of her car when Mike pulled in behind her. He rolled his window down, his eyes flashing with annoyance.

"Is that what you call going slow?" he asked. "I nearly lost you twice!"

"I'm sorry," she said. "I guess I just forget about everything when I get in that car."

"You're lucky I'm not a traffic cop," he answered gruffly. "I clocked you going seventy-five almost all the way here. You could get yourself killed going that fast."

"I notice you kept up with me," she retorted. "You're no slouch yourself, are you?"

He reached through the open window and grabbed her arm. "Listen to me," he said. "You drive way too fast. Were you always like that, or is it the car?"

"It's probably the car. I assure you, I'm usually the soul of conservativism. I'm an accountant, remember?" She laughed. "Are you coming in, or do you want to sit out here and sulk? I won't be but a few minutes."

He turned off the ignition and climbed out of his car. "I'm coming in. I want to see whether you have an apartment or a drag strip in there."

"No drag strip," she said. "I promise."

He followed her into the building and down a long hallway. She inserted the key in her lock and threw the door open. "Voilà!" she announced. "No drag strip. Just one sheepdog—" She stopped as Penny came bounding into the room, obviously delighted to have company. "And many, many plants!" She indicated her plants with a wave of her hand. "This is Petunia, and Porky." She laughed out loud at the look on his face as he stared at the mass of greenery spilling over her coffee table.

"Your plants have names?" He'd never known anyone to name a plant before. There was more to her than he'd thought.

"Sure," she said. "They all do. That's Nancy and Sluggo over there." She pointed toward the ivy on her kitchen table. "And Sheena, Queen of the Jungle." She indicated a massive tiger plant hanging in the corner over a peach recliner. "And Maxwell Smart." She pointed toward a huge rubber plant towering behind the sofa.

He watched while she hooked Penny to her leash and put her outside. He was surprised her dog hadn't come after him. Dogs didn't usually like him. Actually, he didn't usually like *them*, ever since the motorcycle accident when he was nineteen.

One German shepherd running loose, snapping at his heels, and he'd wiped out and wound up with a scar on his face. Dogs knew how he felt about them. They could sense it.

"Does she usually eat first or go outside first?" he asked, nodding toward the backyard where they could hear Penny running back and forth.

She smiled. "It depends. Tonight, however, she definitely goes outside first. It's almost eight o'clock—I'm afraid to take the chance."

"Can I help fix her food?"

"Thanks, but no," she said. "It'll just take a minute. Why don't you just have a seat till I'm done?"

While she mixed Penny's food and put it outside, Mike took a good look around the apartment. Nice furniture. *Very* good quality. It looked as though she'd spent a small fortune furnishing the place. The peach-and-cream sofa alone had to cost more than she made in a month, depending on her salary, of course. He hadn't looked into it yet.

The tables were highly polished solid oak, and there were a lot of them scattered around the room. Polished copper and solid brass bowls, some with plants, some containing magazines. A few multicolored pillows scattered on the floor, all in peach and cream silk that matched the colors in her sofa.

This room had been decorated with comfort in mind. And luxury. Even he could see that.

There were a couple of prints on the wall. He walked over to take a closer look and almost whistled out loud when he saw they were original signed lithographs.

Money. This woman had spent a lot of cash on this place.

The kitchen was the biggest surprise of all. Copper pans hung everywhere. He could see they were all expensive. She hadn't picked any of this up at a flea market, no way. There were kitchen utensils and a full battery of appliances, including a microwave and a large food processor, everything color-coordinated in shades of almond and pumpkin.

Either this woman was a fabulous cook, or someone thought she was. She had every spice he'd ever seen lined up in a solid oak three-tier cabinet.

He was a fairly accomplished cook himself, but he'd never worked in a kitchen like this one. Fixing an elaborate dinner here would be a snap. He wondered if she ever had . . . and who it was for.

"Time to go," she said, opening the sliding door. Penny bounded over to Mike and sat in front of him, grinning expectantly, her pink tongue hanging out.

"She thinks you have a cookie for her," Joellyn explained. "Or she hopes you do."

Mike reached into his shirt pocket. "Here, girl," he said to the dog. "No cookies, but here's a lemon drop. Does she mind the calories?" he asked while Penny plopped down on the floor, munching contentedly.

Joellyn laughed. "Calories are her favorite thing," she said. "Except for being petted."

"We could all use a little of that," Mike murmured to himself.

"What?" She reached for her coat.

"I said, let's go eat," he answered. "French food, eh? Lead the way!"

CHAPTER THREE

JOELLYN SMILED to herself as the maître d' ushered them into a secluded booth next to the massive red brick fireplace in the middle of the main dining room. This was one of her favorite restaurants. Quiet. Wonderful gourmet food. Wine that warmed the soul. And Mike seemed right at home.

Mike looked around. "Very nice," he murmured. "Do you come here often?"

"Not really," she answered, pleased that he approved of her choice. "You'll see why when the check comes."

Deep red flames shot with yellow flickered in the fireplace, casting golden highlights over the deep blue crystal water glasses and the blue-and-white country-patterned china; golden highlights that danced from her eyes to Mike's.

At war with her emotions, she shook her blue linen napkin and placed it in her lap. She didn't want to, but she liked this man. Really *liked* him. But like him or not, she still had to guard every word. She knew why he had asked her out. She was certain it had nothing to do with food.

Mike's fingers toyed absently with the wine list as he watched Joellyn, his eyes reflective. His fingertips still held the memory of their quick brush against her neck. Odd, that they would still tingle like this . . . almost as though he had dipped them in some strange chemical that lingered on and on. He smiled to himself. Sure. Chemistry. That was all it was. Pure and simple chemistry.

"Would you like some help?" she asked. "I'm sure the steward can recommend a good wine."

"Before we choose our entrée? My dear, what would Julia Child think?" he teased.

The waiter hovered patiently as Mike peered through the dim light at the menu chalked on the blackboard, then glanced back at Joellyn. "What do you recommend?"

"The sole is excellent," Joellyn told him. "That's what I'd like to have."

"In that case..." He turned toward the waiter. "We'll both have the ballottine of sole."

"And the wine?" the waiter asked, watching Mike expectantly.

"Château St.-Jean Blanc de Blancs, 1983," Mike said in a no-nonsense voice.

"An excellent choice, sir." The waiter slipped away, leaving a bemused Joellyn to stare at Mike.

So, this was no ordinary bouillabaisse-crepes-suzette man. This man knew what he was doing.

At least the waiter appeared satisfied, having now reappeared and uncorked the wine. He poured a small amount into the goblet and handed it to Mike to taste. When Mike nodded, the waiter filled their glasses, smiled and slipped discreetly away, leaving them alone.

"I hope you realize we may be a while," Joellyn said. "They never seem to hurry here, but we do have to show up for work in the morning. At least I do."

"Oh, so do I," Mike protested. "Vice presidents are expendable, believe it or not. I believe the expression is 'a dime a dozen.'"

"I doubt that," Joellyn replied. "The trick is to find a *good* vice president. How did you happen to come to Chicago? Do you have family here?"

"No, I just happened to know someone who knew someone. You know how that goes."

His first impression had been right. This was a smart woman. She was pulling information out of him. He'd have to turn this conversation around quickly, or he'd wind up telling her all about his childhood.

Not that his childhood had been all that bad, but the reason for this dinner was business, not pleasure. At least that was what had been on his mind when he first asked her to join him. How was he to know he'd find himself sitting by a fireplace, drinking his favorite wine and enjoying himself so much?

"So," he said, pouring a little more wine for Joellyn. "Tell me about yourself."

She watched him pour the wine. Ah, he was going to keep her glass filled, was he? She'd have to sip more water and less wine. "There's not really a whole lot to tell," she said, shrugging her shoulders. "I live a pretty quiet life. My father passed away a few years ago. My mother lives in Miami Beach." She smiled and took a sip of water.

He watched her look first at the wine and then pick up the water, and he almost laughed. She wasn't about to be plied with wine. "Does she live alone?" he asked.

"That depends on what you mean by 'alone.' She has her own condo, but I wouldn't be surprised if she has a boyfriend lurking around somewhere. However, she's pretty secretive about that."

He laughed. "I love it! There's one lady who knows how to live! Do you have any family around here? Any brothers or sisters?"

She hesitated. Well, he'd specifically mentioned brothers or sisters. At least she could answer that. "No," she said. "No brothers or sisters. I was an only child."

"Have you ever been married?" Mike asked, surprising himself. He hadn't meant to ask that.

She gazed thoughtfully into the shimmering wine, watching the way it reflected the firelight and the blue table setting, picturing the past, now shadowy and fleeting.

"No," she answered after a minute. "I got close to it once, but it didn't work out. I seldom think about it now, but it threw me for a loop at the time. You know how hard you take things when you're young." She smiled. "By the way," she said, changing the subject, "this wine's fantastic. How did you know what year to ask for?"

Mike raised his eyebrows. She'd neatly turned the conversation away from herself. "Contrary to popular belief," he replied, "they do have wine cellars in Philadelphia."

"Oh," she protested, "there's got to be more to it than that. You don't learn about good French wine from hanging around someone's wine cellar."

He chuckled. "No, I guess not. I learned it in France."

"In France? Well, that explains a lot. I was wondering how you'd perfected that accent when you were ordering the wine. Did you live there, then?"

Mike toyed with a bread stick. He didn't really want to go into this. He wanted to forget it. But he couldn't see any way out of it, other than flat-out refusing to answer, and he didn't want her to think he was rude.

"I lived there," he answered heavily, "for five years, right after I got out of college. They have a lot of industry. I was offered a job with a company right outside Paris that manufactured automobile parts. It sounded like a good idea at the time. I guess I was looking for adventure."

She smiled. "And did you find it?"

Yes, he'd found adventure. He'd unearthed a plot to divert shipments of small auto parts. That was when his reputation as a troubleshooter had begun.

"I found my wife, Danielle," he said. "My ex-wife," he corrected himself.

"Oh." She hadn't missed his tone. Evidently it bothered him a lot.

"While I was there, before I met her," he said, "I did a lot of research into French food and wine." He smiled. "Especially the wine. The usual things a man does in his early twenties—I ate and drank, had a hell of a good time. And then I met Dani."

"And?" she asked, curiosity getting the best of her.

"And I got married. We had a son, David. We moved back to the States when I got a better job offer." He looked down at the table, his eyes darkening. Damn it, how was she doing this? What was it about this woman that was making him want to tell her everything about himself? He was supposed to be finding out about *her*.

He took a long, slow sip of his wine and glanced around the room, hoping the waiter would arrive soon with the first course. He needed rescuing. He was talking too much about himself. So far he hadn't made a dent in her shell, but she already knew quite a lot about him.

"So you wound up divorced," she said. "What caused it?" Then, appalled at herself, she blushed. "I'm sorry," she murmured. "I shouldn't have asked that. It's really none of my business."

He smiled, a slow smile that made her pulse jump. "Probably not, but I'll tell you, anyway."

She looked embarrassed. "Only if you're sure. I don't mean to pry."

The waiter arrived just then and set a steaming covered basket of miniature croissants and an icy plate of butter curls in front of them. Mike waited until he was out of earshot.

"A lot of things caused the divorce," he said. "We were too young. Or, anyhow, I was. And I was way too ambitious. It was as though I had a fire raging inside all the time." He laughed briefly. "I know that sounds overly dramatic, but it's true. I was determined to make a million by the time I was fifty."

Joellyn grinned. "And you came to United? Bad move."

"Well, I have a few years to go," he said. "Maybe I'll make it, maybe not."

"I can guarantee you won't at United."

"Someone has," he pointed out.

She flushed. "I meant legally." She buttered a piece of roll. "So...your ambition did it," she murmured.

"That, and the fact that my wife fell in love with another man." He forced the words out quickly, hating the sound of them.

Joellyn raised her eyebrows. "Oh? Now *that* surprises me."

It did surprise her. He seemed to be such a strong man; she couldn't imagine him sitting idly by and allowing his marriage to dissolve.

"Too many long hours," he said. "Too many out-of-town trips. And Dani had no family here. She was very lonely. It never occurred to me something like that could happen. It was stupid and naive of me, I know."

He paused for a moment and took a sip of wine, then looked at his half-empty glass. "So she met someone who was around when I wasn't and fell in love with him." He shrugged, trying to shake away the pain that still stabbed through him whenever he thought of those days of stunned disbelief and nights of soul-searching recrimination. "I can't blame her. It was my fault."

He shook his head. "It's the same old story. You tell yourself you're doing it for your family, but you're not really. Eventually you have to face the fact that you're doing it for yourself. But by the time I got myself unraveled, it was too late. We were miles apart, even though we were still living in the same house."

"Did she marry him?" Joellyn asked.

He set his glass down. "Yes, as soon as our divorce became final."

"And you're still in love with her?" Joellyn was surprised to find herself holding her breath, waiting for his answer.

"I don't think so," he said. "It's been a year now. Oh, don't get me wrong. I did love her very much at first. But somewhere along the way it just fizzled out. Maybe that's one of the reasons I left her alone so much."

Joellyn smiled. "Well, it looks as though you're getting your priorities straight now."

"Oh, sure," he agreed. "But it's taken me thirty-five years to figure it all out. And now here I am in Chicago while my son's in Philadelphia getting used to a new father."

Joellyn reached over and touched his hand. "Mike, your son isn't going to forget you. That's your real worry, isn't it?"

Bingo! She'd hit him where he lived. She'd zeroed right in on what was bothering him, forcing him to face it head-on.

He nodded. "I guess you're right."

"Then," she said, "the most important thing for you to do now is keep in touch. Write to him. Call him. And see him as much as you possibly can."

"They're on a trip now," he offered, "but Dani called today. They're going to be in town next weekend. They're dropping David off Saturday night. I'll have him then, and Sunday morning. They're picking him up about noon before they head back home."

She leaned toward him, emphasizing her next words. "Well, when you do see him, make *sure* he knows you love him. And I don't mean by giving him material things. I'm talking about hugs and kisses. The kind of love you *can't* buy."

He was silent for a few minutes, staring down at the tablecloth while the waiter placed an appetizer in front of them. She'd given him plenty to think about. Not that he hadn't thought about it before, but how did she know so much about these things? She'd never been married. She had no children. How could she possibly know about things like this?

He looked up and smiled. "Well," he said, "I think you're in the wrong profession. You have the makings of a great psychologist."

She cut a small piece of pâté while she mulled over his words. A great psychologist. Or a great wife and mother, if that day ever came.

"But that's enough about me," he said. "What about you? What do you do with yourself when you're not working?"

"Oh," she said, "I like interior decorating. I design furniture. I like to cook...."

He poured more wine into both of their glasses. "I gathered that much when I saw your kitchen."

Her blue eyes looked even more liquid in the soft glow of the firelight. He was beginning to hope seriously that she wasn't involved in the mess at work.

That thought jolted him. He'd been sitting here, pouring out his entire life to her and forgetting his original purpose. He *couldn't* become friendly with her. She might be on the other side. His gaze held hers for a long minute before it traveled down to her lips...such soft, innocent-looking lips. He mentally kicked himself under the table. What was he thinking of? Those lips weren't the lips of a little girl, not by a long shot.

"How old are you?" he asked abruptly.

She wrinkled her nose. "Thirty. Isn't that awful?"

"I don't think it's awful at all," he said, feeling unaccountably relieved. "In fact, I'm almost thirty-six myself. I'll be an old man before you know it."

"Well, old man," she said, nodding toward the kitchen, "you'd better put your teeth in. Our dinner's on its way over right now."

They lingered over dinner, mellowing in the warmth of the firelight's glow on the polished wood paneling, the old-world paintings on the walls and the silent, unobtrusive attentions of the waiter.

Finally the meal was over. Mike leaned back against the velvety cushioned booth. "Excellent restaurant!" he proclaimed. "I can't remember when I've had a better dinner."

"It was wonderful," she agreed. "But then, you haven't tasted my cooking."

The firelight had softened her features. Shadowy planes and highlights danced in her hair. He found himself tempted to reach for her hand, but stopped. It was time for questions, and he wanted answers.

He took a sip of coffee. "Joellyn, what do you think's been happening in the plant? Any ideas?"

Joellyn tried not to frown. She'd known he was going to get around to this sooner or later. She hated to see the evening spoiled, but they might as well get on with it.

"I can't figure it out," she said. "It started a little over four months ago—closer to five really. First the inventory balance was down by two hundred thousand dollars, for no reason we could figure out. We thought whatever it was would straighten itself out by the next month-end. Time lags cause discrepancies like that from time to time, so we didn't become terribly concerned about it right away. But next month, when we expected it to go back up two hundred thousand, it went down again. This time two hundred and fifty thousand more. At that point we knew something was wrong."

Mike watched her eyes closely. "Did you do a physical inventory count right then?" he asked.

"No. We probably should have, but we were so puzzled. We thought maybe something had gone wrong with the computer system we were using. It's a fairly new one—up to that time all the work had been done manually, and we thought perhaps a bug had popped up in the program.

"So we started a full-scale investigation of the books, checking all the computer balances, and at the same time the people in inventory control started spot-checking. But they didn't turn up anything. Zilch. Everything was exactly as the computerized records indicated.

"By that time another month had passed and it was time for another closing. We waited until the general ledger came out, and at that point all hell broke loose, because now it was down *another* two hundred thousand."

"So, in three months' time more than six hundred thousand dollars in inventory just vanished?" He sipped his coffee, still watching her through his lowered eyelashes.

"Without a trace," she answered. "By that time Randy and I were looking into everything, and Lanagan was, too. But again, nothing."

She leaned toward him, gripping the edge of the table. "I swear to you, Mike, there doesn't seem to be anything wrong with the books that we can see. I keep telling myself this can't be, but honestly, it looks as though that tubing is gone."

"How can you be so sure?" He leaned back, trying not to notice the way she moved. This was no time to get sidetracked.

"I'm not sure," she said, "but after the third month our outside auditors were called in. They went over everything inside and out. When they couldn't find anything wrong in the books, Lanagan brought in detectives."

She was terribly uncomfortable. Why was she telling him all this? He had to know it already. What could he be thinking, watching her the way he was?

She took a deep breath and went on. "Nobody but Lanagan, Randy and myself knew they were detectives. They watched everything, checked all the shipments, watched them go out the door. They checked all the packing slips as they left the shipping dock. And at the end of the month, sure enough, the inventory went down *another* three hundred fifty thousand."

"So now the total's a million," Mike reflected.

"Yes. The detectives can't figure out how it's getting out the door. The auditors have worked day and night trying to find something, but they're as baffled as we are. Whoever's doing it really knows what he's doing. Now they're thinking of calling in the FBI. Unless you can spot something we can't see."

"The FBI sounds like a good idea to me," Mike said with a hint of a smile. "But can they do that without being sure it's interstate?"

She hadn't missed the smile. It was making her nervous, although why should she be? She hadn't done anything wrong.

"I don't know, but I think anything they can do would be a good idea," she said. "I'm sick and tired of all the suspicion and questioning day after day. We can't do anything but look for the damn tubing. Nothing else is getting done. I'm afraid something else will slip under the wire while we're doing nothing but looking for numbers that just aren't there." She looked at him. "Mike, we can't find a reason. That inventory has just disappeared."

Mike lifted his coffee cup and stared down into the dark liquid. She seemed sincere enough. She appeared genuinely puzzled. But he couldn't imagine anything of this magnitude taking place without her having at least some knowledge of it, or at least some suspicion of who was involved.

He looked up. "I read all the reports this past weekend," he said. "I think it has to be someone in the plant. Someone very, very clever." He regarded her silently for a minute, then abruptly asked, "Do you know the shipping manager, John Terrell?"

Joellyn's heart stopped as the name left his lips. So they *did* suspect Uncle John.

She felt sick. She had hoped his name would never come up, but she'd known all along that was only wishful thinking. Of course they'd suspect the shipping manager. If she were conducting this investigation, he'd be the first one she'd suspect. But then maybe that was because she knew so much about his past. Nobody else at United knew, or at least she didn't think they did.

And it was going to look bad for her, too, if he was involved. Not many people knew he was her uncle, but John Terrell had helped her get her first job at United.

For the time being, though, she wasn't going to discuss him with Mike or anyone else. She needed to buy a little more time until she could see Uncle John alone and talk to him herself. Someplace quiet and private, maybe his house... Damn it, she didn't want to believe he would be involved in this. Everything in her cried out against it, but she had to face facts, no matter how it hurt.

He'd done it before. He could do it again. And if he had, she was somehow going to have to find a way to help him undo what he'd done before he got sent back to—

She averted her eyes from Mike's penetrating gaze. He was sounding more and more like a detective or an FBI man. He could easily be one or the other. This was *awful!* She had to watch every word.

"I know just about everyone in the plant," she answered after a long pause. "I've worked there ever since I got out of college. What about John?"

Mike had noticed the flush on her cheeks when he mentioned Terrell. "I just tossed the name out," he said easily, remembering the conversation he'd overheard earlier. "I imagine I'll be tossing a lot of names out before this is over. His just seemed like the logical place to start."

"But why?" she asked. "John's a nice man. He's been with United a long time. Do you really think he'd have anything to do with this?"

"Maybe not," Mike said with a smile that didn't quite reach his eyes. "I hope not, anyway. I met him, and you're right, he *seems* like a nice enough guy. But do you know of anyone else who might be involved? Even in a small way? What about the other people in the shipping area? Or the plant manager? It could be anyone, you know, even him."

"The plant manager? Al Dobson?" Joellyn frowned. "Oh, I don't think so. Al's a family man."

"Family men don't commit crimes? Well," he teased, "there's a brand-new theory."

"Look," she said, "stop patronizing me. Of *course* family men commit crimes. I just don't think this particular family man committed this particular crime. Al's a very nice person."

Mike reached for the check. "Joellyn," he said, "I'm not patronizing you, but you're going to have to face it. Someone in that plant has very neatly done away with a million dollars' worth of the company's inventory. And I intend to find out who it is. I don't care how nice he is."

"He?" She gave him a cool look. "What if it's a woman?"

"I don't think so."

"Why? Because it's so 'neatly' done? Don't you think a woman could carry off something like this?" She was behaving like a spoiled child and she knew it, but suddenly she didn't like his attitude.

Mike glanced up from the check. "I'll tell you what," he said quietly. "I'll stop patronizing you if you'll stop baiting me." He smiled. "Agreed?"

She didn't feel like smiling back. "Agreed," she said. She reached for her purse. "Look, it's getting pretty late. Don't you think we'd better be leaving? We both have to be at work early in the morning."

"Right!" He slid out of the booth, puzzled by the abrupt change in her manner. The minute he'd mentioned Terrell she had changed. There was something here . . . something he couldn't quite put his finger on, almost as though a curtain had dropped over her emotions.

A few minutes ago they'd been laughing, enjoying a magnificent dinner. Now he was having the uncomfortable sensation of trying to plow through a brick wall.

THE RIDE HOME was quiet, but Mike was very aware of her nearness. He pulled his car up in front of her apartment and switched the ignition off. He turned toward her, surprised to find himself longing to touch that smooth, lovely chin again and take her into his arms. He was going to kiss her. Stupid though the idea might be, he could feel it coming.

He cleared his throat. "How about a cup of coffee? One for the road?"

Joellyn tried not to look at him. She could smell the clean scent of his after-shave lotion. There was a definite attraction here; she couldn't deny it, and she was fighting it for all she was worth. This man was on a witch-hunt that was going to destroy her uncle, if he dug deep enough. And maybe herself in the process.

But maybe they wouldn't find out about Uncle John's record. The detectives hadn't turned anything up. Maybe Mike wouldn't, either. Or maybe they already had and her uncle was being watched. That sounded a little more reasonable.

But in spite of this, she wondered what it would be like to bury her face in Mike's chest, to be close to him . . . just for a moment. In spite of the fact that she was afraid of what he might dig up, she felt—what was it? A pull, a very strong magnetic sensation . . .

She turned toward him, indecision shadowing her face. She couldn't let herself become involved with him even if she wanted to. She didn't really know who he was. She wasn't at all sure about him, or he of her for that matter. She couldn't—but then her doubts were forgotten, drowned out by the roaring in her head, the pounding of a thousand surfs as he bent toward her and his lips met hers.

Her mouth opened as he pressed, his tongue tasting her lips, searching the inside of her mouth. He groaned and pulled her closer as she wrapped her arms around his neck and her tongue answered his.

Her fingers traced a path through his hair and down the back of his neck. Her breath almost stopped from the force of feeling that flowed between them. Her emotions boiled, threatening to spill over. It felt so right. She couldn't understand how it could feel so right, but she knew it was. In the space of time one kiss had taken, her life had changed and would never be the same again.

He was the first to pull away. "Well . . ." he said in a low voice. His gaze moved over her face. "I don't know about you, but I wasn't expecting anything like this."

"Neither was I," she murmured, her voice shaking.

He traced her eyebrow with his fingertips. "How about that coffee?"

"I don't think so," she answered. "I'm going in. Alone. I have to think about this."

He chuckled, a short, rueful laugh. "You're not the only one who has to do some thinking."

She could feel him still watching her. Why wasn't she already out of his car and on her way inside? This was insane. She had to get away from this man and this feeling.

She felt his hand pressing on her shoulder. It was as though an invisible wire were pulling her back toward him again. This couldn't be. They'd only met a short time ago.

He bent toward her again, and she felt herself sinking. Her thoughts drifted as her senses drank in the utterly masculine scent of him, the strength of his arms and the taut skin that felt exactly as she'd known it would.

He caressed her neck with the palm of his hand. "You are one beautiful woman," he whispered. "And I'm going to be seeing a lot of you—I hope." He shook his head and brushed her lips with his, a quick caress that sent an electric shock throughout her body.

"Night," she managed to whisper as she slipped out of the car.

He leaned over the passenger seat. "Hey!" he said softly.

She turned back toward him. "Yes?"

"Would you like to meet my son Saturday night? Just to say hi?"

The air between them buzzed with electricity. "I don't know," she said. "I've got a busy day coming up Saturday. Call me and we'll talk about it."

He nodded, pulled the door shut and switched the ignition on.

Shaken, she watched his car move slowly away and disappear into the black night.

SHE GOT UNDRESSED and took a hot shower, but she still couldn't sleep. She sat on the sofa in the dark, her thoughts traveling back through the years ... back to her last conversation with her Aunt Joy, the only woman Uncle John had ever loved.

Joy had developed cancer, and knew it. None of the family had wanted to talk about it. They had all skirted around the issue and pretended it wasn't there, but Joy had brought it up herself when she and Jo-ellyn were alone.

"I only have a few months left," she said.

Joellyn sat, head bowed, fighting tears, but Joy wouldn't let her grieve. Not now. She had something important to say, and Joellyn was the only one she could say it to.

"I don't know how he's going to survive," Joellyn said. "He loves you so much."

"I know," Joy answered softly. "But he's strong, my John. A lot stronger than anyone knows."

Joellyn shook her head. "He's only been strong because of you. You know how he was before."

"Yes," Joy said, "but that was before. John's fine now. He never loses his temper any more." She smiled. "Or his honesty. Just the other day someone gave him too much change at the drugstore and he drove fifteen miles to take it back. He'll be okay."

"What do you want me to do?" Joellyn whispered.

"Just be there for him," Joy answered. "Just be there."

And Joellyn had, at first. She'd visited John all the time, every chance she'd gotten. And then she'd gone back to college, and somehow the years passed and the visits became fewer and further between until she barely saw him at all, except at the plant, and now her guilt was almost more than she could bear.

Just be there. And now Uncle John was in trouble, or it certainly looked as though he might be, from Mike's subtle questioning. But the subtlety hadn't fooled her. Mike suspected her uncle, and it was tearing her apart. And if she took a long, detached look at the situation, she couldn't really be sure of Uncle John's innocence herself.

JOHN TERRELL STOOD in his darkened garage doorway, estimating the distance between the car and the north wall. It looked as if there would be room. Best to be sure, though. He pulled a metal tape measure off one of the side shelves and began measuring, humming to himself.

Ah, sure. There was plenty of room, a couple of feet to spare, and the shipment wouldn't be here that long, anyhow. It would be in and out of here in a couple of days—it was already sold. This one was easy. Easy to get, easy to get rid of. A hell of a profit this time, too. They hadn't had to touch it this time. He should have thought this up years ago. . . .

He'd have to watch the late hours, though, just like always. He didn't want to disturb the neighbors. They didn't need to be involved in this. Nobody had to know, ever, as long as he and Al watched themselves.

He chuckled to himself. It was getting easier and easier. The more they did it, the easier it got. And the more his bank account was piling up. It looked as if retirement wasn't that far away, after all. He could see himself on that beach now, surrounded by hot sun and piña coladas.

He put the tape measure away, closed the garage door and headed for the house, whistling.

MIKE DROVE slowly home, trying to ignore the hollow feeling in the pit of his stomach in spite of the dinner he'd just eaten.

Show him you love him. Not by buying things, but with hugs and kisses.

How had she hit on that so quickly? How could she have known that for months after the divorce he'd shown up at the house loaded with toys, taken David places, done everything he could think of to make sure his son knew he was loved?

Everything but the obvious. And now... Now he was too far away. Now that he knew what he'd been missing, it was too late. Too late to reach out, to hug, to pull that small body close and bury his nose in the red hair so like his own, breathing in that special little boy scent that was his son... the very breath of life.

How could she have known?

But even more devastating than that—how could *he* have not?

CHAPTER FOUR

"DIANNE!" Jack Lanagan shouted into the intercom, frantically pushing the button five times in rapid succession. "Where the devil is my antacid?" He yanked his bottom desk drawer open with his left hand, scrambling its contents and tossing papers onto the desktop while he jabbed at the button again with his right hand.

"Where the devil *is* that woman?" He glowered across the desk at Mike, then glanced at Randy, who was sitting in the massive brown leather chair on the right side of the room. "Damn it," he barked, "every time I really need her she's off somewhere gossiping."

"Mr. Lanagan." A low, throaty voice purred its way out of the small metal-and-chrome box. "You left the intercom on again. I'm right here. Now what was it you wanted?"

"I want my antacid! What the devil did you do with it?" Lanagan frowned at the intercom, still yanking things out of the drawer and dropping them onto the floor.

Mike leaned over and glanced covertly at the floor, trying to suppress a smile. There were two bags of candy—one full, one partially empty. Miniature chocolate balls rolled onto the deep pile carpeting and under the desk. There was an empty prescription bottle, a box of aspirin, half-empty, a torn cellophane package of tissues.

Apparently the men out in the factory weren't kidding. Lanagan really *was* hyper when he got going! Lanagan's complexion, a fading suntan-olive shade when Mike had first met him, was turning deep burgundy, giving him a dangerous appearance as he waited for his answer.

Mike listened to the disembodied voice—soothing, as though it were calming a hysterical child. "You must have used the last of it yesterday, Mr. Lanagan. I found the empty bottle last night when I straightened up. Now calm down or they'll hear you all the way out in the factory. I bought a new bottle last night. I'll bring it right in."

Mike still hadn't said a word other than "Good morning." He glanced at Randy, wondering how he was taking this display, but Randy was staring out the window, ignoring the whole thing. Not too surprising. Randy had been working for Lanagan for quite a while. He was probably used to it.

Lanagan's face was slowly returning to its normal color. "Damn fine secretary when I can find her," he said to no one in particular. He bent down to pick up the mess he'd made on the floor. "She doesn't know shorthand, but she always remembers my antacid."

"What more can you ask?" Mike murmured as the door swung open. He laughed under his breath. All Dianne needed was a drumroll. She swiveled into the room, hips moving to a silent rhythm. A tall, striking brunette, her red suit fitted everywhere it was supposed to, and some places it wasn't.

The swivel was pretty funny. He hadn't seen anyone do that in years. He liked to see women walk fast, with their heads held high, striding from point A to point B—the way Joellyn walked. There was nothing obviously sexy about Joellyn's walk. She didn't need to be obvious.

Dianne tore the seal off the bottle, uncapped it and handed it to Lanagan. "Good morning, Randy," she murmured, looking straight at Mike. "And, Mr. Walker. I didn't know you two were in here. I guess I must have been away from my desk when you came in."

They both nodded and said, "Good morning."

"Hold my calls, Dianne. Especially if it's my wife. No wonder I drink so much of this stuff." Lanagan took a good healthy swig from the bottle, recapped it and stuffed it into his bottom drawer.

Dianne was still looking at Mike through her lowered eyelashes. She gave him a thousand-kilowatt smile, then turned back to Lanagan. "If your stomach keeps acting up like this, you'd better see a doctor."

"Oh, baloney. I've been drinking this stuff for years. Keeps me going. Just hold the calls, will you? We'll be in here a while."

"Yes, sir." She smiled again, backing out through the door, still looking at Mike.

As soon as the door was closed, Lanagan swung back around and faced the men. "Mike, you've been here a week now. I apologize for not having spent time with you, introducing you around, but I understand Randy took good care of that."

Randy and Mike both nodded.

Lanagan continued. "By now you should have been able to pick up on a few things out in the plant. What do you think? Do things look fairly normal to you out there?''

Mike felt uncomfortable with Lanagan's eyes piercing through him. He'd been wondering himself why Lanagan had left him strictly alone all week. "To tell you the truth, Jack," he answered, "I haven't seen anything that seems directly connected with our problem. A few things bother me, but other than that..."

Mike stared out the window while he considered what he should say next. The trees had begun to bud now that the last of the snow had melted and the sun had been out for two days, on and off. He had cabin fever. He missed the workouts and racquetball games he'd been used to in Philadelphia.

"What's bothering you?" Lanagan asked.

Mike could see the man was waiting for an answer, but he couldn't give him one. Not a truthful one, anyhow. After all, he'd been hired and sent here by the board of directors. Lanagan didn't know his real function, but he *must* suspect something. Even so, Lanagan hadn't seen fit to give him any real help up to now. He'd have to stall for time, for a while, anyway. But not too long.

"Jack," he said, "one week isn't really long enough to know all the ins and outs of our system. Some things that seem loose to me now may not be once I've had time to learn my way around. I just can't tell yet. I haven't had time to fully assess the situation. I've met and talked to a lot of the employees, but so far I've come up with nothing, the same as you."

Mike turned to Randy, who was still sitting in the same position, hands in his pockets and chin resting on his chest. "What about you, Randy? What's your feeling on this? Do you have any suggestions?"

Randy frowned. "I have the same answer you do, Mike. This is a complete mystery to me. I've sat with Joellyn and gone over her work, and I haven't seen anything that could be termed suspicious." Randy bent forward to scratch the back of his knee. "The thing is," he added, "the books *appear* to be all right. It seems to me if it's not an error in the books, then whoever is responsible must be aware by this time that we're looking. I don't know.... I've personally checked everything I can think of."

"Have you checked all of one month's shipments against the billing computer runs?" Mike asked. "Maybe it could be something that's coded in such a way that it doesn't show up on the run. I've heard of such things myself, especially with new computer systems."

"That was one of the first things our internal auditors did," Lanagan said. "Everything was in order there."

"And I've been through every department in the place," Randy said. "For that matter, I see all the invoices that go through the system, anyway, and I haven't seen anything wrong with them. I have to admit, I'm baffled. But I'd sure hate to bring in the FBI. My God, they'd be all over the place, and it's hard enough to get things done now. Don't you think we should wait a few days until we've had one more closing? Just so we can be sure we actually have a crime here?"

"How much more sure can you be?" Mike asked. "And, *will* the FBI come in on it? Don't we have to have proof that this is interstate before they'll move?"

"Nope," Lanagan said. "We deal with government contracts from time to time. They'll come in on it if we ask them. The thing is, we don't really want to ask them if we don't have to."

Randy reached over and helped himself to one of the chocolate balls on Lanagan's desk and popped it in his mouth. "Look," he said, "we'll have a new general ledger out in a couple of days. By then we might find out it's been in the books the whole time. Mike, I don't know how much you know about the office personnel, but the thing is, Joellyn's not all that experienced in inventory control. She's only been in that position a little under a year. There could be dozens of things wrong that we haven't spotted yet."

He looked at Lanagan. "Don't forget, there's more than twenty million dollars' worth of tubing out in that plant. It's pretty hard to keep track of it even if you're aware of all the pitfalls, and Joellyn's not aware of all of them. That takes years of experience."

"Yes," Lanagan said, "but you have to give her credit. She's doing pretty well. You should know that. After all, you're her boss. And you were the one who recommended her for that job."

Lanagan leaned over his desk, lighting a cigar with a cannon-shaped lighter. "And besides all that," he added, "Joellyn didn't install the new perpetual inventory control system. Al Dobson did. Damn it all!" he groused, almost to himself. "I knew we should have stayed on the manual system. Two hundred little old ladies with pencils couldn't be nearly as much trouble as this one computer's been. Or half as expensive."

He glanced at Randy. "And we had the affirmative action people to contend with. You know that as well as I do." He winked conspiratorially at Mike. "Joellyn's our token woman-in-management. But don't quote me, for heaven's sake."

"At least we got lucky there," Randy said. "She sure is good-looking as well as being a brain."

Randy and Lanagan looked at each other and smiled, but Mike's knuckles gripped the arms of his chair. "I don't think Joellyn's looks are the issue here," he reminded them in a quiet voice that made Lanagan's eyebrows shoot up.

Mike caught Lanagan's surprised look. Lanagan and Randy had both just implied that Joellyn wasn't really qualified for her position. If that was true, then why did they give it to her? "She has a degree in accounting, doesn't she?" he asked.

Lanagan nodded. "Oh, sure," he said. "She graduated cum laude from the University of Chicago. Came here right after she graduated."

"How much cost accounting experience has she had?" Mike asked.

"Not much until recently," Lanagan admitted. "Most of her experience was in the other areas."

"Then why didn't you put someone with more cost experience in that spot?" Mike persisted.

"We didn't see any reason to at the time. Joellyn puts in a lot of hours," Lanagan said. "Always has. She's okay. She does her job." His tone of voice dismissed the subject.

Mike stood, walked over to the window and stared out for a minute, thinking. There had been a lot of waffling around with computer runs, but these people weren't even totally sure the inventory was missing.

Although Joellyn had said the inventory had disappeared.... But could he trust her? Who here *could* he trust?

He turned. "Here's what I think. Let's wait as Randy suggested. That'll give us time to gather a little more information. We'll see how the books look this month. Then, since we haven't done it up to now, I think we should hold a full-scale inventory count sometime soon. That'll mean losing a couple of days' production, but it can't be helped.

"That way, if the count shows what the records show, and we still haven't been able to figure it out, we'll have some hard facts to give to the FBI. As it stands now, they might not come in at all. We have suspicion of crime, but we have no evidence. This is almost like accusing a person of murder when there's no body. No body, no crime. I really don't think they'll come in at all at this point."

Lanagan chewed silently on his cigar, eyeing both Mike and Randy. "Damn it all," he said, "I don't even want to think about this. It's all I've thought about for weeks now. What I really want is to go home and shut myself in my den and watch the hockey game."

He laughed briefly. "Funny how the Blackhawks keep overlapping with the White Sox. There's never enough time to keep up with 'em." He switched back to business with surprising abruptness. "I'm really between a rock and a hard place here, you know, Mike. If we even try to bring the FBI in, the board of directors is bound to get wind of it. Then what if we find out it was a bookkeeping snafu all along? You're right about that.

"On the other hand, if we don't bring them in, and more tubing disappears, it'll be just as bad for us. So far we've kept it covered up, but if it gets much worse, it'll be next to impossible to jack up the profits enough to cover all of this. We may not be able to do it, anyway. They read the audit reports, or I'm pretty sure they do. If we show a massive, unexplained inventory shrinkage, they'll be all over our case." Lanagan shook his head. "There's no way we can cover it up. Our profit has been extremely high this year. They're aware of that, but this is going to eat it up."

Mike eyed Lanagan. The board of directors already knew about the shrinkage. That was why he'd been hired in the first place. How could Lanagan not *know* that? He seemed honest enough, as did Randy and Joellyn, but all three of them were definitely under suspicion, although Joellyn seemed to be the only one aware of it.

"*If* there *is* a shortage," Mike pointed out.

"Yes. If. Tell you what." Lanagan tilted his cigar into the ashtray, its blue-gray smoke evaporating into the rarified mahogany-paneled executive suite atmosphere. "We'll wait. But we'll keep looking. If it's still bad when the new general ledger comes out, then we have no choice, board of directors or not. So dig deep, Mike. Do whatever you have to do. And keep me informed."

He stood, dismissing Mike and Randy. As they left the office together, Mike saw Lanagan reaching for the bottom drawer again.

The two men walked toward the stairs leading into the factory. "Come on," Randy said. "Let's go down to the cafeteria for some coffee."

"Sounds good to me," Mike answered. "Look, I've been meaning to ask you. Is there a health club anywhere around here?"

"Oh, sure. Never bother with 'em myself, but the Nautilus is just a couple of miles away, and the Chicago Health Clubs are all over the place. What's the matter? Getting flabby?"

"Not yet, but I'm used to working out a couple of times a week, and I will be if I don't get back to it."

The two men walked down the hallway, quietly joking. As they passed the accounting department, Mike caught a quick glimpse of Joellyn's shiny blond hair covering her face as she bent over a computer run, apparently in deep concentration.

JOELLYN'S EYES were on the computer run, but her mind was far away. She'd been like this for days now, ever since the night Mike had taken her out for dinner. She'd seen him every day since. They would pass in the hallway or out in the plant, but except for a brief flicker of recognition, a quick good-morning, he seemed to be too busy to stop and chat. She was beginning to think she'd fantasized the whole evening.

Well, maybe she had. Maybe he was an investigator. Maybe he did want to see how much she knew and that was all. But... could she have imagined that kiss and the feeling that had shot between them?

She'd dated a few men since Lee, but none of them had even come close to awakening the feelings Mike had. She didn't even want to think about it—the jolt she'd felt all the way down to her toes when Mike's lips had touched hers. Could it have been chance?

One thing she couldn't deny—she'd been engaged to Lee, had come treacherously close to marrying him, but she couldn't remember his kiss affecting her in quite the same way Mike's had. Even so, she would probably have married Lee if he hadn't called it off almost at the last minute.

"It just won't work, Joellyn," he had said on their last evening together. "Our lives are too different. We want too many different things."

Up to that moment she hadn't known there was a problem. She'd gone just that afternoon for a wedding gown fitting.

She'd stared at him in openmouthed astonishment. "What are you talking about?"

"Our *lives*, Joellyn. I'm sorry. This is terrible, but I just can't ... I just don't think ... damn it all, quit looking at me like that."

"And how do you want me to look at you?" All of a sudden he didn't like the way she looked at him? What was going on here? She had no inkling. None at all.

"That's not it. That's not the problem." He looked irritated, anxious to get away.

"Lee ... what *is* the problem?"

"I just don't want to get married. It's not you. It's just the whole idea of marriage. It won't work. Not for me, not now. Maybe never." His dark eyes flashed uncomfortably as he turned away, avoiding the look of hurt in her eyes.

No, he didn't want to see the results of his words, but he'd spoken them clearly enough. And she still heard them clearly today, echoing through the years as though he'd spoken them only yesterday.

But he had been right. She wanted a home and children and security. The house on a hillside with a brook and a white picket fence and swings in the backyard weren't clichés to her. That was how she saw her life; that was how she needed it to be.

She'd been a quiet, conservative person all her life. There was no room in her world for the constant upheavals the wife of a foreign correspondent would have to endure. She should have known from the start it would never work. Thank God Lee had known it.

They were just too different, he'd said.

And now . . . someone had shown up who she didn't know, couldn't trust, but who had touched her to the very core of her being with one good-night kiss. And he'd felt it, too. She knew he had.

But if he had, why hadn't he called her?

She shrugged, annoyed with herself for losing sleep over a man she barely knew and who was now exhibiting not the slightest interest in her.

Well, it wasn't the first time she'd been fooled by her emotions. And it probably wouldn't be the last.

MIKE HAD SEEN Joellyn in her office earlier in the week, but there had been no time to talk. His work had kept him hopping until late in the evening, and by the time he left, she was already gone.

It had been a hellish week. Al Dobson had called him yesterday afternoon with his weekly production report. They needed to talk. There were problems with two of the production lines—the cost variances were out of sight, and he wanted to find out what Al was doing about them.

And he needed to check on the staffing report. There had been too many people standing around doing nothing this morning when he walked through the plant. He wondered why Al hadn't opened the number eight line and put them to work there. They had a huge order of special red tubing to get out by the end of next week. Al had better have a good explanation.

He wanted to talk again to John Terrell and the other people in the shipping department. This was a number one priority.

There was a meeting scheduled with their foreign distributors this afternoon. He'd have to complete his preparations for that. He might have been told by the board of directors to concentrate on finding the tubing, but to all intents and purposes he was still vice president.

For that matter, after this was over, he might just stay on. He was beginning to like it here. Or was this an illusion created by his feeling toward Joellyn?

Not too swift. What if she was the guilty one?

And there was a lot of correspondence to be taken care of. He was beginning to wonder who had been doing all this work before he'd come on the scene. He hadn't replaced anyone; his had been a created position. He stopped in midstep, surprised by the thought that had unexpectedly sprung into his mind.

Who *had* been doing all this work before he'd come on the scene? Dobson? He'd have to find out.

But first he needed to talk to Joellyn.

He'd been putting it off all week, trying to create some distance between them, trying to take the edge off the feeling the two of them seemed to generate every time they came within twenty feet of each other. True, they hadn't come within twenty feet of each other more than once or twice in the past few days, but the times they had stood out vividly in his mind. Once when he brushed by her in the cafeteria and her perfume, faint but compelling, had stayed with him for hours afterward. And once when she passed him in the plant and nodded briefly. The flash of recognition that passed between them had all but undone him.

How could he conduct a realistic investigation when all he could think of was the way her hair looked, and her eyes . . . and the way her lips had tasted?

This was absurd. Totally ridiculous. He wasn't going to give in to this. It was probably only a rebound effect after his divorce. And loneliness. A trip to the health club should take care of that. Lord, how he needed a good workout!

But, in the meantime, the month-end reports were out this morning. He wanted to go through them with her to see firsthand what was in them. There was no time like the present. She wouldn't have had time to go through them by herself yet. He swung around and headed for Joellyn's office.

JOELLYN LOOKED UP when he entered her office and waited for him to speak.

Mike sat down and cleared his throat. "Good morning. I understand the month-end reports are out."

"Good morning, Mike." She kept her tone brisk, businesslike. "Yes, they are. Randy still has them." Her eyes were drawn to the scar by his mouth. How had he gotten it? Well, no matter. She looked away.

"I . . . ahem!" He cleared his throat again. "I was wondering if we could take a look at them together?"

"Certainly," she answered. "Randy should be done with them by now. I'll go get them—"

"Well, no, here . . . let me—where are they?" He started to rise.

"That's okay," she said, already halfway out the door. "I can get them. You just sit there. I'll be back in a minute."

She returned with an armful of heavy computer reports and dropped them onto the desk in front of him. "There they are," she announced. She sat back down and leaned her elbows on the desk, waiting.

He riffled through the first one. "Hmm," he murmured. "These look pretty complicated."

"They are complicated," she agreed.

He bent over the sheets, trying not to notice the faint scent of her hair. Or was it perfume? No, he decided silently, it was her hair. He turned a few pages in the second book, then closed it, frustrated. This was crazy. He'd never seen computer reports so garbled. Could she really work with them?

"Have you looked at the numbers yet?"

"Oh, yes," she said.

"And?"

She looked baffled and worried. "The perpetual is down another two hundred thousand from the book balance."

"Explain that to me," he said. "In words of one syllable or less, if you can. Remember, I'm not an accountant."

She smiled briefly. "Well, Mike," she explained, "we have a separate run generated only from inventory actually removed or added. This runs concurrently with the general ledger, but it's derived from different sources."

"Wait—" he protested, his voice rising "—are you telling me everything doesn't come from the same place?"

"Well, yes and no," she said. "They're *supposed* to be exactly the same because ultimately the sources are the same, but this is where the drop showed up in the first place."

"But *how?*" Mike persisted.

"Because," she explained patiently, "the perpetual is generated from actual removals or additions of the inventory from the storeroom, as I told you. Then it's taken to be processed, and the shipping documents take over from there."

She flinched as soon as she realized she'd said 'shipping documents.' Uncle John again. It was looking worse by the minute. She couldn't hide it from Mike or anyone else. No matter what she said or did, it was looking bad for Uncle John.

Mike saw her flinch. He kept his face impassive and leaned over the books. "It looks as if I'm going to need a little help here," he admitted. "How about if I swing around to your side so we can look at them together?"

"Fine with me," she murmured. "Bring your chair on over."

He brought the chair around and sat next to her. That was a mistake. He'd known it would be a mistake to get so close to her. The pull between them was there again, stronger than ever in the harsh reality of the fluorescent lighting. He felt an old, familiar tightening in his stomach, and he tried to fight off his irritation at himself.

Couldn't he even look at a computer run with her without wanting to slide his hand around her waist and pull her close? What kind of office behavior was this, anyhow?

Joellyn turned the pages, pointing out the different columns and totals and explaining what they meant, puzzled to discover, now that he'd brought it up, that she could see they *were* scrambled.

She'd grown up with the old system, and the way the plant manager had explained the new one to her when he had the reports generated had seemed clear enough. But now she could see why the auditors had been so confused. Now *she* was confused.

Or was it only that Mike was sitting right next to her, occasionally brushing her hand with his as he turned a page or pointed to a number? He wasn't doing it on purpose—or she didn't think so—but it kept happening. And what was the big deal if it did? They were only going through a computer report together.

Her eyes focused on the light red hairs springing out from beneath his blue shirtsleeve.

Business. That was all this was. Business.

They had been looking at the reports for thirty minutes and were no better off than when they'd begun when Mike closed the book. "This isn't getting us anywhere," he said with finality. "There's no way I can tell from these whether the beginning balance is okay or not, and I sure can't see how one thing flows into another."

"I tried to tell you that," she pointed out.

He leaned back and rubbed his eyes. "Yes, you did," he admitted. "And now I believe you."

"I'm so glad to hear that." She turned toward him.

"And you're saying this shows another two hundred thousand down?" he asked.

"Yes, I am. And it does."

Why didn't he just go away? He was *too close*.

"How, I wonder," he murmured, "could two hundred thousand dollars' worth of that stuff disappear between leaving the storeroom and hitting the shipping dock, if that's where the other part of the system takes over? It *has* to be something out there...." He stretched and forced a yawn. "Well, I've got a monster of a day ahead of me, as usual. This isn't getting us anywhere. I'd better get back to my office."

Fine, she thought. Why wasn't he leaving?

He still sat there, looking at her. "Remember I asked you if you wanted to meet my son this weekend?"

"Yes," she said.

"He'll be here tomorrow night," he said. "I thought I'd take him to the McDonald's down the road—the one with the swings and stuff."

"Sounds reasonable," she said noncommittally. "Most kids like McDonald's."

"Yeah." He started to get up, then abruptly sat back down. "Want to go with us?"

She smiled. "To McDonald's?"

His eyebrows rose in surprise.

"I'm sorry," she said. "I wasn't smiling at the idea of McDonald's, really I wasn't. It's just that I was surprised, I guess, that you'd ask me. But I can't go," she added. "I'm busy all day Saturday."

"Doing what?" he asked, then caught himself. "Not that it's any of my business."

"It's not that it's none of your business, exactly," she said gently. "It's just that it's sort of personal. It's something I don't talk about at work. It's just something I have to do."

"I understand," he said, even though he didn't. "Then how about dinner tonight?" he smiled. "I can promise you something a little more to your taste than McDonald's."

"I *love* McDonald's," she said. "But I can't, no matter where you want to go. I'm busy tonight."

That wasn't exactly true. She had nothing to do tonight, but she did want to go to John's house and talk to him. She couldn't talk to him here. Not the way she wanted to, anyway.

He pulled himself out of the chair. "Well," he said, "it was just an idea." He'd be better off if he checked into a health club and got some exercise, anyhow. He had a lot of frustration to work off.

"I have to give you credit for that much," she said. "It *was* an idea."

He laughed. "Is that anything like when you see a really ugly newborn baby and say, 'That *sure* is a baby'?"

"I don't know," Joellyn said in a low voice. "I've never seen an ugly newborn baby."

WHAP! Rivulets of sweat ran down Mike's neck, sliding past the muscles on his back and running down into his blue cutoffs. He swung around as the ball came back at him, caught it and slammed it against the wall, reveling in the satisfaction of winning again, even if it was only against himself.

He was beginning to feel a little more human now— hot, sticky and out of breath, but exhilarated. Three weeks without working out had left him feeling edgy and out of touch. *Whap!* The ball stung his hand as he slapped it in a high arc toward the top of the handball court. This was reality. Yeah! This was a lot better.

He had been in the court for twenty-five minutes now, slamming the ball without stopping. He loved the dank smell of the dressing room, the chlorine odor that burned his nostrils as he padded past the swimming pool area. Even the cold gray stucco walls felt like home to him. This was what he'd been missing, all right.

Work out some of the kinks. *Whap!* Make him forget everything. The plant, David... What was David doing right now? In bed in some motel probably, curled up with that awful brown stuffed toy owl. Had he let his mother wash it yet? The last time Mike had seen it, it looked as if it had been through World War III.

Mike stopped and stared at the wall as the ball ricocheted back and forth, missing him by inches as it bounced, slowing down to a dribble and finally rolling across the floor, coming to a stop in a corner. He was overwhelmed by a sudden vision of his son, a sturdy, red-haired little boy who loved to play outer space games.

Was six years old too young to have such an interest in those things? Mike didn't know, but every time he'd taken David for the weekend back in Philadelphia, David had added another space transformer to his collection.

"Dad, Dad, look in the window. Over there. There's a yellow one!"

"David, you already have a yellow one. I bought you one just three weeks ago, remember?"

"Yes, but that was a different yellow one. I need this one, too. Please, Daddy. Please?"

What was he supposed to do with a six-year-old when he only had him for occasional weekends? There were only so many times they could go to the zoo, although David could stare for what seemed like hours at the bears.

"David, it's time to go now. Your mother wants you home by six."

"Just five more minutes. Please, Daddy? I want to see if he jumps in the water again. Just five more minutes. Mama won't get mad. I promise."

But she always did. Dani was a stickler for being on time. Even five minutes would get her going, no matter what the circumstances.

So he'd taken David to parks, the standard gathering place for all weekend fathers. Mike would sit on a bench with the other fathers, lost-looking men who would keep a wary eye on their kids as the kids shouted and swung and climbed on the monkey bars, while the fathers swapped notes and tried to figure out what to do next with their children.

"Have you tried the zoo?"

"Yeah. Twice last month. How about you?"

"Same here. What about the museum?"

"I tried that last week. He was bored. It's not worth it, listening to him complain about all the walking."

"Yeah. The kids today sure are soft."

"How about the movies? My two like to go there. At least it keeps 'em quiet for a while."

Movies were out. David was too young for most of them, and he doubted whether a six-year-old boy could sit still that long, anyway. So they'd usually ended up at the toy store, with David loading up on toys he would probably never play with after the first day or two.

What good were transformers and train sets that he couldn't be around to set up, laughing and cheering with David as the cars raced around the bend and through the tunnels?

The only way he could really have a decent relationship with his son was to *be* there, tucking him in every night and kissing him on the forehead, even if he did have to kiss the owl, too.

The sudden sting of tears pulled him back to the handball court. Somebody was banging on the door, shouting that his time was up. He grabbed his towel and dabbed at his eyes and neck as he headed for the pool, circling around a group of laughing, jostling young men.

He stretched out in the whirlpool, letting the hot, salty water bubble around every part of his body. It felt terrific after twelve laps around the icy pool. He might be able to sleep tonight, after all. And David would be here tomorrow night.... He needed to see his son. Joellyn had pointed that out.

Joellyn.

Her name sprang into his mind unbidden. What was it about her that kept drawing him to her side? Like a moth to a flame—the old cliché drifted through his mind.

Was that what he was doing? Was he drawn to her primarily because he definitely shouldn't be, especially right now? Was he trying to close himself off from any possibility of a serious relationship because he was still hurting from the last one? Or was it simply that he was new in the area and he knew no other women? He closed his eyes as her face swam into his vision.

It wasn't that difficult. She was right there: those lovely, compelling blue eyes that seemed to look straight through to his soul; the full, soft lips that drove him crazy whenever he thought of their taste; the warm, soft arms that had wound around his neck, pulling him closer...

If she was part of the theft at United, and he was pretty sure it was theft, then he might be in big trouble himself because he needed to hold her close to know he was okay, to feel strong and whole again.

He pulled himself out of the whirlpool. Hot water poured from his shoulders and down his legs into a widening pool on the floor as he reached for the towel, dried himself off and headed for the locker room.

One more day. In one more day he'd see his son, and at least part of his world would be whole again, if only for a little while.

CHAPTER FIVE

JOELLYN EASED the Porsche onto the asphalt driveway next to John Terrell's house. The sky was jetblack and the wind was beginning to roll in short, damp loops. The weather forecaster had said it was going to be warm and sunny all weekend, but maybe he hadn't been counting Friday night. It definitely felt like rain.

John's gray pickup was parked in the driveway in front of his garage. The overhead doors were closed, and there was no light on inside as far as she could tell.

Joellyn swung her car door open and made her way toward the house. Her high heels sank into the damp soil between sparse clumps of grass that had fought their way through the bitter Chicago winter. She shivered as the chilly wind penetrated her coat and blew her hair into her eyes.

The living room window facing the front porch was open about six inches. Apparently John was home, but the house was dark.

Joellyn climbed the front steps and stepped over to the window to peek in. She felt terribly sneaky, but this was no time to bring out the party manners. There were things she had to know. Especially now, because she'd been having the sinking feeling for some time that John might be falling back into his old pattern.

Thirty-five years ago, at the age of twenty-one, John Terrell had been arrested and sentenced to ten years in the federal penitentiary for taking part in a bank robbery.

Fortunately for John, he'd only been driving the getaway car. He'd drawn a shorter sentence than the others and had managed to get two years off for good behavior.

He was a model prisoner, they'd said.

Joellyn hadn't been born yet when he went to prison the first time, but she'd heard her parents discussing it often enough. Just thinking about it made her cringe.

John had been a juvenile delinquent early on, according to her mother. He'd stolen his first car when he was sixteen. Tires, radios out of parked cars—there didn't seem to be anything John couldn't or wouldn't steal.

But none of the people in their small Illinois town had ever pressed charges at first. They'd looked the other way until the day his luck had run out and he'd been caught pulling the big one.

Joellyn was three years old when John got out of prison the first time. The townspeople were polite to him but still suspicious. He'd been a criminal once, they reasoned, he could become one again. But months passed without incident, and people began to relax.

Then one blistering hot August evening John was caught driving eighty-five miles an hour through the middle of town after having just attacked the police chief with a tire iron.

No one ever really understood why John had done that. The police chief would never discuss it publicly, and neither would John. But the gossip swept through their small Midwestern town, swift and humiliating.

So he went back to prison, this time for five more years. When he got out this time, Joellyn was nine years old, and John Terrell was a very quiet man.

He stayed with her parents until he could get back on his feet. This took almost two years, and during this time Joellyn had grown very close to him.

It was so hard to believe all the terrible things she'd heard about him. How could anyone who so gently and carefully helped her patch up the stray birds and animals she brought home possibly have done all that?

But he had. She'd read the newspaper clippings, and she remembered the gossip.

Then Joy came along, and John fell in love. The entire town breathed a collective sigh of relief. At last! John Terrell had settled down.

John and Joy moved to a Chicago suburb and bought a house, and John went to work at United Tubing. They never investigated his past. There was no reason to; he was only applying for a job on the production line. And he was content. He'd put his past behind him.

Then Joy encouraged him to go to night school. Five years later he was promoted to shipping manager, totally responsible for all movement of inventory in and out of United Tubing.

During this time, Joellyn spent part of every summer with them. She adored her aunt. Joy was everything her name implied—carefree, fun-loving, warm. The house echoed with her laughter and her music and her love. Then, the year Joellyn turned eighteen, they discovered Joy had cancer. Six months later she was gone, and the life just seemed to go out of John.

Three years later Joellyn was thinking seriously about her future. A University of Chicago graduate with a cum laude degree in accounting was in hot demand, but none of the job offers she received were in her small town. Most of them were on the East or West Coast. Then John told her about an opening in the accounting department at United.

She thought it over carefully. Did she really want to go to work in the same company as her uncle? John seemed all right. Quiet . . . too quiet. But all right.

So she'd applied for the job, used his name as a reference and gone straight out of college into a terrific job at United. At least it had been terrific then. But now . . . now it was a different story. Now it seemed as though her job and her quiet, insulated world would never be the same again.

The management suspected Uncle John. And who could blame them? Who really knew? Who could tell for certain what was in John's heart and in his mind? She couldn't, and she probably knew him better than anyone else . . . or at least she'd thought so up to now.

A blast of wind swept across the open porch as she peered at her watch in the dim light and shivered again. Eight-fifteen—too early for him to be in bed unless he was watching television. Or unless he was sick . . .

Panic interrupted her thoughts as she felt a hand clamp down hard on her shoulder. Adrenaline racing, she whirled around to find herself looking straight into John's eyes. "Oh!" she gasped. "I didn't hear you come up behind me! Where were you?"

"Ah—" he gestured vaguely toward the backyard "—just out there. What are you doing here this time of night, anyhow, Missy?" His soft brown eyes smiled down at her when he used the nickname he'd first given her when she was a child.

She stared at him in dismay. Every time she'd seen him lately he'd been looking worse. In the dim light his face had a pinched expression, and his hair was even thinner than it had been two weeks ago in her office. What was left of it seemed to have turned gray overnight.

She hesitated, then drew a deep breath, gathering courage. "Uncle John," she said, "I have to talk to you."

He peered at her. "Why, sure," he agreed slowly. "Sure thing. I'm glad you came by. I want to talk to you, too. C'mon in. Don't stand out here all night. You'll catch cold." He held the door open for her and flicked the living room light on.

She was consumed with guilt. It had been months since she'd been here last—more than that. It had been over a year. And nothing had changed since the last time she'd been here. Nothing.

The living room sofa still had a rip in one arm, limp threads still dangled from the jagged, three-cornered piece of maroon fabric. Dark wooden coffee tables still held doilies that Joy had crocheted just before she'd died, and that had once stood proudly under tall ceramic lamps, their starched ruffles surrounding the bases. Now they lay flat and needed washing. Everything in the room needed cleaning, and the fireplace looked as though it hadn't been used at all over the winter. The house smelled musty in spite of the open window.

Looking at this only made her feel worse. Why hadn't she paid more attention to him? They seldom ran into each other at work; they were both too busy.

She had no idea what he did in his free time. But she should have made a point of seeing him at least once a week. Maybe then none of this would have ever happened.

If he'd had anything to do with the thefts at United.

"Well?" he asked, motioning for her to sit down. "What's up?" His eyes looked tired and wary.

"I don't know how to begin," she murmured, looking down at the floor. She couldn't look at him, couldn't bear the look in his eyes. She was sure he knew why she was here.

He reached over and tipped her chin up. "Joellyn, let's not kid around here. Out with it now. What's on your mind?"

Her hands twisted the fingers of her glove. "It's just that... I need to know for sure if... I wanted to talk to you privately, away from—" She stopped.

He tipped his head again and raised one eyebrow. He'd always done that whenever she was trying to avoid telling him something. It had always worked. Always.

"Jo?" he asked quietly, waiting.

She rubbed at her eyes, then blurted out, "I don't want to ask this. It's the last thing I want to ask, but—" She stopped again, unable to go on.

"The tubing," he said quietly. "That's it, isn't it?"

"Yes," she whispered. "I have to know. I just have to hear it for myself. Uncle John, *did* you have anything to do with it?"

"No," he said. "And I don't know nothing about it, either."

"Are you *sure*, Uncle John. Don't you have any idea who might be doing it?"

"No, hon. I don't." He shifted uneasily in his chair.

"But, Uncle John, how could they get it out of the plant without you knowing about it? That's impossible!"

He stood and walked over to the fireplace, jabbing at the dead logs with a poker, silent for a minute. "Do you think I had anything to do with it?"

"I... I don't—no, I don't think so," she admitted. "But if they investigate, if they really go back..." Her voice trailed off.

He finished the sentence for her. "They'll find out about my record. Right?"

"Yes," she whispered.

"And they'll figure it's me, right?"

"They might," she admitted. "They probably will."

He smiled. "And that puts you right in the pickle jar, doesn't it? Guilt by association. Isn't that how it goes?"

"Oh," she protested, "I'm not really worried about that...." But her mind darted back to the words she had spoken to Mike that night in the restaurant.

How do you know a woman didn't do it?

She drew her coat around her, suddenly cold. How could she have made a remark like that? Was that what he'd been thinking all along? Was that why he'd taken her out and asked all those questions? If he already knew about Uncle John's prison record and suspected them both... guilt by association...

"Uncle John," she murmured, suddenly ashamed, "I'm sorry. I don't really think you had anything to do with it. If you say you didn't, I believe you. As long as you say you didn't."

He took a minute before answering. "Well, Missy, I say I didn't. Now whether they're gonna believe that or not is another question. But really," he said, smiling, "what would I do with all that tubing? That's pretty silly, isn't it? Where would I keep it?" He looked around. "Out in my garage? Hell," he said, laughing, "I haven't even got room for my truck out there, much less a million dollars' worth of that stuff." He grinned. "Do you have any idea how much room you'd have to have just to store it?"

"I guess that's true," she agreed.

"Now look here," he said, "you quit worrying about me. I haven't done anything wrong, so go on home now and get some sleep. They'll find out who did it sooner or later. All I know is, it's not gonna be me!"

Joellyn gave him a quick, fierce hug. "I know it's not you," she murmured. "I just had to ask you myself."

"Sure," he said. "Now go on home, Missy, and get some rest." He looked down at her, his dark eyes smiling. "You look like hell. I'm not used to seeing my girl look so bad."

"You're not looking so hot yourself," she said, pausing at the door. "Uncle John, let's have dinner soon, okay? We never have time to just sit and talk anymore."

He nodded. "Sure. That'd be fine. But call first. And I don't want to see any more of those dark circles under your eyes, you hear me?"

She nodded and waved goodbye, heading down the driveway. The light in the living room went out before she reached the car.

She started the car, backed slowly out of the driveway and was half a block away when a thought struck her.

What had he just said?

Hell, I haven't even got room for my truck out there.

Why didn't he have room for his truck in the garage? It was a two-car garage, and he didn't own a car. All he ever drove was the pickup.

She pulled over to the curb and rested her head on the steering wheel for a minute, searching her soul. Either she trusted him or she didn't. She loved him so much... And he *had* changed over the years; there was no doubt about it.

But still... What had he meant, there was no room in his garage? There had always been *plenty* of room in his garage.

Sick at heart, she opened her purse, searching for her tiny red flashlight. She was determined to go back and look in the garage. Just a look, that was all, even though she felt really rotten about it. Her hand pushed frantically into the bottom of her purse while her mind raced. How far did family love go? How far could she trust her instinct when it told her he was innocent? He *had* to be innocent, and at the same time a little voice was telling her it *was* possible. Anything was possible....

She located the flashlight, but she still needed a pin to stick into the door switch so that the car's overhead light wouldn't go on. Lee had taught her that when he first started doing investigative reporting, but she'd never in her wildest dreams thought she'd be using the trick herself, especially doing something as despicable as snooping in her uncle's garage.

Damn it, *where was the pin?* She'd had one earlier today. She fumbled in her haste, her fingers searching the bottom of her purse lining. Okay, yeah, this would do it—a toothpick. She straightened her shoulders and drew another deep breath, gearing herself to do something that went directly against everything she'd ever been taught.

She opened the car door a crack and jammed the toothpick into the switch. Then she slipped out into the darkness and headed back down the street toward the garage, shivering under the heavy mist that drifted down over her shoulders. She reached the door and forced herself to stand on tiptoe, aiming the flashlight's narrow yellow beam into the depths of the garage. And gasped out loud with shock when she saw what was there.

She knew what they were. She'd seen enough of them. She'd been to a hundred antique auto shows with Lee. He'd almost bought one until he'd found out what they cost.

They cost plenty. More than plenty. She'd been astonished at the prices when she looked at them with Lee.

And now she was staring at over six hundred thousand dollars' worth of antique automobiles in her uncle's garage. Even in the faint beam her flashlight provided she could tell they were in mint condition.

On one side of the garage was a white 1931 Mercedes-Benz 190. You couldn't have touched one for less than three hundred and twenty-five thousand dollars six years ago. Now it was probably closer to three-fifty.

And right next to it stood a cream-colored 1928 Deusenberg. That one had to be worth three hundred thousand dollars at least. It had been the last time she saw one, and the price on those cars only increased with time.

Where had her Uncle John found that kind of money?

Nauseated, she headed back toward her car. She glanced quickly back toward the house before she got in, terribly relieved to see that his lights were still off. If nothing else, at least he would never know that she'd found out about them. But why hadn't he told her? If it was all innocent, why had he kept it such a big secret? He'd had plenty of chances to tell her, hadn't he?

She started the ignition and headed slowly down the street. Then she turned the heater on full force, trying to ease the chill that had settled into her shoulders, leaving her numb and cold.

She turned the corner, driving slowly through the darkened side streets toward her apartment complex. Drops of rain splattered against the windshield, tiny prisms of pale blue and translucent silver reflecting the faint glow of the streetlights.

She cursed herself for being so stupid. Of course Uncle John had said he didn't know anything about the thefts. What had she expected him to say?

Had she really thought he'd tell her if he did?

MIKE GLANCED at the clock when the phone rang. Nine o'clock. He thought maybe it was Joellyn, saying she'd like to join him and David tomorrow night, then remembered she didn't have his number. So, in that case, since he didn't know anyone else in Chicago to speak of, it was probably Dani, triple-checking to make sure he'd be home tomorrow night. Securing the world, as usual. Checking every detail down to the last millisecond. As if he'd miss even a minute with his son. He sighed and picked up the receiver.

"Hello?" He was right. It was Dani. He gulped. The last time he'd heard her voice it had been raised in anger, as usual, but this time she sounded warmer, more contented somehow.

"Danielle, how are you? How's the trip?"

There was a pause. "Fine, Mike. We're in Kentucky now. I'm just making sure you'll be home tomorrow."

He'd been right. She hadn't changed that much, no matter how soft her voice sounded. She'd probably call three more times tomorrow, just to make sure. He sighed heavily. "I'll be here, Danielle. How's David?"

"I'll put him on the phone in a minute. We'll drop him off at six tomorrow night, if that's okay. We can pick him up early Sunday afternoon."

Six o'clock! Not 6:05. He'd bet on it. And now she couldn't wait to get off the phone. "Dani, wait a minute. Do you want me to drop him at your hotel later in the afternoon Sunday?"

"No, Mike. We have our plans all set. As soon as we pick him up, we're heading home."

He heard her drop the receiver and call David, and he sighed again. So much for more time with his son. But she was right; he couldn't expect her to change her plans at the last minute. He'd never changed his for her.

"Daddy?"

Mike smiled inside. "David. How are you, son?"

"Fine. Daddy, we saw Mickey Mouse and we saw horses on the way here and there's a swimming pool inside and I'm going to jump in and maybe I can go down the—" He stopped and then continued in a subdued voice. "Daddy Joe says I can go down the slide at the pool. He says he'll stand at the bottom and catch me."

Mike's eyes focused on a coffee stain in the carpeting. Odd, he'd never noticed it before, but there it was—a dark blotch. "That sounds fine," he said heavily. "Whatever your mother and...Joe say. Look, I have an idea. How'd you like to eat at McDonald's tomorrow night? There's a jungle gym there you can climb on...."

David's voice was small, hesitant. "We had McDonald's tonight, Daddy. I already climbed on the jungle gym."

Pow! There went his big plans for the evening. Think fast. There must be something else he liked to do. But what? And where *was* everything here? Damn it, why had he moved from Philadelphia? At least there he knew where everything was. "David, how about this? We can go get a pizza. How's that sound?"

"With pepperoni?" David's voice rose, hopeful. Mike belatedly remembered Danielle had never let David eat pizza, with or without pepperoni. Well, maybe this one time.

"With pepperoni," Mike promised solemnly, smiling at David's excitement, listening while he dropped the receiver and ran to tell his mother. Mike could hear his excited voice in the background.

Dani picked up the phone again. "I hope you're not setting him up for a stomachache, Mike. Remember, we're traveling."

He shook his head. "I'll keep him from eating too much, Danielle. Surely this once can't hurt."

"I hope so, Mike." Why did her voice always seem to hold a threat? It was almost as though she wanted to cut him off from David entirely. Anyway, that was how it always made him feel. . . .

"We'll be there at six, Mike." She hung up the phone without saying goodbye.

He stared at the phone for a few minutes, then picked up the receiver again and dialed Joellyn's number.

JOELLYN HAD BEEN LYING in bed, wide awake and shivering under her electric blanket when the phone rang. She stuck her head out from under the blanket and looked at the backlit hands on her bedside alarm clock. Nine-thirty. Who could be calling her now? No one ever called at this hour. Apprehensive, she lifted the receiver.

"Hello?"

It was Mike. "Joellyn?"

"Yes."

"It didn't sound like you for a minute. Are you all right?"

"Yes." Why were the same people who were making her not all right so concerned about whether she was all right or not?

"Well, that's good." He sounded relieved. "Look, I was just thinking. I might go bike riding tomorrow morning before David gets here, and I was wondering if you'd like to go. Just out in the country for a little R and R."

Bicycle riding in the country? Was he insane? "Mike," she said, "I can't. I'm busy tomorrow."

He sounded disappointed. "All day? Can't you make it for a little while?"

She checked the blanket's temperature control. It was on high—why was she still so *cold?*

"Mike, I really can't," she said. "Besides, I don't own a bicycle. I never have."

He laughed. "Oh, I didn't mean bike as in bicycle. I have a motorcycle. There's plenty of room for two people."

A motorcycle. Well, great, terrific. No way was she going to ride on one of those things. Absolutely not! And besides that, she didn't want to see him.

She shifted under the covers. "Mike," she said sleepily, "I don't, as in do not, want to ride on a motorcycle. Those things are dangerous."

"Oh, come on, Joellyn. Not if you're careful, and I promise I'll be careful."

Didn't he know the meaning of the word *no?* She sighed heavily. "I told you, I can't. I'm going to be busy all day tomorrow. I have to go to a picnic."

"A picnic?" There was a pause. "Alone?"

"Yes, alone," she said. "And I don't want to ride on whatever you call it. Period. Thanks, anyway." She started to hang up the phone.

"Joellyn?"

"Yes, Mike." She gritted her teeth.

"Isn't it a little cold for a picnic?"

Damn it! Now he thought he was her mother. "It's not exactly a *picnic* picnic. It's more of an outing...." She was getting confused. Maybe she was finally getting sleepy. About time, too.

"With food?" he asked, suddenly realizing he'd forgotten to eat dinner. Funny, he'd never done that before.

"With food," she said. "Yes." She felt her body finally warming. Was it the blanket, finally, or was it the sound of his voice?

"When are you leaving?" he asked.

"Early. Early," she said again, acutely aware that she was repeating herself. "About eight or so. Why?"

"Just wondered," he said, chuckling. "You sound as if you're half asleep." There was a pause. "Joellyn, are you still there?"

Yes, she was still there. His words echoed in her mind. She sounded as if she was half asleep? Well, she wasn't half asleep. His voice was coming through loud and clear, forcing thoughts of Uncle John to the background, and she didn't want him forced to the background. She wanted to be sharp and clear, to be able to sift through the rubble of what she'd seen earlier in Uncle John's garage and come up with a clear solution. She'd never be able to do it if she kept talking to Mike. His voice affected her too much.

"Yes, I'm still here," she mumbled. "I'm just sleepy, that's all." That wasn't true. She'd never been more awake in her life. "I'm sorry about tomorrow, Mike. I just can't make it, that's all."

He chuckled again. "Well, maybe we can work something out. Think about it. Maybe I'll see you in the morning."

In the morning? What the heck did he mean, see her in the morning? Didn't he know how to take no for an answer? She said good-night, dropped the receiver back into its cradle, switched out the light and lay in the darkness, trying to think. But no matter how she tried to shut it out, Mike's face hovered in her mind, obscuring her thoughts far into the night.

JOELLYN FORCED one eyelid open, groaned and snapped it shut against the unexpected glare of the early-morning sun. She thought it over for a minute, then opened both eyes and focused on her bedside clock. Six-thirty. What was she doing awake this early on a Saturday morning? She wanted to sleep. Her eyes closed again, then flew open.

Oh. Yes. The sun was shining. Finally! And today was the outing. They were taking a bus load of kids to O'Hare to watch the planes take off and land. Most of these kids probably couldn't comprehend what an airplane was, but they would love the noise and commotion of the airport. And the hot dogs at Frankie's afterward.

She had become involved with the Lakeland Home for Handicapped Children quite by accident a few years back, and she'd never regretted it for an instant.

At loose ends after she and Lee had broken up, she had dropped by one afternoon with an acquaintance who was checking on her sister. Up to that point she'd never been aware there was a home like this one around.

Oh, she'd read articles and seen TV shows about mentally and physically handicapped children and their special needs, but none of those brief glimpses had prepared her for what she'd found when she visited those kids for the first time.

She'd expected extreme misery and sick, unhappy children, and she had found some of that, to be sure, but she'd also found something totally different and far more important.

She had found love. Totally accepting, completely unconditional love.

She'd gone home that first night with wet eyes and an aching heart. The next morning she'd returned alone and volunteered to spend one evening a week with them. It was the one day a week that she wouldn't stay at United after five o'clock. She closed her eyes again. She could stay here for a few more minutes. She was so tired....

She felt a cold, wet nose nudging her bare arm. Apparently Penny wanted to go out.

Joellyn's blanket slid, disappearing down toward the foot of her bed. She groaned and yanked at it, trying to cover herself back up. She was determined not to get up this instant, but the blanket was being pulled slowly and firmly off the bed.

Resigned, she climbed out of bed and reached for her robe. She wrapped the belt around her waist and headed for the sliding door, with Penny dancing around her legs. She laughed and rubbed the dog's head.

What a terrific dog! Penny loved to go outside and she loved to come inside and she loved to eat and she loved to jump on the furniture. Penny loved everything. It must be nice to live such an uncomplicated life.

It was a good thing she was going with the kids today. She needed to get away someplace where she wouldn't have time to think about Uncle John or United or...her eyes widened. Mike! What had he said last night? *Maybe I'll see you in the morning.* She frowned. Surely he wasn't going to come over here and try to convince her to go for a ride on his... bike?

She snorted while she dropped a couple of pieces of bread into the toaster and headed back to the bedroom to dress. Fat chance! By the time he got here, *if* he got here, she'd be gone, anyhow. And besides that, she wasn't getting on a motorcycle for him or anyone else.

Then she remembered a conversation she'd had with her mother.

Her mother had started right in as always.

"Joellyn, when are you going to get married and give me some grandchildren?"

"You have two dogs, Mom. Isn't that enough?"

"Not really, dear. If you don't get a move on, you're going to wind up an old maid."

"Mom, that expression went out with saddle shoes and pin curls!"

Her mother had refused to be sidetracked. "You're going to wind up baby-sitting with children who call you Auntie Jo! Do you want to be called Auntie Jo all your life?"

Joellyn had laughed, but it looked as though her mother's dire predictions were coming true. She was probably entirely too picky, just as her mother had said.

And she was beginning to wonder herself just what the problem really was. She'd do something about it, if only she knew where to start, but she never had time. It had been ages since she'd relaxed long enough to listen to her old tapes—music of the seventies that had once been such an important part of her life. There never seemed to be enough time anymore.

Never enough time for fun.

As it now stood, she felt as though she were stuck in a time warp, floating in space without a lifeline.

At least the astronauts had lifelines.

She reached for her favorite old rust-colored sweater and slipped it over her head, loving the soft whisper of the cashmere against her skin, and eyed her reflection in the mirror, remembering her mother's parting shot.

"Joellyn, all those cashmeres you have aren't going to keep you warm through those cold Chicago nights. You have to take them off sometime, and when you do, there's nothing that can warm you like the body of the man you love next to you in bed."

Her mother was right about that, too. An electric blanket didn't cut it, no matter what the manufacturer said.

She finished dressing and brought Penny in, then reached for her purse. At least she'd be too busy to dwell on her problems today. Nobody could think in all the bedlam those kids created. The noise and commotion would be good for her. She wouldn't have time to think about Uncle John or the missing inventory.

Or Mike. Most of all, Mike.

She was about to open the door when she heard the knock. Trying to hide her irritation, she opened the door to find Mike leaning against the doorjamb with a motorcycle helmet in his hand, his eyes sparkling with suppressed mirth.

"Hi," he said. "Would you like a ride to the picnic?"

CHAPTER SIX

JOELLYN STARED openmouthed at him. "Mike," she said, "I told you no last night."

He smiled, the same slow smile that had knocked her out the first time she'd seen him. And like it or not, it was having the same effect on her right now.

"Well," he pointed out, "there's always a chance you might change your mind. And I just happened to be passing by...."

She sighed. The last thing she needed right now was this man cluttering up her mind and confusing her. She'd been counting on spending the entire day with the kids. Seeing him only reminded her of problems she wanted to forget for one day—only one day. Was that so much to ask? And she certainly didn't have time for his motorcycle nonsense.

She glanced pointedly at her watch, astonished to find she was, as usual, running late. "You 'happened to be passing by' *this early?*" she asked.

"Well, sort of," he said, still smiling. "I really did think you might change your mind."

She was beginning to be irritated. "You thought wrong. Please, Mike, I have to leave. I'm very late."

He chuckled, and she felt her insides knot up at the sound. "Well," he said, "if you're so late, come on out and hop on. I can get you there pretty fast."

"I can get there fast enough by myself."

His helmet swung from his index finger. "But I can get you there faster." He raised his eyebrows and smiled, obviously enjoying himself.

"Not that fast, thank you. I'd like to get there in one piece, if you don't mind. Those things aren't safe."

He laughed and glanced into her living room. "And who told you this?" he teased. "Penny? Hey, Penny! How's the diet?" he called, waving in the general direction of the dog.

Joellyn mentally tapped her foot. She'd never known a man with so much audacity, or such strong-looking shoulders. She eyed his shoulders. He was wearing the obligatory black leather motorcycle jacket and boots and jeans, but on him they looked—somehow—respectable. This was no chain-swinging biker. Just an ordinary man out for a Saturday morning ride.

Ordinary? Who was she kidding? This man was *not* ordinary. What was the expression—'let the buyer beware'? Well, she wasn't buying.

"Mike," she said firmly, "I have to leave. I'll be late if I don't get going. And, no, I don't want to ride to the outing on a—" She glanced past him at the mammoth motorcycle propped against the curb. "Good Lord," she gasped, "what *is* that thing?"

"Hey!" he protested, looking wounded. "Watch what you're calling a 'thing.' That's a 1947 Harley-Davidson Knucklehead. It's a genuine antique." The pride in his voice was unmistakable.

"An antique?" she repeated. Why, all of a sudden, was everyone around her collecting antiques?

He smiled. "I bought it for only three hundred dollars, but I spent five thousand restoring it. What do you think? Like it?"

"I'll tell you what I like," she said. "A thrifty man." She wrinkled her nose. "That looks like something the Fonz would ride."

"Aha!" Mike's eyes lit up. "Just as I thought! You're pretty observant. It's exactly like the one he rode in *Happy Days*."

"I'm not so observant," she retorted. "They all look alike to me."

"Oh." He looked crestfallen.

Joellyn checked her watch. "Mike," she said, "I'm sorry, but I really have to go. If you'll just excuse me..." She walked past him and pulled the door shut behind her.

Mike followed her down the walk. "Are you sure I can't take you? I'm terrific at outings."

"How humble you are," she remarked over her shoulder as she headed for her car. "Thrifty *and* humble. That's so refreshing!" She stopped and turned toward him. "Look, Mike, this isn't an ordinary outing. You probably wouldn't like it."

Mike ran his fingers through his hair and unzipped his jacket halfway. "How do you know? You don't know me that well. Yet," he added.

She stood, undecided, then turned back. "Mike...it's an outing for mentally and physically handicapped kids," she explained. "It's a kind of special day for them. We're taking them to the airport. Most of them have never seen an airplane up close. And on the way home we're stopping for hot dogs. It may not sound like much, but that's what we're doing."

She looked straight at him, waiting but guarded. She had the strange feeling his reaction was going to be important to her.

His eyes opened wide. "You're kidding!"

She shook her head. "I never kid about things like that."

He looked perplexed. "Is one of them a relative of yours?"

"Nope. They're just a bunch of kids who need someone who cares." She shrugged and lifted her arms. "I care."

"Well, I'll be damned," he murmured. "Do you do this often?" He was staring at her as if he'd never seen her before.

"The outings, no," she said. "I haven't had much time lately. But I do spend time with them, yes, every Wednesday evening." She opened her car door.

He put his hand on the door to stop her, but she shook it off. "Mike," she said, her voice rising, "I have to leave."

He looked at her for a long minute, then seemed to make up his mind. "I'd like to go with you," he said quietly. "I may be able to help. I have a child myself, you know. Come on, get in on the other side. I'll drive."

They drove in silence for a few minutes after she gave him directions to the home.

Mike spoke first. "I tried to call you earlier in the evening last night."

"I was out," Joellyn said abruptly. She didn't want to discuss her visit to Uncle John. She wanted to forget about it.

"So I gathered. I was going to invite you to dinner."

"I had to see someone." She prayed he'd drop the subject.

"Oh." He glanced sideways at her.

They rode in silence for a few minutes.

"I went to the health club," he said.

"You said you were going to," she answered, relieved to be on neutral ground once again.

He turned a corner. "Haven't you ever been to one? Even once?"

"Actually, no," she admitted. "I never seem to have the time...." Her voice trailed off.

"I can understand that, in view of what you do with your spare time." He turned and smiled at her. "But working up a sweat a couple of times a week is good for you."

She didn't answer.

"Well, it is!" he insisted, trying to overcome the look of distaste on her face.

"I suppose you jog, too?" she asked.

"Sure. Every morning." He stopped in confusion, watching her eyes glaze over in the rearview mirror.

"*Every* morning?" she asked, astonished.

"Every morning," he affirmed. "Rain or shine."

"Unbelievable," she murmured, almost to herself.

Mike changed the subject. "Tell me about these kids. What should I do?"

"Do?" She stared at him.

"Yes... well, what I mean is, do we carry them, or do they walk? How should I act around them?"

She smiled. That was a valid question. He probably didn't know anything about handling these kids. From what he'd said, his son was a healthy little boy.

"Don't act," she said. "Just be natural. And, yes, we do have to lift some of them. That shouldn't be any problem for you, although after you've lifted a couple of these kids, you'll be wishing you'd gone back to the health club a lot sooner. Some of them are severely retarded," she added. "But you never know. They may understand everything you're saying, so be careful what you say in front of them. Some of them don't give any indication one way or the other that they've heard anything. It gets pretty disheartening sometimes. I hope you can handle it."

"I do, too," he said. "To tell you the truth, I feel honored that you're letting me tag along."

She laughed. "You didn't give me much choice, did you?"

He stopped for a red light and turned toward her. "But now that I am coming with you, aren't you glad to have me along?"

She felt her face flushing. He came straight to the point, didn't he? "I'm glad to have you along, Mike," she answered truthfully. "But I have to tell you one thing."

He turned into the home's parking lot. "And that is?"

"I really need a break. I don't want to talk or even think about United today. Or all weekend, if I can help it."

"You're right," he agreed. "I don't want to think about it, either. Let's both just enjoy this day. There's nothing we can do about the situation at work over the weekend, anyhow."

He followed her out of the car, and they headed toward a group of volunteers waiting outside the building. Joellyn introduced them and then took him inside.

"We'll get Joey first. He's a Down's syndrome child," she explained. "Down's syndrome is almost becoming a thing of the past. There used to be a lot more of it, but now with the prenatal test they do today not many of them are born anymore."

Joey was sitting alone on the edge of his bed.

"Joey?" She spoke softly. "I want you to meet Mike. He's going to help us today."

Mike took Joey's hand and smiled down at him. "We're going to have a good time today, aren't we, Joey?"

Joey's impassive eyes studied Mike's face for a long minute, then something seemed to click in his mind, and his face broke out into the most blissfully innocent, beautiful smile Mike had ever seen.

Joey held his hand tightly. Mike had a sudden flash of David's face as he looked down at Joey, and he felt overpowered by sensations of sadness and frustration. Tears stung his eyes. Why did these things happen to innocent children? And by what miracle, what selective process, was David so healthy and Joey like this?

He lifted Joey and sat him in the wheelchair, tickling him and making him laugh out loud. Then they wheeled him outside and carried him onto the bus, giving him an extra hug as they strapped him into his seat.

As they climbed off the bus, Mike saw Joey's arms reach out to them as if to hold them there. Shaken, he followed Joellyn back into the building.

Joellyn hadn't missed the anguished look in Mike's eyes. She touched his arm and smiled at him. "Joey's my favorite," she confessed. "And I'll tell you, at the risk of sounding overly dramatic, I truly believe these are God's special children."

"Yes," Mike said, breathing deeply and searching in his pocket for a handkerchief so he could blow his nose. "I can see why they're referred to as special."

She led him past a small, brightly decorated room. "This is the CP classroom," she explained. "They're the ones with cerebral palsy. This classroom is for the severely handicapped children who can't go to a regular school. Most of them live at home with their families." She paused, then went on in a low voice. "But the kids we're taking out today don't, for the most part, have homes they can go to."

Mike stopped short in the hallway outside a room with six children in wheelchairs, stunned at what he saw.

"Yes," Joellyn said softly, watching him try to control his emotions. "These are the severely brain-damaged kids. They're completely dependent on their house parents twenty-four hours a day."

"Their house parents?" Mike was shocked at the plight of these children who appeared perfectly normal until he looked into their eyes. And not one of them was more than ten years old.

"We're taking them, aren't we?" he asked, turning away to blow his nose again.

"You bet," she said matter-of-factly. "We sure are. Grab yourself a wheelchair. We've got work to do."

BY FOUR O'CLOCK that afternoon the kids were all back in their home, and Mike was still shaken. This had been one of the most emotionally trying experiences of his life; and, at the same time, one of the most exhilarating.

How had he gotten so lucky? he wondered, wheeling the last child back into the home. His son was whole and healthy. He'd never before this day realized just how lucky he was. And he could see why Joellyn loved these kids. He was beginning to love them himself.

He had watched her gentle hands as she'd fed the ones who were unable to feed themselves, and he'd marveled at the way she'd handled them as though they were her own. She was going to be a wonderful mother someday.

And this was the same woman who, even now, was under investigation for possible complicity in a major corporate theft? There was no way. She was totally incapable of anything like that. He was sure of it now. But the investigation was going on; there was nothing he could do to stop it.

Just as there was nothing he could do to stop the tidal waves of emotion that had been washing over him all afternoon every time their eyes had met or her hand had accidentally brushed against his. Desire was overtaking reason, and right now he didn't care.

They stopped at a drive-in restaurant on the way home.

"Just for a quick cup of coffee," Mike said. He didn't want his day with Joellyn to end just yet, although he was acutely aware of the time passing. David would be at his apartment in a couple of hours. Mike couldn't be late—knowing Dani, she'd just take David and leave and that would be that. But just a few more minutes. It had been such a marvelous afternoon. Almost as though United hadn't existed. Almost as though today, for some unexplained reason, there was nothing but time and space and feeling for this woman.

"Sounds good to me," Joellyn said. "I don't think I could work up enough energy to pour water in my coffeepot."

She'd been watching him all afternoon. He'd been wonderful with the kids. She still could scarcely believe it, but this man had shown all the gentleness and compassion in the world with them. And, oddly enough, he'd seemed to genuinely enjoy himself. She hadn't expected that.

He must really be missing his son, she realized. She had a feeling he was a wonderful father. In fact, she was sure of it.

"So," she said, after their coffee had been brought out to the car, "how'd you like your day?"

He stopped in the middle of a sip. "It was wonderful," he said truthfully. "And you're wonderful. I can't believe how good you are with those kids."

"I was just thinking the same thing about you," she murmured. She averted her eyes and took a sip of her coffee, trying to ignore the warning signals in her head.

She hadn't realized how truly nice he was. And she was beginning to like him far too much, considering... She pushed the thought away. She didn't want to think about it. This day had been special for her in more ways than one. She didn't want to spoil it.

Because somewhere in the middle of the afternoon she'd begun to realize this man was destined to be much more than just a friend.

When had it happened? When she saw him gently brushing back the hair out of an almost sightless little girl's eyes, holding her hands and making the motions of an airplane taking off so that she could "see" it? When he bought a dozen helium balloons at the airport souvenir shop and tied one to the wrist of each child, even the ones who couldn't understand what he was doing? Or was it when he bought them all ice cream and laboriously helped her feed it to the kids, gently wiping their chins after each mouthful, murmuring low words of encouragement?

They had brushed past each other a dozen times during the afternoon, and each time her skin had flamed, responding to a subtle message sent by his, the undercurrent between them so strong that at times she had felt sure everyone else around them must feel it.

How could they not feel it? Every pore in her body was singing, soaking in the nearness of him even now in the middle of a busy drive-in on a Saturday evening with a hundred people milling around, listening to the rock music blaring over the loudspeaker.

His hand moved toward hers in the light of the flickering pink-and-white neon drive-in sign; a hand so strong, and yet, she'd seen how gentle it could be. It moved over hers and claimed it, encircling her fingers and bringing them to his lips, touching each fingertip with a caress of his tongue like the fleeting whisper of a summer rain. Gentle, persuasive, life-giving.

She was stunned by the shock waves that coursed through her body. The light and the sound around them disappeared, leaving only the two of them together in a world of their own.

He moved toward her to take her into his arms, but with superhuman effort she shook her head.

"Let's go home," she whispered.

He signaled for the carhop to take the tray, and they drove home, content for the moment to be sitting side by side in the car, but knowing the moment was coming when they would be even closer, as close as it was possible for two people to be.

INSIDE THE APARTMENT DOOR he took her into his arms. She felt his warm breath as he buried his face in her hair and breathed deeply. "I've been wanting to do this all day," he whispered. "Actually, ever since the other night."

She felt his hand move around to her front.

Yes . . .

Yes.

She wanted him to touch her there. She wanted him to touch her everywhere.

His hand was like a branding iron on her waist. She felt it in every molecule as it moved up, caressing her breast, circling her nipple with his thumb, sending streaks of lightning shooting throughout her body.

She felt his hardness growing as he pressed her close to his thighs, the urgency of his need clear. Every nerve in her body came alive, responding. She pressed closer, moaning softly with pure pleasure as her head arched back and his lips trailed down the front of her throat, leaving a path of fire.

Was it her imagination, or had the clothes between them melted, bringing flesh against flesh, heart against heart?

"I'd like to take a shower," he whispered, searing her soul with the depth of passion she saw in his eyes. "And then I'd like to make long, slow love with you."

Not to her. *With* her.

"Yes," she murmured, although she didn't want to let him go any farther away from her than he was right now. "You go ahead. I'll take care of Penny and I'll join you as soon as I can."

Once more he bent his head toward hers, running his hand up her back and through her hair as he kissed her deeply and thoroughly. His tongue touched hers for an instant, promising so much more to come.

"Hurry," he said. "I don't think either of us can wait much longer." He walked toward the shower, glancing back over his shoulder.

She stood alone by the sliding doors, early-evening moonlight filtering through the sheers and into her hair. And when she smiled at him, a slow, shy smile, the thought flashed through his mind that he was home. Finally, irrevocably home. And then he heard her grandfather clock striking...one...two...three...four...five...

He stopped in midstep. Good Lord, five o'clock! He'd completely forgotten about David! How could he have done that? But now the most important person in his life was waiting, her eyes searching his from across the room. No, he corrected himself, the *most* important person in his life was on his way to his apartment right now.

His jaw had dropped open and his eyes held a look of total confusion. He wanted this woman now, right now. The compulsion to go ahead with it was almost overwhelming, but...

She saw the look on his face, saw him hesitate, and puzzled, asked, "What's wrong, Mike?"

"It's the time," he blurted. "I can't believe this, but I completely lost track of the time. I have to leave right away."

Shock registered on her face. "But *why?*" Then she remembered. "Oh," she said, disappointment cutting through her. "Your son."

He ran his hands through his hair, agitated beyond belief. "Yes. David will be at the apartment in less than an hour. I have to leave right now. Oh, Jo..." He reached for her, and she ran swiftly into his arms. "I'm sorry," he murmured, holding her close and nuzzling his face into her hair. "So sorry. I just...I can't...we can't...There just isn't time."

"I know," she whispered. "It's partly my fault. I forgot, too." She gave him a tiny shove toward the door. "You go on now. I'll see you another time."

He headed toward the door, then turned back. "Look," he said, "I'm taking him for pizza—the place over by the plant. Come with us, please?" His eyes pleaded with her to understand.

She took a deep breath, trying to ignore the turbulence roiling deep inside. "I'll meet you there. But just for a little while. You need to spend time alone with him. That's more important than this."

He laughed ruefully. "I'm not so sure about that right now. I've got a hell of a cramp in my stomach." That wasn't entirely true. The cramp most certainly wasn't in his stomach.

She flushed. "Maybe it's the coffee," she offered, trying to joke him out of his frustration.

He looked straight into her eyes. "Yeah," he drawled. "It's probably the coffee. *Sure* it is." He gave her a halfhearted smile and opened the door. "See you at Shakey's at seven, okay?"

"Shakey's at seven. Okay." She repeated. Although the last thing she felt like having right now was pizza.

THE THICK ODOR of pizza permeated the air. Twelve Different Kinds! the sign on the wall proclaimed as

Joellyn entered the crowded, noisy restaurant, and she believed it. She could smell all twelve kinds.

Normally the odor of tomato sauce and garlic and oregano could send her into a weak frenzy of hunger, but not this time. She was too nervous. She'd had no real experience with normal children, had no idea what to say to one, and was scared to death, although reason was trying its best to convince her there was nothing to be afraid of.

Reason lost. There *was* something to be afraid of, and it was sitting in a booth with its father. Two males, one large, one small, almost identical as far as looks went.

She stared at the two of them from across the room. The little boy was an exact replica of his father. David had the same red hair. The same chin. The same eyes. The same way of staring, solid and serious as she approached the table and he suddenly realized another person was joining them. Another woman, sliding into the booth next to his father where his mother should have been.

He eyed her warily and reached for his father's hand across the table. One small gesture, but the total possessiveness of it cut through her, and an almost uncontrollable wave of jealousy rolled over her.

Mike's son... his son with another woman. How could she ever begin to compete with this? Did she even want to try?

Mike saw her hesitation. "David," he said, "this is Joellyn. She's my friend and she'd like to be your friend, too."

David sat still for what seemed to be an eternity, his eyes wide and unsmiling. Then he looked down at the table, picked up a slice of pizza and took a bite without saying a word.

The battle lines were drawn.

Her heart sank. This wasn't a child. It couldn't be. This was a miniature adult, and she was terrified.

"I'm glad to meet you, David," she said. Then she looked at Mike, her eyes questioning. What should she say next? Her mind was a total blank. The pizza odor was gone. There was no restaurant, no noise, no lights, no people walking back to their tables from the buffet. There were only two pairs of eyes staring first at each other and then at her.

"Your daddy," she stammered, "talks about you a lot." Then her mind went blank again and she couldn't think of a single thing to say.

David chewed silently, his gaze fixed on the tabletop.

Mike shifted uncomfortably. What was going on here? David wasn't talking, and apparently Joellyn wasn't going to be any help at all. Couldn't she even *try?* "David," he said, "why don't you show Joellyn where the pizza and salad buffets are? She could probably use some help."

Joellyn squirmed. She could use some help, all right, straight out the door. This was a mistake, a terrible mistake. She had no business being here with this man and his son, no business at all. Whatever could have possessed her to come here in the first place? The whole day had been a mistake. "Mike," she said, "I think I should be going. Really, I should. I'm awfully tired and I'm not really hungry and—"

He put his hand on hers, trying to ignore the small shadow that fell over David's face. "I'll go to the buffet with you, Joellyn." He glanced over at David.

"Okay, sport? We'll just be a minute." He grabbed her wrist, knocking over a glass of water in the process.

"Now we'll just clean this up," he said smoothly, dabbing at the table with his napkin, "and then we'll get Joellyn's pizza, right, sport?" He gave David a searching look. "We'll be right back." He pulled Joellyn down the aisle toward the buffet.

"What's going on here?" he asked. "I was sure the two of you would like each other."

She reached for a piece of pepperoni pizza. "I don't know what to tell you, Mike. He just stares at me and my mind goes blank."

He grabbed a couple of extra napkins. "There's no reason for that, Jo. He's just a little kid."

She put another slice of pizza on her plate. Suddenly she was hungry. She defiantly added a third piece. "He's just a little kid, yes, but he has grown-up eyes."

"Ah, Jo, that's absurd. He probably just doesn't know what to say."

"He could have said hello."

"Well," Mike said, grinning sheepishly, "he was probably surprised, that's all. I guess I forgot to tell him you were coming."

"You forgot to tell him?" Her voice rose. "You *forgot?*"

Mike coughed. "Well, I sort of . . . oh, hell, I didn't forget. I just couldn't figure out any way to do it."

"You start by opening your mouth, Mike. The words come out easier that way. Try it some time."

"Jo?"

"What?"

"That's six pieces of pizza on your plate."

She looked down. He was right. She had no idea how the last three had gotten there. "Well, I'm hungry."

"And frustrated?" He grinned.

"And frustrated." She smiled back at him. Oh, maybe it wouldn't be so bad, after all. She could go back and make friends with David. After all, she was the adult. She'd figure something out. Maybe she could tell him a story. Her mind darted around, trying to recall one. Ah, yes. The Three Bears. She could tell him about the Three Bears. That might break the ice.

They went back to the table where David was polishing off the last of his pizza. He still remained silent.

"David," Joellyn asked, "would you like to hear a story? I could tell you about—" She broke off when she saw the look on his face.

"David, what's the matter?" Mike asked, leaning toward him with concern.

"Daddy, I feel sick," David said. He bent over, clutching his stomach. "I think I have to—" His words stopped. "I think I have to go home and go to bed. Maybe I'll be all better tomorrow."

Joellyn instinctively reached over to put her hand on David's forehead, but he shrank away from her touch. "Please, Dad," he pleaded. "Can we go home now?"

Joellyn gave Mike a resigned look. "Go ahead," she said. "I'll just stay here and finish my pizza. I'll be fine."

"Are you sure, Jo?" His eyebrows drew together in concern. "I hate to leave you here like this."

David tugged at his sleeve. "Dad, can we go now?"

Mike sighed heavily. "Of course, son. Jo, I'm sorry." He stood and helped David into his coat.

Joellyn and David eyed each other across the table. "I'm sorry you're not feeling well, David. I'm sure you'll be fine in a little while." He'll probably be fine in five minutes, as soon as they get out the door, she thought grumpily, then immediately felt ashamed of herself. What if he was really sick? Well, what then? Face it. She'd be no help. She didn't know the first thing about children, sick or well.

Furthermore, right at this moment, she didn't ever want to. This was all a big mistake. She watched them go out the door, thinking she should be grateful to David for preventing an even bigger one.

DAVID WAS QUIET on the way to Mike's apartment. Mike glanced at him several times, watching to see if he really seemed sick or if he was just faking it. But David stared out the window.

Mike turned a corner. "All right now, son?"

David nodded. "Uh-huh."

Mike drove on for a minute in silence. Then his curiosity got the best of him. "What did you think of Joellyn, David?" he asked quietly.

There was a silence. "I don't like her much," David said.

Mike turned another corner, narrowly missing the curb. "Why not?"

David slid down in the seat. "I don't know."

Mike had seen him slide down like that a million times when he didn't want to answer a question. "Well, David, is it her eyes? Or her hair? Or her forehead?" he joked. "Come on, sport. You can tell me."

David turned toward him. "I don't know, Dad. I just don't."

Mike wasn't going to let it go at that. "Is it because she's not your mama, David?"

David thought for a minute. "Well, why can't you and me and Mama live together like we used to?"

The question exploded in the air like a fireworks display, flashing its light over their faces before it fizzled into the night. This was the first time David had asked that question, and Mike didn't know how to answer it.

"What about Daddy Joe?" Mike asked. "What would we do with him?"

David thought for a minute. "He could live with us. He could sleep in my room."

JOHN TERRELL WATCHED the truck pull away out of his darkened driveway and grinned to himself. Another four hundred thousand dollars; two hundred thousand for him. Easy money. *Real* easy. He couldn't believe how easy this one had been. But they'd have to start looking around for another buyer now. This one was about tapped out.

Too bad Joy wasn't around to enjoy his success. A surge of remorse swept through him at the thought. Maybe if he'd been as smart then as he was now she might still be alive. Maybe he could have taken her to the Mayo Clinic. Maybe to Mexico, where one of those miracle drugs might have worked. You never know. One might have. This money would have come in mighty handy back then.

He pulled himself up the steps to his front porch, longing for Joy almost overwhelming him. She was so sweet . . . so pretty . . . so good for him. If she'd lived, they'd have been retired by now. Not here, worrying about his reputation and his job at United.

Although if it wasn't for Joellyn, his reputation might not be that important. But she believed in him, or anyway he could see she wanted to. Poor kid, it must be tough. Her whole life ahead of her, building a career, and then something like this happens to foul up the works. Well, maybe not. It depended on what they found. If they found anything.

He could retire now. Right now. Probably should, except he didn't want to leave anyone pointing their finger at him, giving him that look.

The mood he was in right now, that look would do it for him. He knew they thought he did it. And so what if they did? They could never prove it, never in a million years. No matter what happened, they could never prove a thing. Not so far as he was concerned, anyhow.

He pulled the door shut behind him and headed for his bedroom. Another sleepless night probably. He'd had a lot of 'em lately. Didn't seem to be worth it. Another couple of months, that was all it would take. Two more months. Then, no matter what they found or didn't find at the plant, old John Terrell was going to call it quits and head for a warmer climate. They'd had plenty of time. If they didn't know what was going on out there by now, they probably never would. Either way it wasn't his problem. He had enough of his own.

MIKE LAY AWAKE, listening to the quiet, even breathing of his son.

His son. Another problem added to an already overloaded list. He tried to visualize a decision tree, a trick taught to fledgling executives in college. A long sheet of paper with a line drawn down the middle; one half for reasons why he should try to further an attachment with Joellyn and the other half for reasons why he shouldn't.

The half for reasons why he should was almost blank, and what reasons there were, were strictly emotional. Bad reasoning, according to his college classes.

Her eyes. Her faint, elusive, clean-soap smell. The way she dressed. The way she looked at him when she thought he wasn't looking, almost quizzical, as though she were formulating a decision tree of her own. She probably was. He could see the negative side of it right now.

He had his own list of reasons to stay away from Joellyn, and the strongest one was lying in bed beside him, sleeping soundly. No more stomachache, of course. That had disappeared like magic the moment they were safely inside the apartment door. Just a little boy who, for some unexplained reason, didn't like the woman his father had chosen.

And what was he supposed to do about that? There was no way he was going to alienate his son. Not after what he'd seen today. Those kids at the home had made him realize how lucky he really was to have a son so healthy, so bright. God, what if it had been the other way? What if David had been born like that? He shuddered to think of it.

He reached for David in the darkness, breathing a sigh of satisfaction when his hand brushed across the small muscles in his son's arms, the sturdy shoulders. No, there was no way. He could never go against David's feelings—especially for a woman who might, at this moment, be planning something he was supposed to be investigating. He hadn't been doing a very good job of it, either. He'd gotten way off the track. But, on the other hand, she was wonderful with the kids at the home. She couldn't—damn it, she *couldn't* be responsible for the thefts. It was impossible.

But maybe not. He'd have to forget about romancing her, for now, anyhow, and concentrate on finding out who *was* responsible. Romance could wait.

He sighed into the darkness. Well, David, at least, would be very happy about that. If he could tell him.

CHAPTER SEVEN

MIKE REACHED for the preliminary Dun and Bradstreet reports on John Terrell, Joellyn and Al Dobson. The others would be arriving soon. He felt like a rat, having had a report run on Joellyn, but... He shrugged. It had to be done, no matter how he felt. And he wasn't too sure at this point how he felt about anything. The only thing he was absolutely sure of was that he was in a rotten mood this morning, and it was getting worse by the minute.

It was bad enough that this was Monday, not his favorite day of the week by any means, but he'd had almost no sleep the night before. Dani had picked David up at two-thirty on the dot the day before; he'd had barely enough time to become reacquainted, much less establish a close relationship with David.

And so David was gone, leaving Mike with the emptiest feeling he'd ever had. Worse than before, much worse. It had been so hard for the two of them to communicate. All morning David had steadfastly refused to discuss Joellyn. He'd just looked down at the floor whenever Mike had brought up her name. After a while, Mike had stopped mentioning her, and then things had gotten easier, but still... Why was Daddy Joe so acceptable, and Joellyn not? There must be something, something he couldn't see....

And this cockamamy job—damn it, nothing in his beer-drinking days at Harvard had prepared him for this. Oh, his business ethics courses had, of course, but the only point ethics had made, really, was that it wasn't nice to be involved in a corporate crime, particularly if you were the perpetrator.

And they'd certainly never offered a course in contending with beautiful but questionable accounting managers. It was just as well. He'd probably have flunked it.

After David left yesterday, he'd taken his bike out and gone for a ride, trying to clear his head. He'd driven furiously for a half hour, found himself in front of Joellyn's apartment, driven off, circled around, parked in front of the apartment, debating whether to go in and try again, given up on that idea, roared off, circled around twice more, then finally packed it in and gone home.

Who would have believed he'd be so pulled out of shape over a woman he barely knew? So they'd almost slept together Saturday—he'd slept with plenty of women. Well, enough, anyway, and none of them had confused him the way Joellyn had. And besides that, almost didn't count.

So he'd been alone again on a Sunday afternoon. He'd hated being alone on Sunday afternoon, but he shouldn't have been bored. He'd had a million things to do.

He washed his car and bike. He made a stab at cleaning his apartment, only to discover he had no cleaning materials, so he drove to the supermarket and bought groceries he didn't need, completely forgetting about the cleansers. He remembered them after he was halfway home.

Then, on the way into his apartment, the grocery bag split open, spilling oranges all over the hallway. He left them where they fell and moped around the apartment, grousing to himself. He didn't need oranges, anyway. He could get all the fresh orange juice he wanted at any good restaurant.

He watched an old black-and-white Laurel and Hardy movie on television, looked for something to eat and belatedly realized he'd just been to the store and bought a dozen oranges of which he had three left, two cans of tuna fish, which he hated without mayonnaise and he'd forgotten to buy any mayonnaise, a package of hamburger buns but no hamburger, a box of chocolate cupcakes and a six-pack of ginger ale.

He wasn't in the mood for ginger ale.

The only things in the apartment worth eating were the cupcakes. He ate three, wolfing them down, then decided to go to the movies.

At the movies he stuffed himself with two chocolate bars, a large cola and a quart of buttered popcorn with extra butter, on which he defiantly sprinkled too much salt.

When he got home, he fell into bed, tossing and turning most of the night, alternately dreaming of German shepherds chasing trucks full of aluminum tubing and waking, reaching out, imagining he could smell Joellyn's hair on his pillow. And through it all, David's eyes, huge and questioning.

And now here he was, sitting in his office on a rainy Monday morning with a sore ankle, indigestion and dark, sagging circles under his eyes, trying to remember what the movie last night had been about. On top of that, he was coming down with a cold. So much for washing his car and bike outside in March. It would be June before he tried that again.

Disgusted with himself and the whole world, he re-opened the folder, sipping his coffee while he read all fifteen pages. Then he closed it and stared at the wall opposite his desk, more confused than ever.

The D and B showed that Joellyn regularly deposited her entire paycheck into her checking account, except for a hundred dollars a month that she always added to her savings account. She had fifteen thousand, eight hundred seventy-two dollars in her savings account. That wasn't bad. She'd been working for nine years. Evidently she saved her money, but the money she had wasn't the kind of money they were looking for, anyhow.

But wait... He did some rapid calculations on his pocket calculator—a hundred dollars a month for nine years was only ten thousand eight hundred dollars, plus interest. Compounded annually at a rough average of seven percent interest, she'd have around fifteen or sixteen thousand dollars, maybe a little more. About what she had in there now.

Where had she come up with fifty thousand dollars in cash? She'd paid cash for the Porsche!

He grabbed the report again, frowning. The numbers were right there in front of him. And the fifty thousand hadn't gone in or out of either of her bank accounts.

She'd simply bought it.

Nothing unusual had happened before or after that, according to the D and B.

He rubbed his forehead. There was no way out of it. In view of this information, things were beginning to look a little different. But he still couldn't bring himself to believe she'd done anything wrong other than refusing to ride on his bike. And that wasn't so wrong... A lot of people didn't like those things. Damn it, now she had *him* calling it a thing.

Still, there were differences between them. Surface differences, to be sure, but differences all the same. Her aversion to camping and exercising, all the things that meant so much to him. She wasn't even worrying about his love of sports. Most of the couples he knew had that problem.

He sat up straight. What had he been thinking? *Most of the couples he knew.*

He snorted. He must be losing his mind. They were far from being a couple. He barely knew her. Or, at least, all he knew was exactly all she wanted him to know... until this.

And he couldn't just drop by her office and say, "By the way, Joellyn, I've been investigating you and everyone else here, and I'd like to know where you got the fifty thousand dollars to buy your Porsche, if you don't mind."

Lanagan's detectives must have something on it. He'd have to see their reports. Then he'd know. Maybe. If not, then he'd ask her.

The reports on Terrell and Dobson were even more confusing. Large sums of money had been flowing in and out of their personal bank accounts in the past year, and oddly enough, some of the amounts that had been withdrawn out of Dobson's seemed to have been deposited in Terrell's either on the same day or within the next two days. And vice versa.

He stared at the computerized sheets, a confusing jigsaw puzzle of deposits and withdrawals, withdrawals and deposits, all huge sums of money.

Where was it coming from? Terrell's salary was roughly thirty-six thousand a year, Dobson's about forty-two. Neither man made anywhere near the kind of salary that would justify these big money transactions, according to this report.

Three hundred thousand dollars had been deposited in four separate banks, two in accounts held by Terrell and two by Dobson. They'd each deposited a hundred and fifty thousand, split right down the middle; seventy-five thousand in each account. This had started almost six months ago. All four initial deposits had been made on the same day.

Almost exactly the same time Joellyn had bought the car.

Before that deposits and withdrawals had been smaller. And there had been quite a few large ones since then, including some within the past week. Mike leaned back in his chair, his stomach churning. This really looked bad. Terrell and Dobson were definitely into something together. Maybe Lanagan could explain it. He picked up his phone and dialed Lanagan's extension, listening while the phone rang four times. Halfway through the fifth ring, the phone was lifted off the hook.

"Hello," a harassed voice boomed into the phone. "Lanagan here!"

Mike smiled. Dianne must be away from her desk again. "Good morning, Jack. This is Mike Walker. How are you?"

"Fine, fine, Mike. What can I do for you?"

"Jack, I have something here that I'd like to ask you about. Could I come up for a few minutes?"

"Ah, Mike, can it wait? I have a meeting here in ten minutes with one of our biggest stockholders. I can't afford to put him off. What's it about?"

Mike drew a long breath. "I have a D and B on our shipping manager, John Terrell—"

"Yes, yes. I know him," Lanagan interrupted. "What about him?"

"It's not just him, Jack. It's Dobson, too. They seem to be into something together. Whatever it is, they're raking in a pile of money. It looks bad. Do you have any idea what they're doing?"

There was a long silence. "No, Mike," Lanagan said, his voice heavy. "I'd sure hate to think—check into it, will you? I'll be tied up here until at least five o'clock. Probably later. I'll try to talk to you then. Find out what you can."

Mike heard the click as Lanagan hung up the phone.

Find out what he could? A big help *that* was! He read slowly through the reports again, making sure of the facts, trying to make sense of the whole thing.

It read the same way. Something was very wrong here, and it looked more and more as though Terrell might be at the bottom of it. Or Dobson. Or both of them. And Joellyn . . .

Where did she get the money for that Porsche?

He lifted the receiver and dialed again.

"Mr. Wagner's office," a soft voice answered.

"Is Randy there? This is Mike Walker."

"Mr. Walker, he just left the office. He's on his way out to the plant. He said something about stopping to see you. Do you want to leave a message in case he comes back here first?"

"No, no. I'll find him. Thanks, anyway."

Mike hung up the phone and swung around as the door opened and Randy walked into the office. "Mike, how are you?" he said, grinning broadly. "How was your weekend?"

"My weekend?" Mike rubbed the back of his neck. "Okay, I guess," he lied. "I joined the health club Friday night. My son was here Saturday night. Other than that I didn't do much. How about you?"

"Oh, my wife and I went to visit her family. Big anniversary dinner. Black tie, the whole route. They really belong to a couple of nice clubs." He straddled the chair in front of Mike's desk and took a closer look at Mike's face. "You look awfully serious for a Monday morning," he commented. "What's up? Anything I can do to help?"

Mike sighed heavily. "I don't think so, unless you want to bring the plant manager and the shipping manager in here and question them for me."

Randy's eyebrows shot up. "Oh, ho! Not me, no way! This is *your* playground. What's the problem?"

Mike crossed his hands behind his head and leaned back. "I'm not sure," he answered slowly. "But I ran a D and B on several people here, and so far it looks bad for two out of three that I've read. And I'm not counting the third one out."

Randy leaned forward, his face lighting up with interest. "Terrell and Dobson?"

Mike nodded.

"No kidding? Who's the third?"

Mike's stomach knotted. "Joellyn," he said.

"Good Lord!" Randy's eyes registered shock. "Why?"

"Well, Dobson and Terrell have been playing with an awful lot of money lately. I'm talking big bucks. In

the hundreds of thousands. I'm going to get hold of
the detectives today and touch base with them. Maybe
I'm misinterpreting what I think I see. If I am, they'll
set me straight.''

"But what about Joellyn?" Randy seemed to be in
a state of shock. "What's she done?"

"Maybe nothing," Mike said. "But she bought a
brand-new Porsche six months ago and paid cash.
Fifty big ones. And it didn't come out of her bank account. She didn't have that much, or anywhere near
it.''

Randy looked completely surprised. "I thought she
financed it.''

"Nope." Mike shook his head. "She paid cash. Do
you have any idea where she could've gotten it?"

"Not a one. Believe me, this is as much of a surprise to me as it is to you. And it's strange about Terrell and Dobson," Randy said. "Neither one of 'em
makes the kind of money you're talking about. I
wonder if, ah, no. Al wouldn't do anything like that.
Neither would John.''

"Well, somebody has," Mike pointed out. "What
I can't understand is why the detectives didn't run any
financial reports on the plant personnel.''

"Maybe they did," Randy said. "But you know,
Mike, there's always the chance that whoever's stealing the tubing never deposited the money in their own
name. Maybe not even in their own bank." He leaned
forward, interested. "Is there any way you can check
on that?"

"I'm not sure how we'd go about it. I guess we'll
have to leave that to the FBI, if we have to call them in.
I'm sure they'd be able to. But we'll see what the detectives have for now and go from there.''

Randy unfolded himself from the chair. "Sounds good. Let me know how it goes." He stopped at the door, his eyes still puzzled. "Did you call Lanagan?"

Mike nodded.

"And?"

"He was pretty busy. He said he'd get back to me later."

Randy laughed and shook his head. "Lanagan's like that. He has a lot on his mind. But he'll back you up, whatever you decide to do." He stared at Mike for a minute. "You know, it's strange about all that money. And I bet there's something else you didn't know. Terrell is Joellyn's uncle. Did you know that?"

Mike's jaw dropped open with surprise. "No," he answered heavily, "I didn't. Are they very close? Some relatives don't have much to do with each other."

Randy frowned. "Um...he was working here quite a while before Joellyn came here. I'm not really sure how long, but we can find out easily enough. I do know he had something to do with her coming here, but as for being close, I really don't know. Joellyn almost never talks about her personal life."

Mike could well imagine that. "What about Dobson?" he asked. "He seems awfully careless for someone who's supposed to be managing a plant. I've caught all kinds of things in the short time I've been here. How long has he been here? Who hired him?"

Randy scratched his head. "Uh...Lanagan hired him, about a year ago." He glanced at his watch. "Listen," he said, "I've gotta run, but keep me posted, hear?" He waved as he rushed out of the office.

Mike rocked back and forth in his chair, frowning reflectively at the door. So Terrell was Joellyn's uncle. This was news, very bad news. Whatever happened, Joellyn was going to be upset, especially if she and Terrell were at all close.

But suppose they *were* close, and she knew, or suspected, John was masterminding the thefts? Now that he thought about it, she had gotten angry when he mentioned John's name that night at the restaurant. Had John give her fifty thousand dollars to keep her quiet?

A new thought entered his mind, chilling him. Maybe the rumors were true. Maybe someone she had been involved with had bought the car for her. And which would be better, the first possibility or the second? If it was the second, who could it be?

Mike sat straight up, astonished at the name that had just flashed through his mind.

Lanagan?

He dismissed that almost as soon as he thought of it. He was just getting himself confused now. Only two days ago he'd sworn to himself she couldn't possibly be involved in anything illegal, and the feeling he'd had then was still with him.

She couldn't. He was almost sure of it. And yet he remembered how long Dani had been seeing the man who was now her husband while she was still married to him.

Yes. He'd been fooled before.

As for Dobson, he'd been here a year. Long enough to get to know the inner workings of the plant. Long enough to have figured out a way to spirit inventory out the door undetected. Or long enough to have figured out a way to get Terrell to do it for him.

Joellyn's face flashed through his mind. Damn it! He'd *known* better than to become involved with anyone here. He'd solved corporate crimes before, but never under these circumstances. He'd really done it to himself this time!

He put the reports away in his bottom desk drawer. He'd made up his mind. He was going to wait for the other D and B reports. They'd take a while to sift through. Then, if nothing else looked suspicious, he'd call Terrell and Dobson in and ask them to take a lie detector test.

And then, if the test turned up what he thought it was going to, Terrell and Dobson would definitely be under investigation for complicity in grand theft. No matter how he felt about Joellyn.

JOELLYN SHIFTED in her chair, scanning photocopies of the last two months' invoices for the fifth time this morning, searching for something, some clue, some simple thing that might pop out or strike her as being unusual.

The top of her desk was stacked with unfinished work. Computer runs littered the floor, taking up space in her interview chair. Her 'in' box was piled high with the latest corporate directives, unopened interoffice envelopes and myriad lists of tasks to be done in order of importance.

But try as she might she couldn't seem to get interested in reading any of it.

Her mind was definitely not on her work, and this was very unusual for her. She had always been a workaholic, even back in high school where she'd studied constantly to keep up her high average.

Her mind was on her mother's words. "Joellyn," she had admonished, "how can a young, healthy girl sit home alone night after night with those books?"

"Mom," she'd pointed out, "you're the school-teacher. I should think you'd want me to study."

"But, Joellyn, studying *all* the time is unnatural! My friends are always complaining about their daughters staying out half the night, running up the phone bill, going out with the wrong boys. I don't even think you know where the phone is, much less what a boy is. It's embarrassing!"

But her mother had hugged her, softening the impact of her complaints. "I'm happy to see you getting straight A's, dear. I just think you should round out your life a little more. There's a lot more to life than homework."

"I know, Mom, I know. And one of these days, when I have time, I'll find it."

"Well, I hope it's soon. None of my friends believe me when I tell them how you really are. They all think I'm hiding something."

But she knew her mother was proud of her. And so had her father been, especially when those hours of homework had earned her a full scholarship at the University of Chicago, one of the highest rated universities in the country.

Joellyn smiled at the thought of her parents. They had been so wonderful with each other, playing golf and tennis together in their spare time, sharing the same interests and loving each other to the almost total exclusion of anyone else except their only child.

Theirs had been a very close, loving relationship—a complete marriage in every way. And the way they'd handled it while her father was alive had looked so easy. They'd had everything in common. It had been beautiful to watch.

She was beginning to wonder if she'd ever have the same kind of relationship with anyone. Certainly it hadn't worked out that way with Lee.

And now here she was half involved with, or probably formerly half involved with, a man who was completely wrong for her. A man whose son could barely look at her without getting a stomachache. A man who was clearly, to her anyhow, looking into a situation that could ruin her Uncle John. *If* Uncle John was involved. Devastating differences, both of them.

And what about the other ones? Harley-Davidson antique indeed! The one man who caused skyrockets to go off, and his primary interests seemed to be jogging, raquetball and that damned machine. And his son.

On the other hand, he did have a nice, safe job. Vice president of manufacturing. She could live with that. At least he wasn't running around the whole world getting himself into dangerous situations.

She shook her head, trying to clear her mind of Mike's image. His face had been haunting all her waking hours, and there had been a lot of those since she'd met him.

When the lights went out at night, there he was, hovering in her mind's eye—his broad shoulders, his long, muscular legs, the hand whose very touch had sent streaks of blazing fire shooting straight through her, streaks of fire that ebbed and flickered even now in the harsh reality of daylight.

And her appearance was showing the results of too many sleepless nights. No amount of makeup could cover the dark circles under her eyes, dark circles she hadn't seen since studying for midterms in college.

She forced her attention back to the invoices, trying to focus her thoughts on the smudged sheets of paper. They really *were* a mess. There seemed to be no control on them at all, although she knew there was supposed to be. But she could see no numerical order, no way of telling for sure whether every invoice was accounted for or not. Why hadn't she noticed that before now?

United had always depended upon the integrity of their key employees, but what if someone had something to cover up? What if the invoices weren't all being turned in to billing the way they were supposed to?

An idea began to formulate—a fuzzy image, nothing she could grab hold of, but if there was no way to tell that the invoices were all there, it would be easy for anyone to walk away with the whole plant. But no, that couldn't be it. There were too many separate computer runs listening these invoices.

The question was, were they being checked?

Thoughts of Mike receded as she pushed herself away from her desk and headed down the hall toward the billing department.

She'd never considered it in quite this way before, but now the flag of suspicion loomed in front of her.

Were all the invoices being checked?

By whom?

MIKE CLOSED the bulging D and B folder, shoved it into his desk drawer and locked it. He'd spent the last day and a half reading them, and by now, red-eyed and weary, he was fairly certain none of the plant employees were involved in the thefts.

Except the original three. And Dobson was on his way in now. He'd called Dobson half an hour ago, requesting a short meeting to talk about plant and production business. Just a short talk in general; he didn't want to tip Dobson off. He barely knew the man, but Dobson was supposed to be second-in-command out here in the plant. A meeting was long past due.

Al Dobson opened the door, whipped off his white hard hat as he walked in and sat down without a word. Mike had the disconcerting feeling they were squaring off, but he shook it away. He wanted to keep it light for now.

Al was around five feet ten inches tall, but his width made him appear massive. Obviously he ate well. His light brown hair had a permanent ridge around the back of his head where his hard hat pressed against it eight hours a day.

Mike knew he almost never took the hat off. He couldn't, according to federal safety rules. Hard hat and protective glasses at all times. Mike didn't envy him. He'd put in quite a few years packing his own hair down the same way. He almost never wore his hard hat anymore, if he could help it.

Dobson's eyes bothered Mike a lot. They were opaque grayish-green whenever Mike was allowed to look directly into them. Half the time they were hooded as Dobson stared at the floor.

Mike sighed inwardly. Lately it seemed to be his lot in life to be faced with people who only wanted to stare at the floor while he talked to them. First David, now Al. Somewhere along the way he must be doing something wrong.

"Hello, Al, good to see you." Mike smiled, watching Dobson closely.

Al looked up. "Yes, sir," he answered.

"Well, Al, I thought it was time we had a little talk."

Al grinned briefly. "Okay. Shoot."

"I wanted to ask you—" he paused "—who engineered the production computer runs? Were they preprogrammed?"

"Nope," Al answered. "I did 'em myself. They didn't have anything that could do the job we needed. Why?"

"Just wondered. They seem pretty comprehensive to me."

"Huh!" Al exclaimed. "I thought so, too, until the tubing started disappearing."

Mike leaned forward, determined to maintain eye contact at least this once. "Do you think it's possible anything could be missing in the program?"

"Nope. It's all there." He rubbed the back of his head. "I can get you copies of the actual programs if you want. They're in my office."

Mike sat up. In his office? Why weren't they kept in the computer department? "Who has access to your office?" he asked quietly.

Al snorted. "Just about anybody who wants to can come in. It's open all the time."

"Don't you think you should have the programs locked up?"

"Sure," Al agreed. "They are."

"Where?"

"In the safe."

Mike nodded, trying to keep his disappointment from showing as his theory dissolved. "Good idea. We don't want anyone messing with your programs. Especially the ones involving inventory."

PLAY
HARLEQUIN'S
LUCKY HEARTS
GAME

AND YOU COULD GET

- FREE BOOKS
- A FREE 20" NECKLACE
- A FREE SURPRISE GIFT
- AND MUCH MORE

TURN THE PAGE AND
DEAL YOURSELF IN

PL

AM

★
★
★

TH
LU
SW

Whe
sen
free !
nove
befoo
them
33¢
pos
mar
ship

Fre
You
pop

Spe
Whe
you
toke

"In case you're wondering," Al mumbled in a defensive tone of voice, "nobody can get into the actual program on the hard disk, either."

"How come?"

Al grinned. "It's password-protected. And nobody but me knows the password."

"Nobody?" Mike was surprised. "Not even the controller?"

Al's eyes flashed for a quick second. "Ah, sure, Lanagan's got it. But that's all. We did it that way on purpose."

"Any particular reason nobody in the computer department has access to it?" Mike asked.

"Sure!" Al exclaimed. "We didn't want them fooling around with the inventory numbers unless they knew what they were doing."

"Do you think anybody has?"

"Nope. Somebody stole that tubing, and I'd sure like to know who it is."

Mike rocked back in his seat and clasped his hands, steadily eyeing Al. "So would I. And eventually I will." He rose. "Thanks for coming in, Al. I'll talk to you later."

Al stood, his eyes flickering with surprise. "That's all you wanted? Just to ask about the inventory programs?"

"That's it," Mike said. "For now, anyhow. Except for one thing." He paused.

"Well?" Al prodded.

Mike cleared his throat. "How do you feel about asking people to take a polygraph test?"

"What people?"

"Everyone, including you."

"Me?" Al exclaimed incredulously. "Why me?"

"I said everyone," Mike reminded him. "Not just you. Everyone."

"Can you do that?"

"I can't force them, of course, but I think it should be done. An innocent employee shouldn't have too much of a problem. Don't you agree?"

"Oh, boy!" Al muttered. "I can see the union now. They'd have us in court in a New York second! Isn't there anything else we can do?"

"Well, we can start with management. The union can't stop that."

"I guess so," Al murmured. "I'm not crazy about the idea, though."

"But you'll do it?"

Al shrugged. "Sure, if I have to. Yeah, why not?" He rose. "But only if everyone else agrees to take one. That's fair enough, isn't it?"

"Fair enough."

Al left, casting a puzzled look over his shoulder. "Let me know what you decide. I want to find that guy as much as you do."

Mike doubted that. Nobody wanted to find out who it was more than he did. Too much depended on the answer.

JOHN TERRELL HAD BEEN waiting outside the door. Mike had asked him to be here at two-thirty, and it was only two-twenty. Well, so he was a little early. He had to do these things when he had time, and right now he had the time. He might not later.

He peered in through Mike's door, where Mike and Al were having a very close conversation. He hoped Al wasn't—nah, Al wouldn't say anything. Al wanted to keep things quiet as much as *he* did. In fact, it had been Al's idea not to tell anyone. Too risky, he'd said. It was nobody else's business. But just the same, when he saw Al lean forward and glance over his shoulder before he spoke, it looked funny—almost as if he didn't want to be overheard.

Nah, that was crazy. Al would never talk. No way would Al ever talk. And old John Terrell wasn't going to, either.

JOHN WALKED in through the door as Al left. Mike watched them both closely, but not a flicker of recognition passed between the two men, other than a quick nod.

John waited by the door. Mike gestured toward a chair. "Sit down, John. We need to have a talk."

"About what?" John asked.

"I think you know what," Mike answered in a no-nonsense voice, and waited.

John frowned. "No, I don't," he protested loudly, banging his hand against the desk as he stood up. "If it's about that missing tubing, I don't know anything about it."

Mike felt the quick charge of electricity in the air. He hadn't said a word about the tubing, but since John had brought it up, why not?

"Sit down, Terrell," he said. "And get this straight. I'm not asking about the tubing. I just want to know where you're getting all your money." He sat back to watch John's reaction.

"What the hell are you talking about?" Terrell shouted. "What money?"

"The money in your bank accounts. All of them."

The two men eyed each other.

"What money in what bank accounts?" John demanded, his eyes flashing.

"Stop playing games with me, Terrell. You know what money and you know what banks, and so do I. Now come on. Where'd you get it?"

John leaned over Mike's desk and narrowed his eyes. "None of your damn business."

Mike raised his eyebrows. "Don't you think the disappearance of over a million dollars' worth of inventory makes it my business?"

John backed up a step. "No, I sure don't. That money's mine, and nobody gave it to me. And I didn't steal anything. I earned it."

"You earned hundreds of thousands of dollars in the past six months? Come on! What kind of business have you got on the side, Terrell?"

"That's none of your damn business, either," John shouted, slamming his fist on the desktop. "I'm not telling you another word. I don't have to!"

"I think you do." Mike spoke in a carefully controlled voice. His eyes never left Terrell's. He hadn't expected Terrell to react like this. The man was behaving exactly as if he *was* guilty of something.

"No, I don't," Terrell argued. He rocked back on his heels, frowning defiantly at Mike. "If you think I did something wrong," he challenged, "prove it. Just prove it!"

Mike heaved a long sigh. "I don't know whether you have or not, Terrell, but I'm asking all management in the plant to take a polygraph test."

John's eyes were flinty with anger and dislike. "A *lie detector test!* Are you crazy?" he shouted. "You know what you can do with your lie detector test, *Mr.* Walker." He opened the door. "You can stick it.

That's what you can do! And you can stick your job, too! You don't have anything on me!''

Mike stood up. "Now hold on, Terrell. I'm not accusing you. I'm only asking you to take a simple test. If you've done nothing wrong, you have nothing to be afraid of. There's no reason to go off like that."

But he was speaking to an empty doorway. Terrell had walked out before the last words had left his lips.

CHAPTER EIGHT

JOELLYN ENTERED the billing department. A long, narrow corridor of a room with six desks lined up in two rows facing the supervisor's desk, it always reminded her of a typing pool in one of the old Tracy-Hepburn movies. Six billing clerks sat at their desks, heads bent over their work.

She glanced at her watch as she skirted the narrow aisle between the desks. It was almost two-thirty, at which time the room was sure to clear out in fifteen seconds flat. But she couldn't complain; they deserved their breaks. They were one hardworking group of women. Not only hardworking, but also very thorough. It would be hard to get anything past them.

The supervisor, Marilyn Norris, was hunched over with her back to her department, whispering into the telephone. She glanced up, saw Joellyn walking toward her desk, raised her eyebrows with a barely audible sigh and said goodbye. Then she dropped the receiver into its cradle and leaned back in her chair with her arms folded across her chest, waiting.

Six pairs of eyes glanced up and quickly back down again. Joellyn was sure each woman was secretly debating the big question of the moment—whether to go on break or stay and listen. There always seemed to be conflict whenever she and Marilyn had business to discuss—guaranteed entertainment for everyone except herself.

It had always bothered her that she'd never been able to win Marilyn over, but it looked as if it was never going to happen. Marilyn just didn't like her. Period.

"Good afternoon, all!" Joellyn said, smiling and nodding to the women as she approached Marilyn's desk.

Six voices murmured "Hello" while their owners glanced up again, then went back to their work.

She felt her insides shrivel a tiny bit, as they always did when this happened. So much for rapport between management and the troops.

"Well, hello there, Joellyn," Marilyn said. "What can I do for you?"

Joellyn smiled, but she was on guard, remembering her confrontation with Marilyn in the ladies' room. "I just have to ask a couple of questions." She eyed Marilyn, hoping to avoid another unpleasant scene but bracing herself for the inevitable.

Marilyn had short, curly, dark blond hair, snapping blue eyes and a medium build. In her thirties, about five-three-and-a-half, today she was dressed in a beige tweed skirt and white blouse. She was a fairly nice-looking woman. And, differences aside, Marilyn did take good care of the billing department. In fact, no one had ever taken better care of it. Joellyn always tried to keep that in mind. One thing seemed to balance out the other; nothing was ever totally perfect in an office.

Joellyn leaned against the edge of the table in Marilyn's cubicle. She didn't intend to stay long enough to make herself comfortable.

Marilyn heaved a long, dramatic sigh. "You have a few questions? I sure hope you can come up with some original ones. I'm getting tired of the same old routine. By the way, if I may ask, what's going on upstairs? They've been having one muckety-muck conference after another up there."

"I don't know," Joellyn answered. "I never get invited to them." She smiled, trying to conceal her annoyance. It was true; she never did get invited to them. But she didn't like being reminded by her subordinates. In her mind it somewhat negated her authority. Heaven knows, she'd had to work hard enough to establish that in the beginning. Keeping it was an ongoing, daily battle of wits.

Once again, and as usual, Marilyn had deftly changed the subject. She was good at that. Sometimes it was so hard just ferreting out the smallest bit of information, but Joellyn wasn't going to allow herself to be sidetracked by this game today. "I need to ask you a couple of questions about the billing process," she said, smiling. "Just to clear up some things in my mind."

"What's the problem now?" Marilyn asked. She picked up her pencil, tapping the eraser end on her desktop in a quick staccato, staring at Joellyn with faintly concealed hostility.

Joellyn's eyebrows knitted together in a frown. "I'm not sure there is a problem. I'd like to find out a few things about our invoicing system. I need to know exactly how the invoicing system works from start to finish."

"From start to finish? Oh, Joellyn, it would take weeks to teach you everything that goes on in this department, maybe longer. You don't really expect me to take the time right now to explain all that, do you?"

"I didn't really mean *everything*," Joellyn said. "Just the basics. I need to know how the system works. And right away," she added firmly.

"You want me to go through the whole process?" Marilyn's voice rose. "Joellyn, just look at my desk. I have enough here to keep me busy for a week, and there's more piling in every minute."

"All right, then, not the whole process." Marilyn should have been delegating some of that work. She had refused to attend a management seminar with the rest of the supervisors a couple of months back, and this was the end result. It was no wonder she was so crabby most of the time. Joellyn purposely lowered her voice. "I need to know if we're sure of the numerical control on these invoices?"

"I don't understand what you mean," Marilyn bristled. "All of the invoices go through here!"

"Yes, but how thorough is the computerized numerical control?" Joellyn persisted. "Is there anything that tells you an invoice has been lost?"

Marilyn's forehead was beginning to turn several shades of pink. "They come straight from shipping to here, then into the computer to be billed. Why? Are some lost?"

"That's what I'm interested in finding out," Joellyn answered patiently. "For instance, if I wanted to track an invoice from beginning to end, could I do it without a lot of hassle?"

Marilyn tapped a pad of paper against the desktop. "Do you know how many invoices we go through in a day, Joellyn?" She waited for the answer.

Joellyn shook her head. "Probably hundreds. Why?"

"Because today we're pretty busy, as you should know. Joellyn, please, *are* some lost, or are we just passing the time of day?"

Joellyn glanced around the department. Sure enough, all six women had stayed through their break and appeared to be concentrating on their work, but she was sure they weren't missing a syllable. Her temper was beginning to rise. Damn it, this happened every time she came in here!

All six women looked up with undisguised interest as her voice sharpened. "Marilyn, I need the answer, and I need it right now. Why are you making this so hard?"

"I'm not making it hard on purpose. I just have a few million things to do," Marilyn answered, "but in answer to your question, yes, there is a numerical control. If an invoice is missing, it would show up on the invoice number run with five stars printed on the right-hand side."

"Have you been missing any lately?"

Marilyn sighed. "Joellyn, these are the same questions the auditors have been asking for weeks. We've been through all this again and again. Can't you ask *them* these questions?"

Joellyn was fighting hard to keep her control. Trying to get one straight answer here or anywhere else in the plant was like trying to swim through a vat of rubber cement!

"Marilyn," she persisted, choosing her words carefully, "*have* there been any missing invoices lately? Any at all you can't account for?"

"In a word, no," Marilyn said. She shuffled through a pile of papers.

"Are you sure? Did any invoices show anything strange at all? Even a little bit?"

"Look, you know perfectly well they're all checked out by Randy before they go out. I'm sure he'd have said something to you if there had been," Marilyn remarked.

Joellyn turned to leave, then swung back. "Is there a run that tells you which invoices are missing, just a short run that lists only invoices that may be held up somewhere? Is there anything like that?"

"If there is, I never saw it," Marilyn answered.

"Thank you, Marilyn," Joellyn murmured. It had been a real pleasure, as usual.

She walked back toward her office, boiling inside. It was so hard not to want to reach out and wring Marilyn's neck. How could the woman possibly expect her to know off the top of her head all the ins and outs of all the different jobs in all the departments? What the devil was wrong with her? She always managed to make Joellyn feel so...so inadequate.

She felt a twinge of something. She wasn't sure what exactly—probably insecurity. Maybe she *should* have learned more than she had by this time. If she'd known more of the finer details, whatever had gone wrong might have been corrected by now.

But then again Marilyn was being run ragged by the internal auditors. She probably thought her precious department was under criticism and was feeling super-sensitive about it.

But there was no reason to feel that way; they only wanted to find out what was going wrong with the system, not the women in the billing department.

There was enough to worry about without creating more waves.

The walk down the corridor took only a few moments. Deep in thought, Joellyn had almost reached the office supply room when a wave of husky laughter floated out through the open doorway.

It had to be Dianne—she was the only woman in the place with a laugh like that, a laugh that was half delighted schoolgirl, half invitation. Joellyn almost walked on, when she heard Mike's voice.

"Why, Dianne," his amused voice murmured, "you *are* funny! How come someone with your sense of humor isn't at home writing jokes for a living instead of sitting behind a typewriter all day at United?"

The bubbling laughter started again. "I don't know, Mike. Why aren't you at home with me, helping me think up funny things to do?"

Joellyn's eyebrows shot up in surprise. Who would ever think Lanagan's secretary would behave like that right here in the office? And Dianne had gossiped about *her* sleeping around? She couldn't begin to match Dianne's track record if this was any indication.

She hesitated outside the door for a full minute, at war with herself, listening to a tiny voice inside.

I have no claim on him. I don't even want one.
Oh?
Not really. Well, almost. But almost doesn't count, remember...

Mike's voice was, even now, causing small ripples of pure pleasure to rush throughout her body, even though his words were directed toward another woman.

So? If he wants to trade small talk with Dianne, that's his business, isn't it?

Probably. She should definitely leave him alone.

Oh? Really? You don't care at all?

No, she didn't. It was impossible. The whole thing was impossible. She was stupid to have even thought of it.

Are you sure it's impossible?

Yes. Absolutely sure. She'd never been so positive about anything.

But what if Uncle John is totally innocent?

There was still David. It wouldn't work.

But you always wanted children.

Her own. Not someone else's.

But at least give it a try. You know no one else ever made you feel the way he does. If you don't give it a chance, how can you ever know?

She shouldn't . . . she knew she shouldn't let it, but the inner voice was winning. Suddenly it didn't matter. Nothing mattered. She didn't care. For only the second time in her life sheer impulse was winning a definite battle with her common sense, and there didn't seem to be any more reason not to go in there and claim her man than there had been not to go back and buy that red Porsche. She took a deep breath and swung in through the doorway.

Momentarily ignoring Mike, she looked straight at Dianne, secretly pleased at the annoyed flush she saw rising on Dianne's face. Then she turned to Mike and smiled. "Hi there," she said. "I thought I heard you in here. How are you doing?"

"Fine, great, just great. And you?" Mike leaned back against the wall, surprised at how glad he was to see her. She didn't appear to be angry. This surprised him, too. He'd been sure she was never going to speak to him again after the past weekend.

His glance sped from the top of her head to her ankles and back up. A sudden, powerful rush of feeling made his breath catch in his throat. God, she was lovely... so lovely.

"I'm terrific," she answered. Her blood sang as it raced through her veins, and her fingertips tingled with excitement. What was it about him that made every nerve in her body feel alive, every pore want to reach out and pull him toward her?

Her gaze traveled over his face, caressing the crinkles at the edges of his eyes. "I've never been better," she added. Out of the corner of her eye she saw Dianne turning to leave.

Joellyn held up her hand to stop her. "Oh, don't let me interrupt your conversation, Dianne. I just thought I heard Mike's voice and popped in to say hello." She turned back toward Mike. "By the way, Mike, since you seem to have such an affinity for Italian food, I'm making lasagna tomorrow night, if you're interested." There! She'd said it.

She smiled innocently, enjoying his discomfort. It was going to be fun watching him get out of this.

Mike was astonished. What was she up to? He pulled at his collar, wondering why it was suddenly so tight. "Not tonight?"

"Not tonight," she said. "I'm always busy on Wednesdays, remember?"

He nodded.

"Besides," she said, "it takes time to cook real homemade lasagna. I have to start it tonight after I get home."

"Tomorrow night's fine," he said. "I'm playing racquetball with Randy tonight, anyhow." He laughed. "I don't want to foul that up. Racquetball partners are pretty hard to come by these days."

She smiled, pure delight shining straight out of her eyes and into his. "Whatever you say," she answered. "You remember the address, don't you?" She glanced toward Dianne, who was now a deep red. If Dianne wanted something to gossip about, she was ready to give her plenty. And at least this time it would be true.

Mike's eyes twinkled with amusement. "I think I can find it all right." By now he was fully aware of what she was doing, and in spite of his reservations, it tickled him immensely.

So she had a bit of a jealous streak, did she? He chuckled under his breath. If she had any idea how she made him feel just standing in front of him, she'd know she had nothing to worry about.

As far as his feelings went, anyhow, he reminded himself. There were still too many unanswered questions for him to just chuck it all, say what the hell and sweep her into his arms here and now, the way he wanted to.

"About seven?" He tried not to look into her eyes. If he looked straight at her, he'd be lost. He was probably already lost.

Joellyn thought for a moment. "Tell you what. Why don't you come a little later, about eight? You did say you like to have dinner a little later in the evening, didn't you?"

Dinner? Did he want to have dinner?

Oh, hell. Yes, dinner. And breakfast. And dinner the next night, and every night after. It was already too late. He couldn't back out now. Not anymore.

"Lasagna at eight sounds terrific," he said. He felt like laughing out loud but settled for a slow smile. "I'll be looking forward to it."

"See you then!" She smiled at Mike, fluttered a tiny wave at Dianne and walked out of the supply room, leaving Dianne alone with Mike.

"Well, she sure didn't waste any time getting to you," Dianne muttered under her breath.

"What?" Startled, Mike turned back toward her.

"Oh...nothing," Dianne said. "Only...well, watch yourself, Mike. You seem like such a nice guy."

He frowned. "What's that supposed to mean? I don't follow you."

"It's only that..." Dianne hesitated. "Well, you're new here. I'm only trying to do you a favor, if you know what I mean."

"Actually, no, I don't know what you mean." He raised his eyebrows. "Why don't you tell me."

She lowered her voice. "Oh, I hate to spread office gossip. I really do. And no one knows if it's true, so I really shouldn't say anything."

"But you will, won't you?"

She squirmed. "Well, like I said, nobody knows whether it's true, but I've heard stories...."

"What kind of stories?" Mike asked.

"The kind I hope nobody has the opportunity to spread about me. I mean, little bits and pieces here and there, but they all add up to the same thing." She stopped and looked at the floor.

"The same thing?" Mike prompted.

"Well, I heard that Joellyn—oh, how do I put this? That Joellyn has been promoted time and time again, but not because she's all that great at accounting. Now—" she held up her hand "—I don't know if it's true. You know how these stories are—how they get started, I'll never know—but I keep hearing it." She averted her eyes from Mike's penetrating gaze. "Just be careful, that's all."

She smiled. "Now I have to get back upstairs or Mr. Lanagan will be wondering what's happened to me." She walked out of the supply room, leaving the heavy scent of her perfume hanging in the air.

Mike was thoroughly baffled. This was twice now he'd heard the same thing, and from different sources. He felt something gnawing in the pit of his stomach. What could have caused this gossip?

And what could he do if he found out it was true? Could he possibly turn off the feelings he already had for her? He didn't think so.

And another thing bothered him. She'd been terribly friendly a few minutes ago. Evidently she hadn't yet heard about his confrontation with John.

Or had she, and was playing a very clever cat-and-mouse game?

And the big question still in his mind nagged at him, tormenting and frustrating him.

The Porsche.

What about the Porsche?

No matter what, he'd ask her again tomorrow night over dinner. Maybe he could phrase it in a way that wouldn't offend her. But knowing his talent for putting his foot in his mouth where she was concerned, he'd have to work on that. He didn't want to make things any worse than they were, especially since John was even now packing up his things in the plant. He'd tried to stop him, but John had adamantly refused to listen.

Well, he'd have to go out back and try one more time before Joellyn heard about it. He sighed and headed back out toward the shipping dock.

JOELLYN HUMMED softly as she picked up a stack of invoices, trying to concentrate on the problem at hand, but somehow Mike's face appeared on every page.

This *had* to stop. She'd lectured her employees about mixing their personal and professional lives; now she was doing the same thing. She was going to have to figure out a way to stop thinking about him when she was at work.

But she could barely breathe whenever she was anywhere near him or even thinking about him. Somehow, in a short span of time, thoughts of this man had invaded every waking moment, dropping in on her dreams, filling a void in her life that a month ago she hadn't even realized existed, creating almost overwhelming problems for them both.

She reluctantly turned her full attention to the invoices. She picked up the first one, scrutinizing every line. Something was very wrong; she could feel it...but what?

Everything looked all right, but she was sure the secret was locked somewhere within these papers, waiting for someone to find the key.

Lost in thought, she heard a soft noise and looked up to see Randy leaning casually against her doorway watching her and shaking his head. "I can't believe you're going through those things again, Joellyn. What are you looking for now?"

"I don't know," she confessed. "I just have the feeling that whatever's happening to our tubing is going to show up in these invoices sooner or later."

Randy sat down and leaned his elbows on her desk. He folded his hands under his chin and looked straight into her eyes. "Joellyn," he said, "you're developing a real hang-up about those things. Marilyn told me you were in her office a while ago badgering her about them. Why don't you just relax and let the detectives handle it? After all, we're paying them a lot of money. Let them earn it."

Joellyn flushed with embarrassment and anger. How dare Marilyn go over her head like that? "I beg your pardon!" she exclaimed. "I'm still accounting manager here, am I not? Is billing supposed to be off-limits? I had some questions and I asked them. What's wrong with that?"

Randy reached over and lifted her chin, a gesture that infuriated her even more than his words. "Joellyn, the thing is, you're wasting a lot of time and energy that you should be expending managing the entire accounting department, not just billing. That's what we're paying you for. Nowhere in your résumé does it say you have to play Nancy Drew, now does it?" He smiled. "We'll find out what's happened to the inventory soon enough. Personally I still think it's something we've screwed up in our accounting procedure, although I haven't yet figured out what it is."

"Neither have the auditors," she muttered.

"That's true," he agreed, "but please try not to antagonize our supervisors. Don't forget. They have a lot of work to do."

"And so do I, Randy. So do I." She watched him walk away, shaking his head.

She shuffled absentmindedly through the invoices, stacking them into separate piles—credit memos in one, invoices in the second, voided invoices in the third. Then she idly wondered what had happened to the other three copies of each voided invoice.

She sat without moving for five minutes, staring at the voids. They looked the same as they always had—just blank white sheets with "Void" handwritten across the front. Come to think of it, she'd never seen the rest of the copies, had never even thought about them. But now everything was important.

Sighing, she got up and headed for billing again. Randy was going to be ticked off at how swiftly she'd disobeyed his orders. Twice in one afternoon. Marilyn would hit the ceiling. But something was nagging at her, and she had to find out what it was.

Marilyn was on the phone again, speaking softly into the receiver. She looked up when Joellyn reached her desk.

"Here I am again," Joellyn said, smiling as Marilyn hung up her phone.

"My, how nice," Marilyn drawled. "What is it this time?"

"Just a short one. What happens to the rest of the void copies?"

"The what?" Marilyn stared at her.

"The other copies of the voided invoices. What happens to them?"

"I don't know." Marilyn looked puzzled. "I never get them. I just get the white top copy that says 'void.' That's all I ever got. What's going on now?"

"You don't have any idea where they go? To the files out back maybe?"

"Don't ask me. We never see them."

"But there are four copies, all typed at the same time. What happens to the ones that are voided?"

"I have no idea," Marilyn stated flatly. "I never even thought of trying to keep track of all that. Maybe they can tell you out back."

Joellyn turned to leave. "Okay," she said. "I'll check out there."

Marilyn stared at her for a moment, her face a mask. "Well," she said, "if you're going to check with your uncle, you'd better move fast. Either he got fired or he just quit. He's packing his personal belongings right now out in the shipping office!"

Joellyn's mouth opened, but no words came out. Her first impulse was to turn and run out of the office, but she couldn't move.

Surely she'd heard wrong. That couldn't have been what Marilyn had said. Her lips felt numb, then words came out slowly, sounding as if they came from far away. "What did you say?"

"I just heard he went into Mike Walker's office a while ago and came out frothing at the mouth. He's getting ready to leave right now."

Without another word Joellyn turned and walked swiftly out of the office, silently cursing her high heels for slowing her down. She ran through the hall, past the entranceway to the factory, through the storeroom, hurrying past the stacks of tubing, their colors blurring into a kaleidoscope of red, blue, chrome, yellow—a videotape on fast forward.

In a dark corner of the shipping dock, lit only by one bulb hanging from a wire, John Terrell was tossing things into a cardboard box. In another part of the area groups of people stood silent, wide-eyed with shock.

She slowed down as she got closer, her breathing ragged and uneven, her palms perspiring.

What could she say to him? What had Mike found out? She couldn't believe it had come to this, and yet she'd seen the cars in the garage.

John looked up as she approached. The overhead light cast long shadows over his face, making his eyes look dark, his thin cheeks even thinner, the horizontal lines on his forehead even more pronounced. His plaid flannel shirt hung loosely on his thin shoulders as he dropped a small radio into the box and hastily searched the desk drawers for anything he might have overlooked.

They eyed each other. For a moment neither spoke. Then John said, "Well, the word gets out fast around here, doesn't it?"

Joellyn's eyes glistened with tears. "Uncle John, what happened?" she asked, feeling sick.

"What happened?" John laughed shortly. "What's it look like? They wanted me to take a lie detector test, and I told 'em to stuff it where the sun doesn't shine!"

"But, Uncle John, why didn't you take it? It would have cleared you!"

"I don't *have* to take it," he said. "I'm sick of people thinking I did something wrong. You should have seen the look on Mike Walker's face a while ago. He thinks I did it, all right. Well, let him think whatever he wants! I don't care what he or anybody else thinks anymore!"

She swiped at her eyes with the back of her hand. "But, Uncle John, you shouldn't leave like this. You should stay here and fight it! Don't you see?"

He snorted. "I'm sick of fighting all the time. I don't need this. I got plenty of money. Don't you worry none."

"But what did he say?" She was frantic. "Uncle John, *please*. Tell me!"

He laughed shortly. "Nothing. He didn't really say anything. He doesn't know anything, either. He just thinks he does."

"But what does he think he found? Please, Uncle John, I can't help you if you won't talk to me."

Her insides bubbled and churned. They'd found the cars. She'd known they would. He was going back to prison.

"I'm telling you, I haven't done anything wrong, Jo, or at least not what they think. To hell with 'em. I can beat this, and I can find another job, too, if I need to."

She was shocked. Was he crazy? What did he mean, he had plenty of money? He *needed* this job.

"*Mr.* Walker did this," he muttered bitterly. "He really thinks I did it." He laughed angrily. "He doesn't know *how* I did it, but he thinks I did. Isn't that a laugh?" He nodded toward the transistor radio in the box. "That's mine, in case anyone wants to know."

Joellyn was frozen. So it *was* Mike. Mike must know John was her uncle. He'd probably always known it. And that was why he'd asked her about John. *Just tossing out names,* he'd said. Sure. He knew. He'd known all along. And he thought she was trying to hide it from him.

But she had been, hadn't she?

"He actually said that?" she demanded, chilled by her next thought.

Mike thought she was involved. He'd been watching her. He'd said he wanted to make love with her, and she'd fallen for it.

Fool! How could she have been so stupid?

"Uncle John..." She reached over and touched his shoulder, her stomach twisting with nausea as she spoke the dreaded words. "I'm only going to ask you one more time. *Is* there anything to this?"

He snorted derisively. "Not a chance. Unless somebody's set me up."

He picked up his jacket and slipped it over his shoulders. "Now look, I don't want you worrying about this. I'll be okay. You just be a good girl and do your job."

"But, Uncle John," she spoke slowly, sick with realization, "they'll think I'm in on it, too!"

He shook his head. "Hush now. They won't think any such thing. Don't worry about it. They can't touch you."

She wasn't getting through to him. "Uncle John, listen to me," she pleaded. "Yes, they will! They'll think I'm in it with you. Don't you understand what I'm saying? If someone's set you up, they could set me up just as easily. Can't you see?"

He tried to grin. "Kid, you always did have an active imagination. Now simmer down and go on back to your desk. Everything'll be all right. Believe me." He leaned over and gave her a quick peck on the cheek.

Joellyn stared past him at the shipping dock. Huge doors clattered, metal screeching against metal as they opened. A semi stacked with tubing pulled out; another shipment ready to leave. Icy wind blasted through the passageway and swirled past her shoulders, making her shiver uncontrollably as John started to walk away.

Then she remembered. "Uncle John," she asked, her teeth chattering, "can you tell me one thing?"

"Sure." He stopped, his expression unreadable. "What do you want to know?"

"What happens to all the copies of the voided invoices?"

The shipping dock workers eyed each other, listening.

John's eyebrows drew together in a perplexed frown. "You mean when they're voided in the sales department? I don't know."

"No, I mean if they are voided out here. If you get a cancellation, what happens to it?"

He shrugged. "I send it up to billing. Everything goes there. Why? Did you find something?"

"No," she said. "I just wondered." Her heart sank as she watched him walk away. Her worst fears had been realized. They thought Uncle John did it. Or Mike did.

Mike.

Thoughts of him raced through her mind, images of their short time together blending into one soft and lovely watercolor scene, the edges blurred by her tears.

She heard a soft noise behind her. She whirled around to find Mike standing behind her. He reached out to her. "Jo..." he said, his eyes pleading.

She shook his hand away, her eyes narrowed. "Don't touch me," she whispered. "Don't ever touch me again."

She turned from him and ran back through the factory, her mind churning.

Had she been wrong in defending John, blinded to his true character by her childhood memories of a gentle, loving man? Why hadn't he ever mentioned the antique cars, if everything in his life was on the up-and-up? How *could* it be? John didn't have anywhere near the kind of money it took to have even one of those cars, much less two!

Did Mike have something substantial to go on, or was he the sort of man who could wreck another's life without giving it a second thought? How could he have seemed to care for her when he knew he was getting ready to do something like this, and even this afternoon accepted when she foolishly asked him to come for dinner? And how could she have been naive enough to have fallen for him so quickly, allowing the spark they'd both felt to turn into a raging fire burning almost out of control?

Almost . . . but almost didn't count.

Haunted by the memories they'd made together, one thought lingered in her mind.

How could she not?

CHAPTER NINE

JOHN SWUNG his pickup out of his driveway and headed west toward Interstate 57, which would take him down through Kentucky and south toward Florida.

At least it was warm in Florida, not like this god-forsaken state where it was either snowing or raining or so damn hot and humid a man couldn't breathe. There didn't seem to be any in-between.

The rain pelted against his windshield, and the wind sluicing across the prairie made his pickup shudder.

But he'd be out of this weather soon. A couple of days traveling, then he'd spend a few days visiting his sister, then he'd have to get in touch with their Florida contacts. Al had given him the phone numbers this afternoon, right after—but he didn't want to think about this afternoon. It was over and done with, and not a minute too soon, either. It was time to get away. He should have done it a lot sooner.

He pulled out onto the interstate and headed south.

South. Just the sound of it made him feel better. Too bad Joy wasn't with him now. She'd always loved Florida. Loved the sun, always lifting her face to catch every ray, the same rays that killed her, or so they said. One last trip to St. Pete, and right after they'd gotten home he'd seen the spot on her back. A few months later, in less time than it took to save for the trip, she was gone...gone...

Almost blinded by sudden, overwhelming grief that stung the back of his eyes and had him fumbling in his pocket for a handkerchief, he barely saw the semi bearing down on him. The shrill whine of the air horn drowned out the sound of its massive engine as the driver downshifted and tried to avoid the pickup that had suddenly, inexplicably swerved into his way, but it was too late.

John felt a horrendous crash and felt himself rolling, rolling, and the last sound he heard was his own voice crying out, "Joy...I need you...Joy..."

MIKE HUNG up the phone, shaking his head in disgust. It was getting harder and harder to bridge the chasm between himself and his son. At first Dani had adamantly refused to put David on the phone.

"Mike, he says he doesn't want to see you for a while."

Mike couldn't believe his ears. "What?"

There was a pause. "He said something about a lady...." She paused again, waiting.

He felt his blood pressure rising. "What about the lady, Dani?" Why was it all right for *her* to remarry *and* become pregnant again right away, but he couldn't even share a pizza with someone without David withdrawing completely? What the devil was going on here?

"Well, he didn't say much, Mike, but I gather he doesn't think too much of her."

"I could tell that," he admitted, "but I sure as heck can't see why. They never said more than a dozen words to each other."

"Maybe that's one reason why," she said.

"I don't understand this at all," he said. "What's that got to do with me flying up there to see him this weekend?"

"Mike." She gave an exasperated sigh. "You can't just expect to 'fly up here' at the drop of a hat and see David. We have plans for this weekend."

"Well, then, what about next weekend?" he asked.

"That's out, too. We're taking him to the Ice Capades next Saturday night. We already have tickets. Really, Mike, you'll have to give me a little more notice. We have our own lives to lead, too, you know."

"All right, all right," he sighed. "In three weeks, then. Either I'll fly there, or you can put him on the plane and I'll meet him here. In the meantime, may I at least say good-night to him?"

"I don't want you upsetting him, Mike."

"I'm not going to upset him," he said, controlling himself. "I only want to say good-night!"

There was another long pause. "All right. But make it quick."

"Sure," he muttered to himself as she went to get David. "I'll make it quick. Real quick, so Daddy Joe can tuck him in."

David came on the phone. "Hello, Daddy."

"Hi, son." Mike felt the quick rush of love he always felt at the sound of David's voice. "How about I come to see you in a couple of weeks?"

"Okay, Daddy." There was a silence.

"Or," Mike said, "your mama said maybe you can fly out to see me. Would you like that?"

"All by myself?" David's voice was an excited squeal.

"All by yourself, sport. I'll meet you at the airport. How about it?"

David giggled. "Maybe I can watch a movie on the plane," he bargained, fully aware his movie-watching hours were severely restricted. "Can I do that?"

"Sure can," Mike said, making a mental note to make a reservation on a flight with a decent movie.

"Can I eat dinner on it, too?"

Mike chuckled. Kids were terrific. The smallest things could make them happy. "You can eat dinner on it, too," he promised.

He heard the receiver tumble as David jumped with excitement. Dani picked up the receiver again. "Well, you managed to get him in an uproar right at bedtime, as usual. Thanks so much, Mike." She hung up without saying goodbye.

Damn! He shook his head. No matter what he said or did, it looked hopeless. Almost as though no matter how many steps he climbed, there was an even longer, steeper set waiting at the end.

This, on top of the day he'd had. First John's totally unexpected outburst, then his walking off the job, not to mention Joellyn's refusal to listen to a simple explanation. But he owed her one. Even if she didn't want to listen, he probably should call her.

He lifted the receiver again, dialed her number and listened to it ring, then remembered this was Wednesday night. Her night at the home. Pictures of her with the kids filtered through his mind—kids who needed so much, and there she was, a woman who had so much to give. It was so confusing. What could have happened between her and David? Whatever it was, how could he have missed it?

Jealousy probably. A common characteristic among children of split marriages. Although David didn't really have any reason to be jealous, not now, anyhow. But he did want to talk to Joellyn away from the office. Just to explain.

Maybe if he drove over there, she'd be home. She should be home early. She'd said she had to make lasagna. No, strike that, she probably wasn't going to makc it now. Not after what had happened today.

He thought it over for a few more minutes, then made up his mind, grabbed his jacket and headed out the door.

Just a few minutes of her time. That was all he wanted. What he needed was something else again.

JOELLYN HAD BEEN in her apartment for ten minutes when she heard a knock on the door. When she looked through the security peephole and saw who it was, anger rushed through her body, clouding her mind.

Anger at Mike for being so overbearing and suspicious. Anger at John for whatever had caused him to quit his job and go heaven knows where. She'd been on the phone trying to call him when she heard the knock, but he hadn't answered his phone.

And she was very angry at herself because of the way, even now, the sight of Mike affected her.

She opened the door. "What are you doing here this time of night?" she asked, frowning.

His glance flickered over her, and she saw the briefest hint of a smile, a look of pleasure. "I wanted to talk to you."

"No," she said. "Forget it, Mike. Let it go. Whatever it was, it's not important anymore." She started to close the door, but he held it open with the tip of his toe.

"Just give me a minute," he said. "Then I'll go."

She sighed with resignation. "All right," she agreed. "One minute, that's all. It's late."

He walked in and swung around to face her. What was it about her eyes that seemed to be drawing him closer... closer... ?

He found himself walking toward her, then before he could think twice about it she was in his arms and his face was buried in her hair. "Ah, Jo," he whispered, "what are we doing? There has to be a way to straighten this out." He tipped her chin up toward his face and felt the same gauzy feeling her nearness always caused. Her lips drew closer, her eyes were pools of unfathomable depth, and the scent of her, that wonderful scent, was rapidly overpowering his reserve.

He bent toward her. She opened her lips, and he felt a drowning, sinking sensation. It felt so right, so utterly right.

"I don't know, Mike," she murmured. "Everything just seems to be working against this. I know how I feel, and I think I know how you feel, but—" She broke off as the phone rang.

"Damn!" he whispered. "Let it ring, Jo."

"I can't," she said. "Nobody ever calls this late. It might be important." She made a move to draw away.

"No," he whispered. "Let it ring. Please, let it ring. We have to talk."

She pushed him away. "No, Mike, I *have* to answer it." She lifted the receiver. "Hello? Yes, this is she." He saw her eyes widen with shock. "When?" Her hands were trembling. "What happened?" she asked.

"How is he?" She listened intently, avoiding his eyes. "Yes, I'll be there as soon as I can. About thirty minutes. Yes. Thank you for calling."

She hung up the phone and turned to him, her face a white mask. "Uncle John's had an accident. A semi hit his truck and rolled it into a ditch on the interstate. They said it's bad." She began trembling violently. "He's unconscious. I have to leave right away." She looked around frantically, trying to locate her purse.

"Jo," he said, "let me go with you—"

"No!" she cried. "You've done enough! This is your fault! Go away!" She grabbed her purse and headed for the door. "You caused this, you with your digging and your questions and your constant suspicions."

She stood with her hand on the doorknob. "Listen, Mike, John Terrell is the closest thing to a father I've got. I love him. I *know* he's innocent!" She opened the door. "Do you *hear* what I'm saying, Mike? John Terrell did *not* steal that tubing!" She turned away from him and headed down the steps.

He ran down the steps behind her and followed her to the car. She started the engine, then turned to look at him one more time. Eyes flashing, she rolled the window down. "And I'll tell you one more thing, Mike Walker. If he dies, I'll never forgive you. Never!" She revved up the engine, and was gone.

THE NEXT DAY the news was all over the plant. Mike spent most of the morning in his office, agonizing over a decision he hated to make, but one he had to. He'd gone too far to let it rest now, no matter what.

By noon he'd heard that John hadn't regained consciousness, was still in intensive care, and Joellyn had come in about eleven after spending the night at the hospital. Randy had said he'd keep him posted on John's condition, but so far there was nothing new to report.

Not as far as Randy knew, anyhow. Mike's eyes involuntarily strayed to the note he'd received in the intercompany mail a few minutes ago. He felt worse about this than he'd felt about anything since his divorce. Joellyn's eyes, when he reached out to her and tried to explain the unexplainable, had haunted him all through the night. And he couldn't blame her a bit. He'd have felt the same way himself, given the same circumstances.

He wondered what John had said to her earlier. Had he told the truth and admitted he'd lost his temper and stormed out of Mike's office? Probably not, judging from the way she'd reacted.

By noon he'd read and reread the note at least a dozen times. Sighing heavily, he unfolded it again.

"Mike," he read silently, "forget about dinner tonight or any other time. Joellyn."

That was it. No hesitation, no warmth, nothing. She'd sliced through what had almost been between them very neatly.

A clean cut. No sutures needed.

He wondered if he should call and try again to explain, but what good would that do? She was aware of the situation, of John's tenuous position as well as her own, he was sure. Probably better than anyone else. She had to be; it was the only explanation he could think of for her behavior.

Such a puzzling woman. Her reactions seemed to be jumping from one extreme to another. He'd wondered about that when she sailed into the supply room like Admiral Farragut with a definite "damn the torpedoes, full steam ahead" look in her eyes, laughing and flirting with him right in front of Dianne. She must not have known about John when she invited him over.

But she knew now.

This seemed to be another extreme reaction. Surely she couldn't be blaming him for John's accident? And yet maybe she *did* have something to cover up. He hated to think this, but had she become involved with him to cover up her involvement in the theft? How involved *was* she?

Fleeting memories shot through his mind. Joellyn's gentle touch as she'd taken care of the kids at the home. The way her eyes had looked the night he'd been about to head for her shower. It seemed so long ago. But the look in her eyes that night was no put-on. She hadn't been acting then.

How had he gotten himself into this situation? Here he was half in love with—

He stopped, stunned by the enormity of what had just hit him.

Half in love?

Only half?

He leaned back in his chair and stared at the hair that had all of a sudden stood straight up on the back of his wrists, an unmistakable manifestation of his emotional trauma. It told him all he needed to know about his own feelings.

Yes. He was lost. It was already too late.

He couldn't believe she'd done anything wrong. But if she had, he'd have to find some way to help her. He stared at the wall opposite his desk for a long time, fingering the stack of Dun and Bradstreet reports, delaying the inevitable.

None of the D and Bs on the other plant personnel had shown anything suspicious. He hadn't really thought they would.

There had been a few overdrawn checking accounts, a few lawsuits, one bankruptcy, late child support and alimony payments—all the things otherwise intelligent people manage to inflict upon themselves at one time or another during the course of their lives. But nothing in them even approached the level of suspicion Al's and John's reports had generated.

Not to mention the fifty thousand dollars for Joellyn's Porsche. He found himself almost hoping someone else *had* bought it for her—at least that would explain where the money had come from. But one thing was for sure. Now was not the time to ask her about the Porsche.

Damn it all! Why couldn't she have settled for a secondhand Chevy like everyone else?

Remembering the volume of late child support payments he'd run across in these reports, he grabbed his calendar and almost whistled with relief when he saw he still had plenty of time to get David's check off. He couldn't forget about that, no matter how many problems he was running into here.

And—he looked at the calendar again—he had fifteen more days before he was to meet David's plane at O'Hare. And he couldn't wait. He wasn't going to let anything here interfere with that, either. David came first.

But for now it looked as though no matter how he felt about Joellyn, and no matter what condition John was in at this point in time, he was going to have to have Lanagan's detectives run a full investigation on all three of them. John and Al and Joellyn.

He shook his head, dismayed. She was too much in the picture—too many things concerning the missing inventory centered around her. And John couldn't tell them anything now. Maybe never.

There was only one way to find out for certain whether or not Joellyn was involved in the theft. Frowning and apprehensive, he reached for the phone.

"HEARD ANYTHING YET, Joellyn?" Randy stood in her doorway, chewing on his unlit pipe, his head tilted in concern.

"Not really, Randy." Joellyn pushed a stack of papers to the side of her desk. It was pointless going through them, anyway. She was finding it impossible to concentrate. "I talked to the doctor a few minutes ago. He said they won't know anything until he wakes up." She drew a deep, shuddering breath. "If he wakes up."

"Now don't think that way, Jo. He'll wake up." Randy tapped his pipe on his hand. "Anything broken?"

"He has some internal bleeding," she said. "They took X rays last night. They're being read now. But they don't want to move him to set anything if they don't have to. Not yet, anyway."

Randy nodded. "Jo, if you want, you can leave and go back to the hospital."

She shook her head. "Not now, Randy. Maybe later. I'll wait till I hear again from the hospital. I can't do anything there, anyhow. I might as well be here."

"You're probably right about that. Let me know if you hear anything." He started to leave. "Oh, before I forget," he said, "guess who's dropping in at Beautiful Downtown United this afternoon?"

Joellyn barely managed to cover a yawn. "You've got me. Who?"

"Irv Harris."

Joellyn grimaced. "Harris?"

Randy nodded. "One and the same. The big corporate CEO. There's a meeting scheduled in Lanagan's office at two-thirty."

"Are you going?"

"Of course! We're going to discuss the next strategy wave, or whatever you want to call it. The next plan of attack." He stretched. "The modus operandi, if you will."

"Who else is going to be there?"

"Oh, Mike. Myself. Lanagan. Harris. And a couple of new detectives. Lanagan says they're former FBI men, so they should be pretty sharp. He nearly flipped when he found out Harris already knew about the missing inventory. He's been chugging down the antacid like you wouldn't believe."

He had her full attention at last. "Former FBI men? Are you sure about that?"

"Not really, if you want the truth. They could be finally slipping the real thing in. Why they haven't up to now is beyond me."

She turned back to her work as soon as he left the office, memories of the previous night washing over her in desolate waves as she turned her attention to the newest stack of papers on her desk.

She sighed and slipped the first letter out of its envelope, trying to ignore the nagging sensation of guilt that shot through her every time she thought of the terse note she'd written to Mike.

Well, he was probably expecting it. He had to be. He had to know there was no way the two of them could ever repair the damage that had been done. No way.

It had almost looked good. But almost didn't count.

AT TWO-THIRTY her phone rang.

"Joellyn, this is Dianne. Mr. Lanagan would like you to come to his office right away. He wants you to attend a meeting in progress. Can you make it?"

Joellyn was surprised. She'd never before been invited to one of the top-level meetings. Something major must be going on. She spoke into the phone. "Of course, Dianne. Tell him I'll be there within five minutes."

She entered Lanagan's office as unobtrusively as possible and slipped into the nearest vacant seat, nodding hello to everyone, trying not to look directly at Mike.

Jack Lanagan had stopped talking when she entered the room. He waited until she was settled in her chair, then spoke, indicating Joellyn. "For those of you who might not know her, this is Joellyn Keene, our accounting manager. Joellyn, I think you know most of the people here, with the exception of the two gentlemen on your right, Doug Macy and Brice Woodfield."

"Gentlemen." Joellyn nodded, still trying to ignore Mike.

"I'm sure you know Mr. Harris, our chairman of the board."

"Yes, sir," Joellyn answered. "Good afternoon, Mr. Harris."

Irv Harris nodded her way and grunted. Clearly this wasn't the way he wanted to spend his afternoon.

"Joellyn," he said, "this meeting is top-priority and confidential, understood?"

"Yes, sir. Understood." Her face turned pink. Did he think she was going to run out and call the *Tribune?*

Harris motioned toward the two men. "Joellyn, we've called these two in as a last resort. This last closing was a disaster, as you're aware."

Joellyn nodded.

"I want a full physical inventory taken. This should have been done long before now," he said, glaring pointedly at Lanagan. "However," he continued, "it wasn't, so I want it done immediately. Randy, can you handle that? How soon can we have this done?"

Randy shifted in his chair. He pulled his pipe out of his pocket and stared at it as if he was considering lighting it, then stuffed it back into his jacket pocket, glancing toward Joellyn. "Joellyn handles most of these things. How about it, Joellyn? How fast can we get it ready?"

This was what she'd been dreading all along. An interim physical inventory, the most horrendous job she could imagine. "Probably a month. Maybe three weeks. It depends how fast we can get the inventory cards printed. I think we can do it in three weeks, if we have to."

"We have to," Harris stated. "No question about it. This has gone on far too long already. I think you'll all agree with that. Even if you don't, the rest of the board is screaming bloody murder because of this mess, and you know what that means. If they start unloading their stock, there goes United. Now Doug and Brice are on the payroll for the duration. I want you all to give them your full cooperation. They'll be working for Mike Walker and reporting directly to me."

"Are there to be any preliminary counts?" Joellyn asked. "Do we want people to know what's coming?"

"No to both questions," Harris answered. "Jack, do you think we can keep this quiet until the day of the count?"

Lanagan chewed on his third chocolate kiss and stared at Joellyn. "Sure. The only ones who know about it are right in this room. If it gets out, at least we'll know who leaked it."

"I see no problem with keeping it quiet, Mr. Harris," Joellyn agreed. "But what about Doug and Brice? Exactly what are they going to be doing?"

"Shipping," the CEO said. "They're going to be watching the shipping dock."

"We already tried that," Randy interjected. "And nothing turned up. I'm still betting on a book error. I bet when we do the physical we'll find a million dollars more than we show on our books right now."

"I hope to hell you're right, Wagner," Harris said. He stood, stalked toward the door, turned the knob and yanked the door open. "And the rest of you had better hope he's right, too!" He walked out and shut the door behind him with a definite, firm click.

There was a long silence while everyone digested what their chief executive officer had just said.

Randy broke the silence. "Three weeks. Just three weeks! Can you believe that?"

Lanagan reached down into his desk drawer and pulled out his antacid. "I'll tell you what we can believe."

"What?" Randy asked.

Lanagan unscrewed the bottle cap. "He wasn't kidding." He lifted the bottle to his mouth. "We can believe he wasn't kidding."

JOELLYN COULDN'T remember ever having spent a more miserable week. Not that her comfort was the most important thing on her mind right now, but it seemed as though things were going from bad to worse with alarming rapidity.

John had been moved from intensive care and was now in a private secondary-care room. At least he was now and again drifting in and out of consciousness—that was one bright spot at least. Two broken ribs and a concussion, the doctors had said. He should recover, but so far, although she'd been at his bedside every evening and far into the night, he hadn't been able to manage more than a couple of words. But that should improve soon, they'd assured her, unless there were other complications.

But nothing was going right at United. Nothing. Two of her accountants were still out with the flu. The auditors were back, dismantling the entire office. The printer's office had only halfheartedly promised the inventory tags in three weeks. They'd told her they might take up to five, and Lanagan had been livid. To top it all off, she'd gained six pounds in as many days.

Six pounds might not seem like a lot to some people, but she was only a size eight to begin with. Six pounds to her meant that the clothes she'd had tailored to fit her measurements precisely were now getting tight.

Between rushing to the hospital every night and racing home to get at least a few hours of sleep, she'd had nothing to eat except a combination of hospital food and junk food, and it was hard to tell which was the most damaging. To compound her misery, she was constantly hungry.

What an unbelievable eating spree she'd gone on! A truly staggering combination of pepperoni pizza, hot fudge sundaes, Swiss steak, mashed potatoes and gravy and ham-on-rye sandwiches in the hospital cafeteria. But no matter what she ate it didn't taste right. It was never what she wanted, so she'd grab something else on the run, something different, something that sounded terrific until she got it halfway down and discovered it wasn't terrific at all; it was only junk food, and she was still hungry.

Her hunger was running rampant, and she knew it, but she didn't care. All she wanted to do was eat and sleep, and there was no time to do either properly. This lapse into weakness might have been laughable under any other circumstances, but as it was, she felt perfectly horrible. And exhausted. And fat.

She hadn't seen Mike all week. Not even a glimpse. Not that she cared. She never wanted to see him again anyway. Unless . . .

Unless he was right, and John was really guilty. And probably not then. No, strike that. *Certainly* not then. If that were true, then Mike had probably gotten all he needed from her. End of case.

Unless *she* was right and he was still looking....

Every night she'd fallen into a restless exhausted sleep while Mike's face and voice drifted in and out of her dreams.

Anguished, she fought against remembering the warmth of his arms and her relief at being enfolded in them right before the call came from the hospital.

How long could the bittersweet scent of his aftershave linger in her mind? What would it take to pry him from her subconscious? Would she ever be able to stop thinking about him every minute of every day?

Somehow she doubted it.

It wasn't food she wanted, she suddenly realized as she dropped a half-eaten stale Girl Scout cookie into the wastebasket under her desk. What she was craving was something far more elemental than food.

It was too late to forget about Mike.

It had been too late the minute she'd whispered, "Let's go home."

MIKE HAD AVOIDED Joellyn all week. He knew John was improving; Randy had kept him informed. But he was keeping his distance until the reports came in. There was no point in starting something he couldn't hope to finish. Hope. There was an overworked word. What hope was there?

The days and nights had been long. Too long. Phone calls to David were less than satisfactory. The only thing keeping him from total insanity was the knowledge that David would be here in another week.

But this was this week, and he was alone.

He drummed nervously on his desktop, eyeing the clock. It was Wednesday night again, Joellyn's night at the home. But he knew she was heading for another vigil at the hospital. It wasn't hard to keep track of Joellyn. Randy came in every day and kept him informed. And just the fact that she would skip her night at the home told him something he'd been trying to avoid thinking about. She *was* close to her uncle. Obviously she must really love John.

And, in that case, at this point she probably hated *him*.

Well, another long evening was coming up. He glanced at his watch. Five-thirty. He couldn't call David again. He'd called four times already this week and he was running out of things to say.

What could you say to a six-year-old boy day after day? How was school? Did you do your homework? Any problems with your reading? The answer was always no. David never had problems at school, or anyplace else for that matter. He was a smart kid with no problems. While those kids at the home had nothing *but* problems....

The kids at the home. Mike felt the hair rise on the back of his neck as an idea began to form.

Nah. He shook his head, embarrassed. He couldn't do that.

But why not? She wasn't going to make it tonight. They needed *somebody*.

Nah, that was a crazy idea. He couldn't just blast in there and—

Sure he could. They knew him. They'd love to see him, especially Joey.

He grinned. Joey. Joey loved his stories. Laughed at all the right places, listened to every word whether he understood all of them or not.

Yeah. He'd do it. Do them some good, and it would probably do him a whole lot of good. Sure. It was a *terrific* idea! And Joellyn didn't even have to know.

He grabbed his jacket and headed out the door, smiling. It was doing him good already. This was the first time he'd smiled and meant it in weeks.

JOELLYN SAT by John's bed, holding his hand and watching the evening news on the overhead television monitor. It was a good thing they had television in here. It gave her something to do besides looking at the pale face lying in the bed, asleep.

He was almost never awake, but he *was* coming out of it. Slowly. The doctors had told her his recovery would be slow because of his age. But that was okay. At least he was going to recover. Whether it would be a full recovery remained to be seen.

The world news was depressing, as usual. Seven commercials, then back to the news. Sports this time. Mike's face flashed through her mind. Was he watching the news? Probably hanging on to every word of the sports segment. Her thoughts drifted in and out. A segment on the run being held in downtown Chicago. Would he run in it? He'd told her he jogged every morning. Maybe he did long-distance running, too. She didn't know—there was so much she'd never had a chance to find out.

"Jo?" John's weak voice jolted her out of her daydreams.

"Uncle John!" she said. Relief coursed through her. His eyes looked clear, lucid.

"How's everything down at the plant?" he asked.

"About the same. Now don't tire yourself too much trying to talk. How are you feeling?"

"Feeling okay, considering," he said. He closed his eyes for a minute, then opened them again. "Find that tubing yet?"

She shook her head.

"Jo..." His eyes closed again, and he opened them with great effort. "Guess I had a run-in with a semi, didn't I?" He laughed weakly at his own joke.

She smiled. "Guess you did, Uncle John."

"The other driver okay?"

She nodded and squeezed his hand. "He's fine. Not a scratch."

"Jo?" He was looking intently at her, trying to tell her something.

"Yes?"

"Don't blame Mike Walker," he said. "Wasn't his fault. You know me and my temper." His eyes closed again.

"It was so his fault!" she said. "If he hadn't been harassing you—" She stopped. His eyes were closed again.

He forced them back open. "He's just doing his job, honey," he whispered. "All he did was ask me about the money. It's true. There's an awful lot of it...." His voice drifted off.

"Uncle John?" She shook his hand, trying to keep him awake. "What money? What are you talking about?"

But he couldn't answer. His soft snores told her he had fallen into a deep sleep again.

CHAPTER TEN

INSTEAD OF MAKING steady progress, John slipped backward. For days, every time he seemed to be waking, he'd fall back into a deep sleep before Joellyn had a chance to question him again. The doctors told her this was common enough with a deep concussion, that she had to face the fact he was in and out of coma and the best thing for him was to let him rest. When he was ready to awaken, he would. In the meantime she should try to get some rest herself.

She tried. She slept late Saturday, cursing herself for being so careless when she bolted awake to find it was nearly noon. She rushed to the hospital only to find John *had* been awake but had drifted back to sleep again.

So she went to the office and tried to catch up on some work, but she couldn't concentrate. She gave up after a couple of hours, drove home and fell into bed again. It didn't matter, anyhow. There was no point in going over and over the reports until they had a firm physical count. And that was at least two weeks away.

Sunday was almost a repeat of the previous day. John would open his eyes, mumble a few words, nothing that made a lot of sense, then he'd lapse again into unconsciousness, and she was left to wonder— what money? What did John, and probably Mike, know that she didn't?

She was away from her desk Monday when the phone call came. She'd walked back with an armload of unbound computer runs and a thick folder full of financial reports, spied the note and dropped the papers on her desktop while she read it.

"Mr. Walker called," she read. "He wants you to call him back as soon as possible."

Call him back? She shook her head and reached for the folder. No way. She didn't want to talk to him. Not now, not ever. If he wanted anything more from her, he was going to have to scratch for it. Maybe she'd call him back tomorrow or next week. And then again, maybe not.

EARLY THE NEXT MORNING, in the ultimate gesture of defiance, she broke her own cardinal rule and wore slacks to work, just a pair of black slacks with a red short-sleeved sweater, nothing special. To heck with the professional look. She didn't feel professional. She didn't feel anything.

She almost left the apartment like that, but she stopped and took a critical look at herself in the hallway mirror, then walked back into her bedroom and added a string of pearls and earrings. A little better maybe, but what difference did it make? Nobody really cared how she dressed. Besides, the slacks were the only thing in her closet that fit decently.

At seven forty-five she walked into her office just as the phone began to ring. She lifted the receiver, but before she could say "Good morning" she heard Mike's voice.

"Don't you return your phone calls, Joellyn?"

Her heart sank. He sounded so...businesslike. Her answer was crisp and unemotional. "I've been busy, as you should know."

"Too busy to return a simple phone call?"

"Sorry," she said. "If I'd known it was a *simple* call, I'd have returned it sooner."

He ignored her remark. "I need to see you right away. Will you come to my office, please?"

"Mike, I'm busy. Can't it wait?"

"I know you're busy," he said. "So am I. But, no, it can't wait. Please be in my office in fifteen minutes."

His no-nonsense voice was beginning to annoy her. "Mike, are you pulling rank on me?"

There was a pause. "Would I do that?"

"Apparently."

"Well, then, I guess I'm pulling rank on you. I'll see you in fifteen minutes. Be here." He hung up the phone before she could argue any further.

She fumed silently. Of all the nerve—ordering her around like that! No "How's your uncle?" or "Good morning" or anything. Just "Be here in fifteen minutes." Automatically she reached for her mirror and checked her face and hair, sorry now that she'd worn slacks and a sweater. She'd always said if she was going to get bad news, she wanted to be dressed to the nines. From the tone of his voice, she should at least be wearing mink.

Well, too bad. She dabbed some perfume behind her ears. She couldn't look like a *Vogue* model every day. She brushed her hair back from her face and stood up. He'd said fifteen minutes. That was when she'd be there. Not one second sooner.

JOELLYN GLANCED at her watch as she approached Mike's office. It had been exactly fifteen minutes. She drew a deep breath and tapped twice on the frosted glass door.

"Come on in," he called. "It's open."

She opened the door slowly, barely able to conceal the surge of feeling that shot through her at the sight of him, but apprehensive. He'd sounded awfully formal on the phone. Maybe she'd been reading something into this whole thing that had never been there. Maybe she really had misinterpreted his intentions. Maybe she was in serious trouble, as she'd thought before.

He sat hunched over the desk, his hands folded in front of his chin, watching her as she walked into the room and stood silently in front of him.

"Sit down," he offered, his face impassive. He motioned toward the chair in front of his desk.

"No, thank you," she answered. "I'd rather stand. I can't stay long."

"You might as well sit," he said. "This is going to take a while."

She sat down on the edge of the chair and crossed her arms. "Why? What's this all about?"

He leaned back, laughing inside. He knew his body English. So she was going to cross her arms and try not to listen, was she? She really was stubborn!

He fumbled in his shirt pocket for a box of lemon drops, stalling for time. He shook one out of the box and offered the box to her.

She shook her head and waited for him to make the next move. Her gaze never moved from his eyes.

He crunched on the lemon drop, still watching her.

She shifted uncomfortably in her chair. Her gaze dropped to the indentation on his chin, then quickly back up again. She was surprised to find she could feel her lips nestling into it and her tongue tasting it. Wasn't he ever going to say anything? Why was he looking at her like that?

The silence lasted another minute.

Finally he spoke, his voice softer than she'd remembered. "I saw your uncle last night."

"So?" Her eyes were still stony.

"It was kind of late. He was asleep, but the nurses said he's doing fine."

"It must have been late. I was there until eight-fifteen."

"I got there at eight-thirty."

"It was nice of you to visit him. Is that all you wanted to tell me?" She rose, preparing to leave.

"Sit down, Joellyn," he said. He waited for a moment until she was again settled in her chair, then spoke. "Joellyn, in view of evidence that's now come to light, evidence we had no knowledge of before, we're no longer considering your uncle a possible suspect."

She was surprised. "But—what happened? I don't understand! I thought you were convinced he did it."

"He doesn't have any reason to be involved that we can see. Not anymore. I've been pretty busy this week, Joellyn. We know a lot now that we didn't know before. Your uncle's completely exonerated, in view of what our detectives' report shows. Look, for what it's worth, I'm sorry about this whole mess, but if he'd been open with us from the beginning, a lot of this might have been prevented. Including his accident."

She could understand that. She knew John had a vile temper, although she hadn't seen him exhibit it in years. "He said the same thing," she confessed.

He was surprised. "When?"

Her eyes were downcast. "A few days ago, the one time he was really lucid and carried on a halfway intelligent conversation with me."

"What did he say?" He leaned forward with interest.

"Just that I shouldn't blame you, that there *was* a lot of money. Then he fell back into the coma, and he hasn't said much since."

"He said enough." He smiled.

"But what about the report?" she asked.

"For one thing, we finally know where the money came from." He watched her eyes closely.

"What money?" she asked. "The two of you are driving me crazy! I keep hearing about 'the money' and I have no idea what anyone's talking about. Uncle John doesn't have any money, or I thought he didn't, but then how... ?" Her face was a rapid kaleidoscope of emotions.

"You really didn't know?"

Was that a look of astonishment on his face, or one of relief? She began to relax. "Maybe we're discussing apples and oranges, Mike. How about letting me in on the secret?"

"I will in a few minutes, but first I have to tell you this. I had to do something else, too. You're not going to like it." He paused.

"What do you mean?" she asked, suddenly afraid. "Mike, what are you trying to tell me? What did you do?"

He leaned back in his chair, wishing for the first time in his life that he smoked. Maybe a cigarette would help him through this. The lemon drops certainly weren't helping.

He cleared his throat. There was only one way to do this, and that was to get it over with quickly.

"Jo, please try to understand, this was partially in progress before we...before we—"

"What was in progress?" She stared at him. "What are you getting at?"

"Jo," he said flatly, "you were investigated by a private detective agency. The investigation had already begun before we started seeing each other, but there were so many unanswered questions that I had to see the reports."

Joellyn's jaw dropped in disbelief. "Why on earth would you do such a thing?" she demanded. "I haven't done one thing wrong. Not one *thing*, Mike. What possible reason could you have for thinking that I—"

She stopped. Of course. She'd been right. They thought she was masterminding the thefts.

Her gaze moved up over his face, that wonderful, sexy face, and she pushed the thought away. "Are you telling me you didn't trust me?" The hurt showed in her eyes.

"It wasn't a matter of not trusting you, Jo."

"Oh, no? Well, let me ask you point-blank. *Did* you trust me?"

He felt sick. "Not at first," he answered heavily.

"Do you trust me now?" she demanded.

"With my life," he said. "Yes."

"What made the difference?" she asked.

"A lot of things. To begin with, the investigation started as a general thing—a lot of people were checked out, including your uncle and Al Dobson." He saw her flinch at the mention of John's name. "At first the D and Bs were run. That was when we got onto Terrell and Dobson."

Uncle John again. Her heart sank.

He held up his hand. "Hold on a minute, Joellyn." He frowned, puzzled. "Surely you knew they were being investigated? You had to know just about every person in the plant was."

"But *why me?*" she asked. "What could you possibly think I had to do with it?"

"Nothing," he said, trying to smile. "Until I saw your D and B."

"What about my D and B?" she demanded furiously, shaking her head in disbelief. "You've got a lot of nerve. You really have! Prying into my personal life, checking out my entire life history. You *did* check out my entire life history, didn't you? Was it interesting?"

"Joellyn," he protested, "listen to me. This company paid a lot of money to have that done. And, yes," he added, "it was interesting."

"Oh, they paid a lot of money! And that makes it right?" She stood to leave. "I don't care what you found out on your little spying trip. I resent this. I really do."

He jumped up from his seat and strode toward her, grabbing her wrist. "Damn it, Jo. Sit down."

She shook her head. "I'm leaving!"

"If you leave, I'll follow you and we'll have this little talk in your office. Do you want that?"

She shook her head and sat back down, seething.

"Jo," he said, "this is important. It may be one of the most important discussions we'll ever have. Please." He looked into her eyes, nearly drowning in the hurt he saw there. "It was my job, Jo."

She drew a deep breath. "Then you are really an FBI man?"

He smiled. "I guess I can't blame you for thinking that. But it's time for the truth between us, although what I'm about to tell you has to be strictly between us. Nobody here knows, not even Lanagan. Nobody except the board of directors. Nobody *can* know yet, and for a very simple reason."

"Yes?" She regarded him strangely.

"It's because everyone else in this plant is still under suspicion. Everyone. Jo, I'm exactly what I told you. Vice president of manufacturing, but I'm also what they call a corporate troubleshooter. I just happened to unearth a couple of things in previous companies, and the word got around. The board of directors has known about this a lot longer than Lanagan thinks. One of them knows someone who knows me, and that's how I got here."

"Does this mean after it's over you'll probably be leaving?" Her heart sank. It was Lee all over again. How had she fallen into this twice?

"I don't think so, Jo. This one's about done me in. I think I've had enough intrigue for a while."

She began to relax. "Did your investigation turn up anything?"

Mike leaned against his desk. "It turned up just about everything except what I thought it would. But it did explain your Porsche."

She jumped up again. "My *Porsche?* What about my—" She stopped, sudden realization dawning in her eyes. "Oh, no," she murmured, almost to herself. She shook her head and laughed ruefully. "Well, I brought that on myself, didn't I? A fifty-thousand-dollar car on my salary? It must have looked odd now that I think of it."

"Yes, it did," he said. "At one point I was even hoping someone here had bought it for you."

"Oh," she murmured. She looked down at the floor. "You've heard the rumors...."

"Yes," he said simply.

She raised her eyebrows and shrugged. "Well, there's not much I can do about them."

"Do you know who started them?"

"No, and I don't really care," she said. "They're not true."

"Aren't you forgetting something?" he teased.

She frowned, puzzled. "No... what?"

His voice was low. "There's a very strong possibility the rumors may be true now."

She reached for his hand. "Maybe so. In that case, let them talk all they want. But, in the meantime, what *did* you find out?"

"Want me to read the report?" he asked.

She sat back down. "Please do," she said. "I'm not sure I like this. But go ahead, read it."

He raised his eyebrows. "Every word?"

She settled back in her chair. "Yes. Every word."

Mike reached into his desk drawer and pulled out a thick manila folder. His eyes flickered over her, desire for her even at this moment causing his nerves to tighten. "Sit back," he said, "and relax while I read to you the ongoing saga of one Joellyn Keene.

"Joellyn Keene. Age thirty. Lives alone," he read. "With assorted plants and one sheepdog," he added, smiling. "One mother in Miami. So far so good. Bank accounts, checking and savings—is this embarrassing you?" he looked up anxiously. "If it is, I'll stop."

She shook her head. "Not so far," she said.

"Good. I'll plow ahead then. Current checking account balance, seven hundred seventy-five dollars and some odd cents."

"Six hundred fifty-five," Joellyn muttered.

"What?" Mike asked. "I didn't hear you."

"Six hundred fifty-five," Joellyn repeated. "I just bought some groceries. Go on."

Mike pursed his lips. "Savings account, fifteen thousand eight hundred seventy-two dollars. Pretty good. According to this, you've been saving it over a period of years, no unusual deposits or withdrawals." He looked up at her. "That's what got me wondering."

"Porsche, six months old," he continued. "Bought and paid for with proceeds from a trust fund set up by your father just before he died, to be collected by you on your thirtieth birthday, not before. Jo..." He looked up at her and put the folder down. "Look, do you really want to hear the rest of this stuff?" He gestured toward the folder.

"Oh, sure," she said. "We might as well get the record straight once and for all."

He leaned back and smiled as he read on. "Cum laude graduate, University of Chicago." His eyes shone with admiration. "All your classes and grades are here. I had no idea you were so good at so many things. You've planned your life well, it seems."

"Not well enough," she retorted. "Strange things seem to be happening, and I can assure you I didn't plan any of them."

"Well, that's one thing we have in common," he murmured. "Now—" he grinned wickedly "—the really interesting part starts."

He turned his attention back to the paper in front of him. "Engaged at one time to Lee Bronsky." He looked puzzled. "Where have I heard that name before?"

Outwardly Joellyn was perfectly composed, but inside she was simmering. "He's a foreign correspondent with the *Sun-Times*."

Recognition dawned on Mike's face. "Of course! That's a pretty famous byline, even in Philadelphia. How'd you meet him? And what happened?"

"You mean it's not all there?"

"Yes, it's here," he admitted. "I just want to hear it from you, unless you'd rather not discuss it."

"No...it doesn't bother me anymore," she said. "I met him in college. I was young. I had my career ahead of me, and he had his. I just didn't want to spend my life running around the world with him. His job was too dangerous."

"Didn't he win a Pulitzer last year?"

"Yes, and I wish him all the best. I really do. But he wanted the danger and excitement his job gives him. He loves to go out late at night, any night, and party. He especially loves to party in France, London, Spain—anywhere but home. His idea of fun is to cover a coup in South America or a bombing in Lebanon."

She thought for a minute. "The truth is, I never could understand him. For instance, look at the nightlife in Chicago. There's enough excitement here for anyone, but not for Lee. I wanted to stay here and develop my career and someday have a home and a family. But it just couldn't work. We were too different." She shrugged. "I lived through it. And I'm stronger because of it."

Too different, Lee had said. And now here she was falling into the same trap again.

He saw the guarded look in her eyes. "Are you sure you're over him?" he asked gently.

"I've been over him for a long time," she said. "That wasn't what was on my mind."

"What was?"

She raised her eyebrow, leaned over and tapped the folder. "Check in there," she challenged. "I'm sure you'll find it."

He cleared his throat and picked up the folder. "That's about all that's in here," he said. "A few more odds and ends. Your Wednesday nights at the home." He paused.

"Yes," she said. "You ought to try it some time."

"I have something to confess," he said.

"Yes?"

"I *did* try it. Last Wednesday night."

She was giving him the oddest look he'd ever seen. "And?" she asked, holding her breath, waiting.

"And I liked it," he said simply. "I could get used to those kids real fast."

She nodded to herself, as if something had been settled in her mind.

"It's funny," he murmured, "how much an investigation like this can tell you about a person's life."

"Ah, but it's misleading sometimes," she said. "Isn't it?" She looked pointedly at him. "I still don't understand—if nobody here knows what you're doing, how come you have access to all these records?"

He shrugged. "I asked for them. Don't forget. I *am* the vice president!" He laughed and rubbed his head.

"You haven't heard the best part of it yet. Wait till you hear the report on your uncle! I think you're in for a big surprise. I know I was."

"So surprise me," she said grimly. "I could use a couple of good ones for a change."

He pulled out two more folders. "To begin with, his and Dobson's are a lot longer than yours. They're some pair, those two."

"John and Al?" she asked, puzzled. "What possible connection could they have?"

Mike fidgeted, pulling at his collar and his shirt cuff. This wasn't going to be easy, but nowhere near as hard as it might have been if...

"Stop stalling," Joellyn said. "What's he been up to now? I'm sure the investigators have unearthed his prison record, but, Mike, that was so long ago."

Mike coughed. "Well, first of all, I doubt if you know this, but that's where John and Al met."

Joellyn's eyebrows shot up. "You're kidding!" she exclaimed.

"I'm not kidding. They were both in prison at the same time. They recognized each other when Dobson came here last year. The company knew about Dobson's past record, but not John's. So they kept their friendship quiet, met away from the plant.

"Jo, I hope you understand how this looked. We knew they were in on something together. The D and Bs showed a tremendous amount of money going in and out of their personal bank accounts. Big money. We thought...we all thought they were stealing the tubing and selling it. What other reason could there be for a thirty-six-thousand-dollar-a-year man to be running hundreds of thousands of dollars through his bank account?"

Joellyn thought back to the antique autos in John's garage. She leaned forward, waiting.

"Did you know John knows all about restoring antique autos?" Mike asked.

"Restoring them?" Joellyn looked blankly at him. "No. He was always interested in cars. That's what got him into trouble in the first place when he was younger. But, oh, my God!" she exclaimed. "That's what he was doing with those—" She stopped.

Mike regarded her for a moment. "Those what?"

Joellyn looked at the floor, shamefaced. "I saw two cars in his garage," she admitted. "I knew they were expensive. He had over a half-million dollars' worth of autos in there. I used to go to the shows downstate with Lee, and he taught me a lot about them. But I thought...when I saw them I thought—" She stopped again.

"You thought he was in on the thefts, didn't you?"

"Yes," she admitted in a whisper.

"And you didn't tell anyone?"

"No."

"Not even me."

She raised her eyes. "Mike, especially not you."

Mike took her hand. "I think, Jo, we've both learned a serious lesson about trust."

She nodded. "I was thinking something along those lines myself."

"Let's just hope settling the rest of our differences won't be quite as hard on us," he said, smiling.

She smiled. "We can't let them. I can barely squeeze into my clothes now."

He took a quick peek through the frosted window and leaned forward, brushing her lips with his. "You look wonderful to me," he murmured. "You always do."

"And you to me," she said, touching his face. She smiled, thinking about the days to come. And the nights. But then she remembered.

"What about Dobson?" she asked.

"Evidently he and John started talking. John told him he'd found one of those old cars—I think the first one they restored was an Auburn." He opened the folder and scanned the pages. "Ah, yes, here it is. An Auburn. John had found it in some farmer's garage. He could buy it for fifteen thousand dollars, but he needed another fifty to restore it. He knew he could triple his money, but he couldn't raise that much.

"Apparently he'd spent the major part of the insurance policy he inherited from his wife. He mentioned the Auburn to Dobson, and Dobson went in on it with him. They bought it, spent six months restoring it and sold it for a cool hundred and fifty thousand.

"They paid off the parts, split what was left, bought a couple more and fixed them up. Those were the ones you saw. According to the detectives, they're both already sold. And you're right about the amount. They just split over half a million dollars."

"But, Mike, where did Dobson get the money?"

"Good question. But our detectives found that out, too. His wife's family is very wealthy. Her father lent it to them."

"You're sure of all this?" she asked, relief washing over her.

"I'm sure of all this," he said. "Yes."

"But, Mike, why didn't John tell you any of this?"

Mike smiled. "He has a bad temper, like someone else I know."

"Well, I can sure see how he felt," Joellyn said.

Mike laughed. "Jo, if you'd see the D and B, you'd have seen how *I* felt. I never saw so much money going back and forth! It really did look bad."

"I guess," she admitted. "Mike, what about his job?"

"When he recovers, if he still wants it, it's his," Mike said. "He'll need quite a while, though. Jack and I talked about sending him to Florida to stay with your mother for a while."

She nodded. "That's probably where he was headed when the accident happened."

"Probably," he said. He rubbed his forehead. "I feel terrible about the whole thing, Jo, I really do, but the evidence all pointed straight at him. I was absolutely convinced he had to be involved."

"And that I had to be involved, helping to spirit a million dollars' worth of inventory out of here, in between sleeping with heaven knows who."

He leaned toward her, looking deeply into her eyes. "Joellyn, please, forgive me. I've made mistakes where you were concerned, and I'm sorry. Can we start all over and go on from here? I think we have something worth exploring, don't you?"

Joellyn looked down at the desk. They'd both made mistakes. It took a big man to admit he'd been wrong, and she hadn't been very rational about it herself. A slow smile began to dance in her eyes. "As far as the two of us are concerned, no problem. No major ones, anyway, except for one."

"My son?" he asked quietly.

She nodded. "Your son. Mike, children make a big difference in a relationship. We've already seen that. And to tell you the truth, I don't know if we can hurdle this one. He just doesn't like me!"

"Eventually, Jo," he said, "he will. Just as I—" He paused, and the silence lengthened between them as those unspoken words hung in the air.

After a minute, she said, "Look, okay, we'll give it a try." She drew a deep breath. "How'd you like to have that lasagna for dinner tonight? Seven o'clock okay?"

His eyes danced. "Is it ready? I know you have to do quite a bit of advance preparation for lasagna."

"It's ready," she said quietly. "It's been ready in my freezer for quite a while."

He reached over and brushed her cheek with the back of his fingers and murmured, "I'll be there at six-thirty."

Joellyn stood to leave and walked slowly toward the door, lost in thought. She turned back, puzzled. "Mike, the thing is—" she looked straight at him "—if it's not Uncle John, then who is it?"

He rocked back in his chair, hands clasped behind his head. "I don't know," he answered. "It looks like we're back to square one."

"Well, at least we're on square one together." She waved as she slipped out the door. "See you at six-thirty."

"Six." Mike's voice followed her. "Make that six."

IN ALL THE TIME she'd worked at United, Joellyn had never left the office early. Somehow it had never seemed like the right thing to do, no matter what the circumstances.

But today was different.

Strange...everything felt different now. Her orange chair, instead of annoying her with its jarring vinyl brightness, seemed at last to blend in with the rest of the office furniture. Her employees chattered and joked, their voices floating over the partitions in waves that undulated toward her, rolled past her and moved on. She didn't hear the words. She was hearing secret, unspoken words meant for her ears alone.

Mike's voice whispered, echoed in her mind and her heart, and the day sped by, uninterrupted except for one quick phone call from him a little after one.

"Hello? Joellyn here."

"Hi!"

"Oh...hi, yourself."

"I noticed there seems to be a full wine cellar in your apartment...."

She laughed softly. "Well, don't spread that one around. My people already think I'm a little odd."

He chuckled. "Especially lately?"

"Yes. *Especially* lately."

"Well, let's not encourage an office revolt. I called to see what I should bring."

"Really?"

His voice softened. "Nah, not really. I was just sitting here thinking about you."

"Not getting a whole lot done, are you?"

"You're right. Is it possible for one accounting manager to single-handedly wreck the entire career of one vice president?"

She laughed again. "What accounting manager? Do we have one?"

"Probably not today. Look, the other reason I called is, I just talked to the head nurse on John's floor. He's been awake and talking most of the day. She said she's sure he'll be sleeping later on. Do you want to stop by the hospital, anyhow, or do you want to skip it for tonight? I'm just asking," he added hastily.

Joellyn thought for a minute. "He's awake? Really awake?"

"That's what they told me." He waited.

"Well, maybe I should stop by for a minute at least. Just in case he's still awake."

"You can, but he probably won't be," Mike said.

"I'll call in a little while and check."

"Sure. If he's awake, leave early. That way you can see him and still have dinner ready by five-thirty."

"Five-thirty!"

"Did I get the time wrong?" he murmured in an innocent tone of voice.

"Well, just a little! I still have to get home first and, honestly, Mike, I can't really leave here until at least four-thirty."

"Jo?"

"Yes?"

"Haven't you ever heard of playing hooky?"

Joellyn smiled. For once that didn't seem like such a bad idea.

CHAPTER ELEVEN

SURE ENOUGH, John was asleep again when Joellyn called.

"Don't bother coming in tonight unless you really want to," the head nurse told her. "He's doing fine, but he'll be sleeping the rest of the night. And, by the way, we're moving him to a room with two other men. He needs someone around in the daytime to talk to. He's been driving us crazy today!"

Joellyn laughed, vastly relieved to hear John was finally out of the coma. Tomorrow she'd go to see him, tell him about the developments here. And probably gently chew him out for not telling her about the antique cars. She still couldn't understand why he hadn't told her—but tomorrow was another day. Today she had other things on her mind.

Amazing how easy it was to slip her coat on and walk out of the office at three o'clock in the afternoon. Her fingers brushed over the sleeve of her wool jacket. Had the texture always felt this nubby?

Her sharpened senses quickened as she inhaled deeply. Had the air outside always smelled this clean and beautiful, as though a million flowers had burst and released their perfume at this precise moment in time? And where was the music coming from as she drove home? She hadn't turned her car radio on.

She wandered around her apartment, arranging and rearranging the magazines on her coffee table, aligning them first in a neat row, then spread out in a fan shape, then back into a row again. She polished the wineglasses as she set the table, then checked the time on the kitchen clock. Had the clock always been that gauzy shade of peach? She couldn't remember.

She opened the oven door to check on the lasagna, sniffing deeply, savoring the warm oregano-parmesan aroma. Yes. It was perfect. She had never made anything that smelled this wonderful before.

She checked the salad, green and crisping in the refrigerator, then picked up the small copper ramekins of *crème brûlée,* shaking them to make sure they were firming up the way they were supposed to. Was it her imagination, or was this the first time she'd ever been able to get the tops perfectly browned from edge to edge?

Satisfied that dinner was going to be as delicious as she could make it, she drifted through the living room. Light from the brass floor lamp cast soft shadows over her face as she moved around the room, plumping and straightening nonexistent wrinkles on the oversize peach-and-brown sofa cushions.

She walked into the bedroom and stood in front of her mirror, unsure of her outfit now that she was taking another look. When she first put them on, the light blue velvet pants and overblouse had seemed like the perfect thing to wear for a casual evening at home. Now she wasn't sure; she'd noticed white dog hairs on her leg just below the knee.

She started to strip the shirt off and had it halfway over her head when the buzzer sounded. Sighing with resignation, she pulled it back down, smoothing her hair as she walked toward the door. He'd have to see her as she really was, dog hair and all. If he didn't accept her by now, he never would. The time for illusions was past. She reached down to pluck a couple of the hairs off, then opened the door to let Mike in.

He'd been home and changed. The suit and white shirt he usually wore at work were gone, and with them the business executive. Now he was wearing a thick white sweater with a deep blue sport stripe around each arm and a pair of dark blue slacks that outlined every bulge from the waist down.

He leaned casually against the doorjamb, holding out a bottle of Piper-Heidsieck and a bottle of Amaretto di Sorrono. "I wasn't sure which to bring, so I compromised. I brought them both." He walked into the apartment and put the bottles down, stared at her, bemused, for a minute, then reached for her, drawing her close.

"You look so beautiful," he murmured, kissing the tip of her nose. "And you smell wonderful. What kind of perfume is that?"

"Probably lasagna," she answered, laughing softly.

"Ah, lasagna—my favorite kind." His hand caressed her back and he inhaled deeply. "You should always wear it."

She flushed with pleasure. "I'll get some ice and fix us a couple of these." She held the amaretto up. "We can have the champagne later. Oh-oh. Look out. Here comes man's best friend."

Penny lumbered into the living room and, tongue lolling out with pleasure, headed for Mike. She sat on his foot and rubbed against his leg, silently demanding her share of attention.

Joellyn glanced down at his leg. Sure enough, there were white hairs on his pants now. "Well," she said, "look at that. Sheepdogs aren't supposed to shed, but she sure is."

"Maybe she's in love," Mike offered. He rubbed Penny's head affectionately.

"If that's what does it," Joellyn said without thinking, "I should be bald by now." She clapped her hand over her mouth, appalled. The words had rushed out before she could stop them.

Mike glanced at her as though he were seeing her for the first time. "So should I," he agreed, stunned by what they'd both just said.

He scratched behind Penny's ears. "I hate to bring up practical matters, but when's dinner? I'm starving. I haven't been eating right for weeks."

Her cheeks flushed as she took the salad out of the refrigerator and placed it on the table. "I've been having the same problem." Ice cubes clinked as she filled two glasses and handed them to him. "Here, you pour."

He poured the amaretto and sipped his drink, watching Joellyn toss the salad. Suddenly his appetite was gone, replaced by an even more insistent desire. His heart hammering, he set the glass down and walked over to her. He took the wooden salad forks from her hand and dropped them onto the table, wrapped his arms around her and pulled her close. She felt so warm... so soft. She smelled so nice....

"I think we have some unfinished business, you and I," he murmured.

She buried her face against his chest. "So do I," she confessed. The blood began to race through her veins. She felt his hand at the small of her back, warm, insistent, moving down to the end of her spine and back up again.

"You're always with me," he whispered. "Always. Twenty-four hours a day. I can't get you out of my mind." He groaned as his hardness swelled against her. "I don't want to get you out of my mind." His hand caressed her cheek, her forehead. "I haven't been able to think of anything else since the day I met you."

"I know," she murmured. "I know...I keep thinking about you, too. Even when...even after... Mike, every day, whether I want to or not, I've caught myself looking for you in the hallways at work. I can't sleep at night. And the days have been disasters."

Mike drew back far enough so that he could look full into her eyes, his gaze searching. His breathing was ragged as he bent toward her, his lips pressing, demanding until hers opened and his tongue moved slowly inside, meeting hers.

Her breath began to come in short, quick gasps, and her fingers dug into the back of his neck as she drew his tongue in even farther. The primeval, faraway sound of a waterfall echoed through her head as love for this man pushed away all doubts, replacing them with the warm certainty that this was right. This was absolutely right. It had to be, no matter what.

She was barely able to breathe; her body cried out for fulfillment, pulling him closer with invisible fingers. "I love you," she murmured over and over again as her warm breath branded the space under his chin.

"And I love you," she heard him whisper through the forest of desire.

His hand roamed up and down, caressing the small of her back, then drew slowly around to her front, under the velvet waistband of her blouse. His fingers moved in a deliberate, circular motion—gentle at first, but becoming more insistent as his hand moved slowly upward, covering her breast. His thumb moved in lazy circles around her hardening nipples, and her head arched back as she moaned with ascending desire. Her breath caught in her throat when he stopped, his jaw set with determination, and reached around to unhook her bra.

"Mike," she whispered. Her fingers dug fiercely into the hair at the back of his neck. "What about dinner? It's almost ready."

"Turn the oven off," he said. Need for her boiled and thundered throughout his body; he could barely force the words out. "Dinner can wait. This can't."

With almost superhuman effort she moved away from him and turned the oven control all the way off. Then she slid her arm around his waist and drew him into the bedroom, closing the door behind them.

Hands and bodies moved slowly, silently. Buttons slid through their openings. Her fingers undressed and caressed his chest as he pulled her shirt up and over her head. Every movement was done carefully, both looking into each others' eyes all the while. She pulled his shirt off, then reached down to unzip his trousers. She took him into her hands, loving the warm, hard, throbbing pulse of his manhood.

He moaned, pulling her closer, then moved back a little to look at her. Somehow—he wasn't exactly sure when—her slacks and his trousers dropped to the floor. He drew her down onto the bed.

He pulled her slippers off one by one and bent down to kiss the arch of her foot. His lips moved up past her ankle, behind her knee, trailing tiny kisses along her inner thighs; an electric wire dancing in the storm, shooting sparks of desire everywhere he touched. His lips met the soft mound that was damp and waiting for him and his tongue tasted, teasing, worshiping, then moved on.

He reached again for her breasts. His lips covered first one and then the other until he heard her moan and felt her fingers kneading through his hair.

His fingers moved slowly, expertly over her body, touching all the secret places she'd been longing for him to touch, causing every nerve in her body to sky-rocket. His fingers moved inside, exploring even more, making her gasp when he finally reached the secret place and stayed there gently pressing, his lips now covering hers.

Time and space were one as he brought her closer, closer, the sound of her own heartbeat and breathing roaring in her ears. Then her hands reached down, encircling and guiding him until he entered her.

He moved slowly at first. She rose to meet him, moving in perfect harmony with him as their bodies created their own symphony, a brand-new song never before heard anywhere on earth.

They made love slowly, lazily, savoring every sensation new and old. She reveled in the tautness of his body, the wonderful clean smell of his skin, the feel of the hair on the back of his neck and his shoulders and his chest.

He delighted in the smoothness, the absolute perfection of her breasts that swelled so softly and firmly, the warm taste of her nipples that moved with him every time his tongue slid over them.

In perfect tune with each other they made love un-til they were both sated, then fell asleep, his body curled spoon-fashion around hers, his hands cupping her breasts, their ankles intertwined.

THE MOONLIGHT SLIPPED through the blinds quietly so as not to disturb the new lovers. Joellyn awakened, feeling soft and lazy and wonderful. Mike was still asleep, one arm thrown up across his face. She reached out tentatively, fingering his chin, teasing him awake until he opened his eyes and saw her watching him.

He smiled and stretched. "Hello, you. What time is it?"

She stroked his eyebrows. "Umm...it's about one-thirty. And I'm starving. The lasagna's still in the oven. Want me to warm it up?"

"Sure," he murmured, nuzzling her elbow. "I'll even help."

"Only thing is," she said, "I can't guarantee it now." She swung her feet over the edge of the bed. "I've never left lasagna in the oven for seven hours before."

"It'll be terrific," he answered. He watched her reach for her robe. "Hey!" he protested. "Why are you putting that thing on?"

She turned pink. "I need something, don't I?"

"I can't imagine why. I like looking at you."

Mike lay with his head resting on his arms, watching her. She let the robe slide to the floor as she stood and walked toward the door. She glanced back at him. "Hey," she asked, "what about you?"

"What about me?" he teased. He threw the covers back. "Race you to the champagne!" he called, already past her and into the living room.

"It ought to be good and cold by this time," she remarked. "I can heat the lasagna in the microwave. You pour while I get it ready."

She walked into the kitchen, blushing as Mike stood against the doorway eyeing her with undisguised appreciation. "You've got one hell of a body," he murmured. "Everything's just right."

"Thank you very much," she answered. "You're not so bad yourself." She watched him out of the corner of her eye. He *was* perfect. All that jogging and whatever else he did really had him in good shape.

Mike walked over to the refrigerator, took out the champagne and opened it with a loud pop, laughing when it spewed out and onto her shoulders.

Ten minutes passed quickly. Joellyn set the steaming lasagna on the table. "Looks like we might have to throw out the salad," she said, eying the limp vegetables with distaste.

Mike lifted his glass to his lips, savoring the pungent, dry bubbles while he watched her lift the slotted spoon to serve the lasagna, her breasts rising and falling with her movements.

She glanced up and saw him watching her. Then she put the spoon down and reached toward him. "Mike..."

Desire flooded through him again, and he took her hand. "Forget the lasagna for now, Jo. All of a sudden I'm only hungry for you again."

And holding hands like two young lovers on the way to the movies, they walked together back into the bedroom.

"ARE YOU HUNGRY NOW?" she murmured at 6:00 a.m.

"I've never had lasagna at six in the morning, but I guess there's a first time for everything." He rolled toward the edge of the bed and threw the covers off again. "But, yes, I *am* hungry now. I'll run it through the microwave again while you start getting dressed."

Joellyn headed for the shower. She had turned the water on full blast and was standing under it, loving the warm, pulsing spray that poured over her skin, when she heard a loud laugh from the kitchen. A minute later Mike's face appeared around the edge of the glass shower door.

He stepped in, reached for the soap and began lathering her shoulders. "You can forget about the lasagna," he said, still laughing. "Man's best friend already ate it."

"SO JOHN'S GOING to be okay, eh, Joellyn?" Randy perched on the edge of her desk, a horizontal yellow flame spurting ineffectually out of his lighter as he attempted once again to light his pipe. "Damn this thing!" he said, frowning and flicking the spark wheel. "It never wants to work when I want it to."

"You might have better luck if you tried using a pipe lighter," she answered. She didn't want to think about Randy's lighter right now; she wanted to think about the sexy spot inside her ankle that Mike had discovered last night.

"Do you think he'll be coming back?" He drew on his pipe, gray curls of smoke evaporating into the air as he blew the smoke back out.

Joellyn studied his face. "That's anybody's guess. I'm going to see him tonight. Maybe he'll give me a clue then."

"It's amazing," Randy said. "I have to admire the guy, starting that nifty little side business. Mike tells me he's been making a small mint. Imagine redoing antique cars and selling them! I'd like to see one myself. I'm pretty relieved, though. Up to now it looked as though John and Al were going to take the fall for the whole missing million. Did you know what they were doing?"

Joellyn shook her head. "No. I can't believe they were into something like that without anyone here knowing about it. He didn't even tell me."

"Well, they were hauling in a bundle with it. They probably didn't want the word to get around."

Joellyn stared at him. "Obviously. But I wonder why not?"

He smiled. "Income taxes probably. Didn't you learn anything in Accounting 101?"

Her eyebrows flew up. Of course! John had been angry at the U.S. government ever since Korea. She shook her head. That *would* explain his silence.

"If that's what he's been thinking," she said, "then he's being very stupid. He'd be a fool to try to get away with cheating the government for any length of time."

Randy smiled again. "Well, you're entitled to your opinion, but odd things do seem to be happening around here lately, don't they?"

Joellyn yawned. "Odd things always seem to be happening around here. What's one more?"

"Let's hope not too many more happen. My adrenaline can't take it." He rose. "I'm meeting Mike for coffee in a minute. Want to come along?"

"Thanks, but I have a lot to do here. The printer called and said the cards'll be in by the end of next week. I need to get ready, and I want to get finished early. I have to have a talk with Uncle John when I leave here today."

Randy left, and Joellyn went back to her thoughts. A short talk with Uncle John, and then she could get back to Mike. They still had a lot of things to work out. No matter how they felt about each other, there was still David.

"STAY A FEW MORE MINUTES, Randy. I need to talk to you." Mike sat across from Randy in the deserted cafeteria, sipping a cup of coffee.

Randy leaned back and smiled. "Sure. I didn't want to get up just yet, anyway." He lifted his mug in a wry salute. "What's the problem? Job got you down already? Couldn't blame you, the way things have been going here."

"Oh, no, nothing like that. I was just thinking about that meeting in Lanagan's office the other day. Did anything seem odd to you?"

Randy scratched the side of his neck. "No, not really, other than the fact that Lanagan called Joellyn in. He usually doesn't. But it's only right. After all, she's the one who does the major part of the work on the inventory."

"That's true," Mike agreed. Then he frowned. "Randy, I'm getting more concerned about this missing tubing by the minute. We keep running into all these dead ends. You haven't turned up anything, have you?"

"Nope. Zero. But just like I said, I still think it's a ledger problem. I seriously doubt anything's really happened at United. I think we'll find it's been here all the time."

"How could it be? Haven't you and Joellyn gone over the books a couple of dozen times already?"

"Ah...yes and no," he answered. "You know how it is. She doesn't really have time to sit down and go over it with me."

"But the auditors have looked at everything, haven't they?"

"Oh, sure. And then some. But things can slip through. I've seen it before. Just one entry done wrong month after month. It builds up. But—" he shrugged "—whatever's happened, we'll find it. I'm going to go over everything myself in a couple of days, no matter what."

Mike's eyebrows lifted. "You mean you haven't sat down by yourself yet and looked at the figures? How come?"

"Oh...things keep happening. You know how that goes. The auditors have been here for weeks, and I didn't want to get in their way. And then Lanagan had the books for a while. I couldn't get at them then, either. He ought to stick to his stocks and bonds. When we got the books back from him, they were a real mess. Joellyn said she'd get 'em all straightened up again, but so far she hasn't had time."

He stood and stretched. "Guess it's about time for old Randy to take over. Show 'em how it's done." He grinned. "Want to stop for a drink after work? All the guys meet across the street. Might do you good." He raised his eyebrows, waiting.

Mike looked at his watch. It was four o'clock. He was supposed to pick up steaks on the way to Joellyn's apartment. "Maybe some other time, Randy. I have something very important I have to take care of this evening."

When Mike walked back into his office, the phone was ringing.

"Mike?" It was Joellyn.

He smiled. "Uh-huh. What can I do for you?"

"I'm just curious. Are Doug and Brice *really* former FBI men?"

He pulled at his collar. "Uh, not exactly," he confessed.

"What, exactly, are they?"

"Jo, I don't think we should discuss this over the phone. Let's talk about it tonight, okay? I'll tell you all about it then."

There was a pause. "Okay, then. Don't forget the steaks."

He smiled. "I'm not likely to. We both missed dinner last night, remember?"

She laughed softly. "How could I forget? See you later, after I get back from the hospital. We'll talk then."

"Yes, ma'am. We sure will." He hung up the phone, whistling.

JOHN WAS SITTING UP in bed wide awake when she got to the hospital. Joellyn laughed silently at the sight of him—he was surrounded with newspapers, working a crossword puzzle, looking as though nothing unusual had happened.

She leaned over the puzzle and took a look. Ah, it was three-quarters finished! He *was* okay, just as they'd said. "I'm glad to see you're recovering so nicely," she remarked.

He smiled. "Looks like it. The doctor said I can get out of here in a day or two. Then I'm heading down to Florida to see Sis for a while."

She frowned. "You're not driving, I hope."

He shrugged. "Gotta do it sometime, kitten. Why not start now?"

"Your truck was totalled," she pointed out.

"There are other trucks," he argued. Then he took pity on her and laughed. "I'm flying, kitten. Don't worry so much. I'll be fine."

She exhaled a soft breath of relief. "Want me to make reservations for you?"

He shook his head. "Mr. Lanagan called just before you got here. He offered to send me on the company plane, and I took him up on it. Always wanted to fly on one of them little Lear jets." He laughed. "Now's my chance." His pencil rolled down onto the floor. "Get that, will you, hon?"

Joellyn reached down, scooped up the pencil and handed it to him. "Uncle John, did he say anything else?"

John smiled. "Sure. He told me I was cleared. Not that I wasn't expecting it, but it was nice to hear all the same."

"He told you why, didn't he?"

"Yep. Those bloodhounds did a good job of sniffing it out. Always figured they would sooner or later. I wasn't going to help 'em any, though."

"Uncle John, why didn't you tell me about the antique cars?"

"Didn't figure I had to, kitten. I saw you come back and look in my garage that night. I figured you knew what they were doing there." He gave her a Cheshire cat smile. "You did, didn't you?"

Joellyn gulped, embarrassment flooding her face. "I thought—"

He reached over and patted her hand. "Sure, kitten. I know what you thought. You thought I got the money for the cars by selling that tubing, didn't you?" He smiled quietly. "And you didn't tell anybody." He shook his head, bemused. "Just goes to show you, blood's thicker than water anytime, isn't it?"

The old cliché drifted through her mind. Thicker than water. Evidently it was. And, if so, what about Mike's blood tie to his son? Could she possibly overcome that? If she couldn't, what hope was there for the two of them?

JOELLYN COULD SEE by the green glow of the luminescent dial on the nightstand clock that it was eleven-thirty. She rolled toward Mike, comforted by his nearness.

He lay awake, staring into the darkness and gently stroking her arm.

She rubbed her cheek against his shoulder. "Can't sleep, either, hmm?"

"Who wants to sleep?" he answered.

"If this keeps up, we're both going to have to wear makeup under our eyes to hide the shadows."

"I hope it does," he answered. "I want it to last forever." He propped his chin on his hand and drew circles on her stomach with his finger.

"So do I," she whispered.

"Joellyn . . . I never thought I'd say this to anyone again, but I do love you. You believe me, don't you?"

"I hope so. I'm not accustomed to falling into bed with just anybody."

"Are you sure you feel the same way?" He peered through the darkness, trying to see her eyes.

"Yes," she whispered, "a thousand times yes."

Her body arched to meet his again. The moonlight outlined the two of them as their lips and bodies joined in joyous celebration of their love.

"'This is the female form,'" he whispered a few minutes later. "'A divine nimbus exhales from it from head to foot. It attracts with fierce, undeniable attraction.'"

"'I Sing the Body Electric.' Walt Whitman," she answered with surprise. "How'd you come up with that?"

He smiled into the darkness. "Business law wasn't the only thing I learned at Harvard. I learned a few other things, too. Poetry was one of them."

She smiled. "At least you had a well-rounded education. I still can't believe what you did to that steak tonight. Don't tell me you learned that at Harvard. I'll never believe it."

"Nope, not Harvard. My father did all the gourmet cooking in my family. He really rolled it out when we had company. And don't forget, I lived in France for years. I just watched and learned. Got pretty good at it, too."

"Is there anything you aren't good at?"

"Yes," he answered gruffly, reaching for her again. "Restraint."

JOELLYN WAS STILL awake at twelve-thirty, although she could feel herself drifting, lounging on an imaginary raft somewhere in the middle of a warm ocean, waves rolling around her, gently rocking her to sleep.

Mike caressed the side of her cheek, at peace with the world. "Jo?" he whispered.

"Umm?" His voice soothed her, lulling her even closer to sleep.

"Are you as surprised as I am about you and me?"

"Yes and no," she answered after a moment. "Yes, because of the strong feeling between us. No, because I felt it right from the start. Does that make sense?"

"As much sense as anything else, I suppose."

"You sound confused," she said. "What's bothering you now?"

"Nothing really. I'm just...surprised about all this. A serious relationship was the last thing on my mind when I came to United. I guess the wounds were still pretty fresh from my divorce, and I miss my son terribly. And, by the way, speaking of that, I forgot to tell you. He'll be here Friday night."

"Umm...*what?*" She bolted straight up, wide awake.

He laughed. "Relax. He's just a little boy. He can't hurt you."

"Oh, but, Mike—"

"Oh, but Mike what?" He propped his head up and smiled. "You sound terrified."

"I'm not terrified. Yes, I am. No, I'm not. Well, maybe I am." She switched on the lamp so that she could see him. "Mike, what are we going to do? He doesn't like me!"

That had been bothering him, too, but he didn't want her to know how much. "Are you kidding? He's my son, isn't he? As soon as he really gets to know you, he'll love you." He traced little hearts on her arm with his index finger.

She was astonished at the physical reaction she was having at the prospect of seeing his son again. Her heart was pounding, and she felt cold. She drew a deep breath. "How's he getting here?"

"Dani's putting him on the plane Friday afternoon. I'm meeting him at O'Hare, and on Sunday night I'll put him on the plane again and she'll meet his flight. A little tricky, but it can be done."

Joellyn felt a rush of relief that his ex-wife wasn't coming, too. But still... "Mike?"

"Yes?" He was smiling.

"What do you do with a normal six-year-old boy besides take him for pizza?"

He laughed. "What a question! If you *really* want to wow him, you take him to the Palmer House and buy him a porterhouse and a couple of margaritas, then you hit the discos on Rush Street, and after that—ouch!" he protested, laughing as she pummeled his chest. "I don't know," he confessed. "Whatever you do with a five-year-old or a seven-year-old, I guess. Now stop worrying. He'll come around as soon as he gets to know you better."

He had his fingers crossed. He wasn't sure of this at all—he'd seen David's stubborn little chin jutting out that night on the way home from the pizza parlor. But at this point he was determined to make it work.

"What are you getting so wound up about?" he asked.

"Well...we don't have any toys. Or candy. Does he like candy? That's a dumb question. Of course he likes candy. What about popcorn and chocolate milk and carrots and—"

"Whoa!" He placed his open palm against her mouth. "Slow down! This is one little boy, not the United States Navy! We can buy toys on the way home from the airport, but we're really not going to need many."

"Why not? He'll be here almost three days." Her brow furrowed. "We'll need—"

"Joellyn."

"What?"

"I have something to tell you."

"You're up to something. I can tell."

"Well...yes, but nothing all that terrible." He drew a deep breath. "I promised I'd take him camping."

She stared at him, astonished. "You what?"

He smiled and shrugged. "You heard right the first time. We're going camping."

"Mike..." She closed her eyes and shook her head. "It's only the end of March! Don't you know what that means here? It's *still cold.*"

"Ah—" he waved his hand "—we're used to it. We used to do it all the time. No problem. I have all the gear, except we have to get another sleeping bag and pup tent for you. As long as it doesn't rain or snow, we'll be fine." He looked anxiously at her. "You *will* come, won't you?" He smiled and reached for her.

"As long as it doesn't rain or snow, we'll be fine," she repeated. "That is what you said, isn't it?"

"Yes, ma'am."

"Does your ex know you're taking him camping?"

He nodded. "Yes, ma'am. Can we go to sleep now?"

"Mike, I don't see how I can go. Even if I wanted to, I couldn't."

"Why not?"

"The physical inventory is coming up. I have about a million—"

"Things to do," he finished for her. "Listen to me, Joellyn. I learned this the hard way, and I know what I'm talking about. That company will lump along just fine without you over the weekend." He leaned toward her, his eyes serious. "I mean it. You need to get away from that office and relax. And not just this weekend, but *every* weekend. You've been working too many hours out of your week."

"I don't think I work too hard," she objected, even though she'd thought so many times.

"Sure," he said. "I can still hear myself saying that to Dani a long time ago. That's what broke up my first marriage, and I'm not letting it happen to us. End of lecture. Now, you know what we need?"

"No, but I'm sure you're going to tell me. What do we need?"

"A camping trip," he said. "Two days in the country with fresh air and food cooked outdoors and—"

"Bugs and things that go bump in the night," she finished triumphantly.

He laughed. "Jo."

"What?"

"That's one nice thing about camping in March. There are no bugs."

They lay side by side in the darkness again. She felt herself drifting... drifting...

"Jo?"

"Umm?"

"I was watching you with those kids. You'd make a terrific mother. Or are you one of those 'career only' women?" he teased, half joking but waiting for her answer.

"No way," she murmured, wishing she could see his eyes. "I always planned on having six kids."

"Six?" He smiled in the darkness. "Only six?"

"To start with," she answered. She could tell he was smiling by the tone of his voice.

"Do you really want that many?" he asked after a minute.

She chuckled. "Probably not, but I want some."

"Would you give up your career?"

"Would I have to?" she asked, aware they were now crossing over from general conversation into delicate negotiation.

"I don't see why unless you wanted to," he answered. He stared at the shadowy ceiling, realizing something important had just been settled between them.

They were quiet for a few minutes; sleepy new lovers unwilling to let this day slip by, wanting this moment of quiet happiness to last forever.

She touched his arm. If he was asleep, she didn't want to wake him.

"Mike?" she asked softly. "Are you still awake?"

"Um," he answered. "I think so. Why?"

"I'm curious about something."

"Um?"

"You told me over dinner that Brice and Doug *are* actually FBI agents, not *former* FBI agents."

He was momentarily jolted out of his drowsiness. "Yep. Why?"

"Just wondering. No reason. Go back to sleep."

There was silence for a moment. "Jo?"

"Yes?"

"Why did you ask that?"

"I was just wondering . . . do you really, truly intend to stay here once this is over? You're not going to do this anymore?"

"Yep. This time I'm baffled. I know the stuff is gone and I have no idea how they did it. I went out and spot-counted the tubing myself, and the count's way off. The physical count Irv Harris ordered will give us an accurate indication of the loss. I talked to him today and told him the tubing's gone all right, even though Randy doesn't think so and Lanagan seems to want to go along with him."

"Wishful thinking," Joellyn murmured.

"Yep. Jo, a huge crime has been committed here, and we need the FBI. The reason I wouldn't discuss it over the phone is, who knows? The receptionist may be in on it. We've got to be very careful now."

"Uh-huh."

"No more discussing this with anyone at work. Anyone. Answer questions only if you have to, but that's all, hear me?"

Joellyn heard. She lay curled against his side, her head snuggled against his shoulder. After a few more minutes, her even breath caressing his chest told him she was asleep.

THOUSANDS OF PIECES of paper floated through radiant currents of air, gliding, soaring like eagles high over the Arizona canyons—white copies, yellow, pink, blue, green, always just a little out of reach.

She tried over and over to catch them, but they slipped past her, eluding her grasp, drifting silently toward the floor. As she bent over to retrieve them, they moved on, tormenting her with their secret.

Muted factory sounds echoed far away. Machines moved, and shadowy people took large, lumbering steps in slow motion, as though they were treading over the moon's desolate surface.

A kaleidoscope of color engulfed her as she tried again and again to comprehend what everyone was trying to tell her, but the sounds whispered past her ears. Lips moved slowly, pronouncing words with great effort, but no sounds that she could understand came out.

Stacks of yellow tubing burst through their wire bonds and hurtled past her in the air, clattering down onto the floor, narrowly missing her as she jumped out of their reach. Then red, then green, then silver, coming at her so fast that she knew she couldn't keep dodging them much longer.

Faces floated in and out of her field of vision, people she worked with—Dianne and Marilyn and Lanagan and Al and Randy. She looked around, frantically calling Mike's name and reaching for him, but he was walking out through the shipping dock doors toward a waiting plane and a tiny boy who refused to look her way. Beads of perspiration froze on her forehead as she tried to run after him, but her ankles were held down by lead weights. She couldn't force her legs to move.

John Terrell sat in a hospital bed; only the stark white sheets were visible in the shadowy mist. He bent over a stack of papers, writing furiously as Al Dobson stood beside him, tapping on a deep red piece of metal. The muted *tap, tap, tap* of the rubber hammer on metal were the only sounds she could recognize.

The paper flew faster, faster, tormenting her, whipping through the air, their edges curling away as she strained to read the writing on their surfaces. They allowed a peek, only a fast, hazy glimpse, just enough to tell her... nothing... but wait... there was something... no...

There was nothing.

The scene before her dissolved into a heavy mist, taking her into a deep sleep from which dreams never surface.

CHAPTER TWELVE

ON THURSDAY NIGHT Mike and Joellyn stood in front of the pup tent display at SportMart. Mike pointed to a display. "I like the round one, don't you?"

She sighed, resigned. "I suppose so. It matches the sleeping bag." She indicated the wildly striped orange-and-yellow double sleeping bag they had already stashed in the cart. "But I thought pup tents were supposed to be long and narrow."

"Only for long and narrow pups," he joked. "This one's just like the one we already have."

"Except yours is khaki," she protested. "Standard camping colors. I remember Girl Scout camp..."

"Ah!" His eyes lit up. "Then you *have* been camping before!"

"I'd forgotten about it," she admitted, "until you brought your stuff into my apartment. That brought it all back."

"Bad memories?" he asked.

"Well...not really bad, I guess. I just remember being very homesick and eating strange food and—" She giggled. "I know this is silly, but I hated it. I had latrine duty five days out of fourteen."

He laughed. "Joellyn! What did you do to deserve that?"

She blushed and ducked her head. "I was bored. And the leader who slept in our tent snored. A lethal combination, I'm afraid."

Mike was fascinated. "And?"

"We taped her snoring and played it back the next night, full blast, just as she was getting ready to go to sleep."

He laughed out loud, delighted to be getting a glimpse of the carefree little girl she had once been. "Well," he said, "I'm relieved to hear you do kick it out once in a while."

"But, Mike," she protested, "I put it all out of my mind the minute I got home and I never went back."

He cupped her chin in his hand, trying to look serious. "Jo, I promise you won't have to clean the latrines."

"In that case," she said, "I guess I'll give it another try."

He laughed. "Wait till we get to your apartment. I'll show you how to set this thing up. You'll love it."

"That's wonderful," she muttered. "Just what I need. A tent in my living room."

JOELLYN LAY in bed Friday night, thinking about the evening. David's plane had been a half hour late. Apprehensive, she had paced with Mike while they'd waited in the terminal. But finally the plane had landed, and David had walked out of the concourse, escorted by a smiling stewardess.

"Well, I can see the right person is meeting him," she said as Mike swooped David into his arms, laughing and tickling him, making the small boy shriek with delight.

Joellyn stared at the man she loved and the small boy who was fighting their relationship for all he was worth. So far he hadn't looked directly at her, but she knew he was aware she was there.

Finally he looked up at her, his face sober. He glanced at his father and then back at her.

Mike saw his hesitation. "David," he said, "you remember Joellyn, don't you?"

David stood still for what seemed an eternity, his eyes wide and unsmiling as he stared at her. "My daddy's taking me camping tomorrow," he announced.

The words, "And you're not coming with us," hovered in the air, unspoken but clear. He'd set the stage and the next lines were hers, but for the life of her she couldn't think of what they might be.

She drew in a deep breath. "I know he is, David. Your daddy—" Her tongue stumbled over the word, "Your daddy's taking me camping, too," she said, the words rushing out before she could stop them.

He looked up at his father. "With us?"

Mike laughed. "Yes, son, Joellyn's going with us."

"Why?" David asked, coming right to the point.

Mike smiled. "Because she's a nice lady and she likes children and she hasn't been camping before. At least not the way we do it, right, sport?" He hugged his son.

David looked down at the floor. "I guess so," he said in a small voice. "But I bet it'd be more fun if just us guys went."

MIKE HAD DROPPED Joellyn off at her apartment. He and David had gone on to his apartment, and now it was late and David was in his bed, curled against him.

"Daddy?" David moved restlessly.

"Yes, David?"

"Can we turn the light on for a minute, please?"

"Sure!" Mike switched on the light.

David scrambled up to a sitting position and looked his father straight in the eye. "Does that lady have to go with us, Daddy?" His voice was mournful and uncertain. "Does she?"

He looked so serious that Mike had to choke back a laugh. "Well, she doesn't *have* to, David, but I thought you and she should get to know each other. You'll like her, I promise. Joellyn is very nice."

"But I don't like her, Daddy." His eyes were round and solemn.

"Why not?"

"Well..." David fished around for an answer and finally came up with one. "She has no children. You said she likes children, but she doesn't have any."

Mike's heart went out to him. "If she had children, do you think you'd like her?"

David considered that for a minute. "Do you think she might sometime?"

Mike suppressed a smile. "I think she might sometime, yes. How do you feel about that?"

David eyed him warily. "Would he be my brother?"

Mike shot up, astonished. "What made you say that?"

David's jaw jutted out again, reminding Mike of a picture of himself at that age. "Because Mama says when she has her new baby it'll be my brother or—" he grimaced "—yuk, sister. And Daddy Joe will be its daddy, and I don't see why I have to have two mamas and two daddies and sisters and brothers...." He stopped for a minute, then drew in his breath and went right to the heart of the matter. "Is this lady going to be my other mama?"

Mike hugged him. "That's looking pretty far into the future, son. Don't worry about that right now."

David thought for a minute. "But why can't you and Mama just live together and we'll have babies together instead of with other people? Why can't we, Daddy?"

Mike's heart ached for his small son, who was far too young to understand this, but he had to take a stab at explaining it. "That's a hard one, son. Sometimes people love other people—" He stopped. This wasn't going well. He closed his eyes for an instant and tried again. "Your mama loves Daddy Joe now, right?"

David nodded solemnly.

"And you do, too, don't you?"

David nodded again.

"Well, then, you see...you can love more than one person, can't you?"

"I guess so...." He looked at Mike and waited.

Mike sighed. "Well, I admit it's not the greatest situation in the world, son, but no matter what, we *all* love *you.*"

David stared, disbelieving, at his father. "Even that lady?"

Mike drew a deep breath. A lot depended on this weekend; he could see that. "Yes, even Joellyn, David."

David thought for a moment, then scrambled down under the covers and turned away. "You can turn the light out now, Daddy."

Mike shook his head ruefully and switched the light off. It was apparent he hadn't made too much headway.

They lay there for a minute, then David spoke through the darkness. "What should I call her?"

"What do you want to call her?"

David's small body moved, and Mike heard a tiny sigh in the darkness. "I don't know, Daddy. I guess I'll call her Joellyn." He was silent for a minute, then he said, "If I *have* to talk to her."

JOELLYN WOKE Saturday morning to the sound of thunder and pouring rain. She lay in bed, listening. Rain sliced against her bedroom window, making the windows rattle. It sounded like hail or sleet. Probably sleet, she realized. She reached drowsily for Mike, then remembered he wasn't there.

Joellyn shivered and looked out the window. The sky was dark as far as she could see. Not the swift, blue-black darkness of a spring thunderstorm that could pass in an hour and leave the sun shining and the grass sparkling; this was a low, gray rain that obviously intended to stay with them for some time.

There would be no camping trip this weekend.

Well, she'd tried to warn Mike about spring in Chicago. She shrugged. He'd believe her now. She hadn't wanted to go, anyhow, but now...she was surprised at her disappointment. The phone rang and she picked it up, still staring at the sky.

"Have you looked out the window?" Mike demanded without preamble.

"That's what I'm doing right now," she said.

"What are we going to do?" he asked. "I've got the rest of the stuff ready here."

"What rest of the stuff?" she asked, eyeing the huge bundles by her front door.

"The food. The rec box with all the dishes and cooking utensils. Damn!" he exploded. "What kind of weather is this, anyhow? It's supposed to be spring!"

She didn't have the heart to say, "I told you so." Instead she said, "We can always take him to the museum."

"Aw, Jo, that's so... so boring."

"Well, we can always take him to the Palmer House for a few—"

"Damn it, Jo, be serious! What can we do with a six-year-old in an apartment on a rainy weekend?"

She was incredulous. "You're asking *me?*" She thought for a minute, a completely unexpected idea beginning to form in her mind. Then she laughed out loud, the excitement in her voice unmistakable.

"Bring him on over," she said. "You'll find out."

He hesitated. "Shall I bring the food, too? We might as well use it up."

"Oh... I guess so," she answered nonchalantly. "Sure. Bring it. And give me a couple of hours. Make that three hours. See you at ten!" She hung up, giggling, before he could question her any further.

WHEN MIKE AND DAVID walked into the apartment, she was already exhausted. She had never moved as fast in her life as she had in the past three hours, but the look in their eyes was worth every minute of it.

"Gosh!" David breathed. "Look at that!" He looked up at her, his eyes questioning. "And look, Daddy! She has a dog!" he squealed as Penny bounded over to him, her eyes dancing and her tongue hanging out of the side of her mouth, wildly happy at the sight of someone her own size.

"Ah, Jo," Mike murmured, shaking his head in disbelief at the sight that had met his eyes when he walked through the doorway. Tears stung the back of his eyes as he pulled her close. He would never understand how she had done it alone in only three hours, but her entire apartment had been transformed into a campsite.

All of her furniture was pushed against the walls and both tents were set up. He prodded the sides of the tents and shook his head, grinning. They were solid. She really had been paying attention the other night when he showed her how to set them up, unrolling the fiberglass tubing and forming the round canvas covering over them.

The sleeping bags were unfolded and laid out inside the tents, two in one tent and one in the other. Her dining room furniture was stacked in one corner. In its place was a huge blanket, and the propane stove was set up on top of a huge metal pan right by the sliding glass door, waiting to be placed outside and lit.

There were large picture books scattered all along the floor in a little path. Mike walked over and looked down at them. Three on animals. One on plants. A couple on trees. He glanced at Joellyn, his eyes questioning.

"For our nature walk," she explained. "I saw them in the store recently, but I never thought—" She stopped, her cheeks turning pink from the adoration in his eyes. "I ran out and got them a while ago," she finished.

A card table and three chairs had been set up. There were coloring books, crayons, paints, clay, construction paper, three pairs of round-edge scissors, paste, and two boxes of model cars to be put together. Da-

vid walked around, touching everything, glancing up
at her from time to time, the beginnings of a smile
hovering around his mouth.

"There's more," she said, smiling. "Go look in the
bathtub."

David ran into the bathroom with Penny lumbering after him, and they heard a shout of laughter.
"Look, Daddy!" he shouted. "We're going fishing,
too!"

They followed David into the bathroom, laughing
at his excitement. Two small toy fishing poles were
propped by the tub, which had been filled with water.
And in the water floated a dozen yellow, green, blue
and pink polyfoam fish and turtles. "That's what took
the most time," she said. "I couldn't find any toy
ones, so I got sponges and cut them out myself."

David was already casting his line into the water,
aiming at a pink turtle.

"There's only one thing missing, as far as I can
tell," she added.

Mike looked around the apartment, puzzled.
"What could possibly be missing? Surely you don't
want to set swings up in here."

She smiled. "Bugs. We need bugs. Why don't you
two sit down and cut some out of that black construction paper while I start breakfast? You did bring
bacon, didn't you?"

He shook his head, still astonished at what she had
done for his son. "Yes," he said, looking her full in
the eyes. "I brought the bacon. And I always will."

"WASN'T HE FUNNY when he wanted to fry the fish he
caught?" Joellyn asked after they put David back on
the plane late Sunday afternoon.

He squeezed her hand. "You were just as funny, pretending to fry it."

Her eyes sparkled. "How'd they taste? You had to pretend to eat them."

"Like sponges," he said. "But don't tell David."

"And this crazy weather," she said. "Honestly, isn't this just like Chicago? Pouring rain one minute, then just as we get to the airport, the sun comes out."

"Yeah," Mike agreed. "And it's warm. Good biking weather," he said, looking at her sideways.

She ignored that remark. They watched the plane take off, then walked in silence toward the car. Mike was hurting, she knew. And she could see why. Who would have ever believed one small boy could have entrenched himself so firmly in her heart in only one shared weekend? But he had. He was so like Mike that her heart had ached every time she'd looked at him.

The son of the man she loved, on his way back to his own mother. . . .

Mike wasn't the only one hurting right now.

Maybe it was a good thing she had to talk to him. What she had to tell him might help take his mind off the tiny figure that had held a flight attendant's hand and walked down the long concourse toward the waiting plane. It might help to clear away the haunted look in his eyes.

"Mike," she said after a minute, "I have to talk to you."

"Sure," he said. He unlocked the car door. "What's up?"

She slid into the seat. "Don't start the car yet. This is going to take a few minutes."

He slid in beside her. "You look so serious all of a sudden. What's wrong?"

"I was lying awake for hours thinking last night," she said.

She reached for his hand. "Mike, I hate to spoil this weekend, but . . . I think I know how the tubing could have been stolen."

He stared at her. "Are you serious?"

She searched his eyes for a minute, then took a deep breath. "Mike, this could cost me my job . . . and maybe more. If I'm right, it's going to cause a lot of trouble at United. It has to."

"United's trouble has already been caused, Jo, and not by you," he pointed out. "Tell me what you think."

"Mike, remember last night when David was playing office?"

"How could I forget? He was having a wonderful time, especially when you let him use your stapler."

She smiled at the memory. "I was watching him while he was doing his 'office work.' He had all these little stacks of paper. And he kept saying, 'These go here and these yellow ones go there and these blue ones don't go anywhere.' Do you remember?"

"Sort of. He was doing all that while I was watching the Burt Reynolds movie." He frowned. "What about it?"

"I kept hearing him say, 'These stay here and these go there.' And all of a sudden I realized that could be it."

He shook his head. "You're way ahead of me. What could be it?"

"You're going to think I'm crazy, but listen. If someone has a four-part order form—are you with me so far?"

He nodded.

"And they wrote 'void' on the white copy and sent it through the regular channels, it would be considered void, just as it always has."

He nodded again, his eyes puzzled. "Go on."

"And if that same person, or persons, wrote out an order on the rest of the copies, it could get shipped out the door and nobody would ever know."

"How could that happen?" he asked, incredulous.

"Because the other copies are used as packing slips. The white top copy is the only one that gets processed by the billing department. It gets entered as an order, and that's where the billing and all the shipping reports come from. That's basically where all the inventory records flow from, as far as shipments are concerned. Except for the perpetual. Don't you see, Mike? This could be the missing link! This could be why the perpetual is so far off from the book!"

"I see what you're saying, Jo, but if this is true, there would have to be quite a few people involved."

She shook her head. "Not necessarily, Mike. Now hear me out. Suppose, just suppose, this *was* what was happening. If this were true, the people in shipping would never know about it. They're doing their job, getting the order on the trucks for shipment. The people in packing are doing their jobs, packing the order up and getting it ready to be shipped. Everyone's doing their job right on schedule. The tubing could go right out the door, past the shipping people, past the guards and the detectives and heaven knows who else, and nobody would ever know it."

"But—wait a minute." Dumbfounded, Mike stared at her. "What about the freight bill? Doesn't someone check that out?"

"Not if there is no freight bill, Mike."

"How could there be no freight bill?" he demanded.

Her gaze held his. "There would be no freight bill if someone on the other side is receiving the tubing collect."

He frowned and rubbed his head. "Run that past me once again, slowly this time."

"Okay. Now listen. If someone in the freight company knows to make sure we never get any kind of billing on these shipments, if it's all sent collect to the other company, if the other company pays all the freight charges, then as long as the bottom copies of the voided invoices are sent out with the merchandise, how could it ever be checked out here?"

Joellyn wrung her hands, suddenly cold. "And how would our shipping people ever know? Mike, this is the only way I can think of that the tubing could get out the door without anyone suspecting a thing. They'd have a valid shipping copy. The guards could look at it fifty times and it would still be a valid shipping copy. Look how simple it is. All the paperwork goes with the merchandise. Nothing would stay at United. Nothing!"

"You're telling me," Mike said slowly, looking dazed, "that someone could write an order, just write it on all the copies except the top copy?"

"Yes. They could. I'm not saying they have. I'm only saying it's possible."

"Then they could take the top copy, the one that goes to billing, and write 'void' on it?"

Joellyn shivered. "Yes."

Mike whistled. "I'll say this much for you, Joellyn. You sure have an imagination!"

"I've heard that before. I guess I can't blame you for thinking that, but, Mike—"

"My God!" he broke in. "Give me a chance to get my breath back. It's hard to comprehend any of this. It's too incredible."

"I know," she murmured. "It's almost impossible to believe. I'm not sure I believe it myself. I'm only saying it could happen that way. It *could.*"

Mike leaned back, covered the lower part of his face with his hands and stared at the far end of the garage. "It would have to involve another company," he reflected. "And the freight company—I'll buy that. But who would be smart enough to dream up a scheme like that?"

"I don't know," she said. "But I know how we can find out."

"How?"

She leaned back in the seat, emotionally exhausted but not ready to give up. "We can go out and look at the voids. Right now."

He looked at his watch. "Now? That's crazy," he said. "It's five-thirty! Why can't you look tomorrow?"

"We can't look when there are people around," she said. "We don't know who's involved...if anyone is. If you're worried about getting in, the guard knows me. I often go there on weekends to work."

He snorted. "You *used to* go there on weekends."

"Mike," she argued, "I think we should try it just this once. I know there are voids. I've seen them. I want to take another look. I know everyone's handwriting, at least in the accounting departments, and some of the others. I just never really looked at them in this light before. Please, Mike. We're not doing anything else right now."

He turned the key in the ignition, and the engine roared to life. "We could be," he said, pausing for a moment to give her a meaningful look. "It's been a long two days."

She rested her hand on his leg. "Three, and two nights. But please, this is important. I'm sure we're onto something. I'll make it up to you later. I promise."

THE SUN'S LAST RAYS shot over the horizon as they pulled into United's parking lot an hour and fifteen minutes later. Mike switched the ignition off and turned toward Joellyn. "Ready?" he asked.

She slid down on the seat, her hands in her pockets. "All of a sudden I'm scared," she confessed.

He put his arm around her shoulder and squeezed. "That's normal enough." He smiled to mask his concern. "After all, how many times have you done serious espionage work before now?"

"Never, thank goodness." She shivered. "I don't like it, either. It seems as though the whole world is dark and threatening."

Mike laughed briefly. "It's a good thing it does. I don't want any surprises." Trying to reassure her, he smiled. "We should be all right. Everyone else is at home watching *America's Funniest Home Videos.*"

"Murder, She Wrote," Joellyn contradicted.

"I should have known," he muttered, shaking his head ruefully.

She opened the door and slid out. They hurried to the building's front entrance, and Joellyn stopped in surprise as they pushed through the door to the reception room. A guard she'd never seen before stared up at them, a half-eaten doughnut poised over his steaming coffee mug.

He put the doughnut down on the desk. "What can I do for ya?" he asked warily.

"We work here," she said.

"Oh?" He raised his eyebrows. "Well, let's see your identification then."

She pulled a plastic card out of her jacket pocket. "This is mine. Mike . . . do you have yours?"

Mike fished through his wallet for his card. "Here we are," he said with relief as he handed it to the guard. "Thought I'd forgotten it for a minute there." He smiled. "This is a hell of a time to be dropping in at the office, isn't it? But she remembered some things she had to pick up for an early-morning appointment, so we came on over."

The bored guard glanced at the IDs. "Yup," he agreed. "But at least it stopped raining."

He picked up his doughnut and dunked it into his coffee, leaning over the cup to stuff it into his mouth. Then he wiped his mouth on his sleeve. "Yeah, at least it stopped raining," he repeated. "Just sign in here."

He pushed a clipboard toward them and bent over to dunk his doughnut again while Mike and Joellyn signed in, glancing at each other. They'd both forgotten about the sign-in sheet.

Mike took Joellyn's arm and pushed open the doorway leading into the first-floor office area. It was eerie in the half-light with no people milling around, no machines blasting in the background, the thick hum of the furnaces the only recognizable sound.

Long shadows snaked ahead of them on the floor and halfway up the dark wall as they made their way down the hallway toward the finance offices.

Joellyn's heart raced as they passed Randy's desk. His massive leather chair loomed in the darkness almost as though he were sitting there watching them.

She shivered. "If this is what crime is like," she whispered, "I'm glad I never tried it."

Mike was apprehensive, too. Something about this just didn't feel right. His lips felt stretched and dry as he tried to joke. "What's the matter? Didn't you ever read Nancy Drew when you were a kid? This is the way you're supposed to feel."

They reached Joellyn's desk. "Well, where do we look first?" he asked.

Joellyn looked at him. "I don't know," she confessed.

"All right," he said, "let's go straight to the source. Where are the voids kept?"

"Somewhere in billing," she whispered. "I don't know exactly where."

"Joellyn?"

"What?"

"Why are you whispering?"

She managed a shaky laugh. "I don't know that, either."

Mike frowned. "Well, cut it out. It's making me nervous. Let's get on with it and get out of here. I don't like this. We could always wait and let Doug or Brice do it."

"Oh, sure. And what if I'm wrong?"

"Then you're wrong."

"But, Mike..."

"Yes?"

She looked at him, her face white. "What if I'm right? What then?"

He heaved a long sigh. "I suppose you have a point. But let's get through billing and then get out of here."

"You've got it," she said. "This way."

They walked down the long hallway into the billing area, their shoes making a hushed clacking sound on the floor. They opened file drawers, riffling through crackling sheets of paper.

Mike frowned in the dim light. "Damn!" he swore. "I can barely read this stuff." He located a switch on the wall and flicked it on, creating strange patterns of light in the hallway beyond the office. He pulled first one drawer open and then another, stopping to check each paper. Joellyn worked her way through a table in the back of the room. Her pulse jumped at every imagined sound. It seemed as though an eternity passed while they looked through the papers, searching for the one word that would explain everything.

"Mike, let's hurry," she whispered. "What if the guard catches us?"

"There's no point in doing this if we don't do it right, Jo. Here, you take this drawer. We can be finished in a few more minutes. I'll check the desks."

He scanned the tops of the desks. The were clean and neat, with no papers in sight.

But Marilyn's desk was exactly as he'd heard it described—a jungle of unkempt piles of paper, chewed pencils and half-straightened paper clips. He riffled through the papers.

Nothing.

Then he opened the middle drawer and pulled out a handful of papers, rapidly scanning the contents for each sheet.

Nothing.

He was reaching for another stack when his hand froze. "Joellyn," he whispered, "do you hear anything?"

They both looked toward the doorway, their ears straining to catch any sound, but all they could hear was their own breathing, ragged and uneven.

He tried to laugh. "There's nobody here but us. I guess I'm getting nervous in my old age. This place sure looks different at night, doesn't it?"

"It never did before," she whispered shakily.

They returned to their search, their ears tuned to catch any sound.

Joellyn's skin prickled. "Damn!" she muttered. "How can there be so much paper in this place, and none of it what we're looking for?"

Mike lifted a folder of papers from the desktop. He flipped through a few papers, then stopped and pulled one out.

"Look what I found," he said quietly.

She looked at the paper, then up at Mike, stunned.

It was a handwritten invoice, partially filled out with what would have been a shipment of tubing, with the name of a freight carrier on it, and it was marked "collect."

The items to be shipped had been hastily scratched out, and the word *Void* handwritten over the face of the invoice.

Joellyn shivered. "That's Marilyn's handwriting."

"Does she normally void invoices?" Mike asked.

"No," Joellyn answered in a low voice. "Never. Her handwriting was the last one I expected to see. I thought for sure it would be someone in shipping or sales."

He let his breath out in a heavy sigh. "Well, we'll take it with us. In the morning we'll turn it over to Doug and Brice and let them handle it. We've done enough for one weekend, don't you agree?"

She nodded, sick at heart. "I agree, but I'm not happy about what we found."

"I'm not, either. Especially in view of one other thing."

She looked at him. "What?"

He flipped the light switch off. "I don't see how she can be doing it alone. There's got to be someone else here in on it."

Her eyes widened. "But who?"

"Take your pick. Your guess is as good as mine."

CHAPTER THIRTEEN

MIKE WHISTLED softly as they entered Joellyn's apartment. Nice night. It had cleared up. The moon was out in full force, a vivid white-yellow without a hint of a cloud in the sky, and the temperature was close to seventy. A perfect night for a bike ride, if he could talk her into it.

He needed it. Needed to clear his head. Needed something to take his mind off the little redheaded boy walking toward the plane... It would probably be a month before he saw him again. And he was sure there was a rough day coming up tomorrow at United, if they'd found what they thought they had at the office.

He was keyed up beyond belief; not a bit tired now, not at all. And Joellyn seemed distracted, too. Understandable enough. He watched her cross the room and open the curtains. Moonlight filled the room, warming them both.

"Jo?" he asked.

She turned, smiled and walked toward him, holding out her arms. "Ready for me to make that trip to United up to you like I promised?" She wound her arms around his back, slid her hands down and cupped his bottom. "Did I ever tell you you have a *great*-looking bod?" She nuzzled under his neck. "Listen," she murmured, "I have a great idea." She moved seductively against him. "We could both use a shower right about now, don't you think?"

"A shower?" He gave her a blank look. What did a shower have to do with riding a motorcycle?

"A shower," she affirmed. "And then..." She moved away from him, toward the bedroom door, humming softly. She turned and flashed him a seductive smile and unbuttoned her blouse, slowly, one button at a time, moving as she hummed. "And then," she purred, "I'll teach you what spring nights are *really* for."

"But, Jo—" He watched helplessly as she peeled the blouse down over her shoulders, revealing her smooth upper arms and the firm, round breasts he'd grown to love. He felt himself stirring, and thoughts of his motorcycle virtually vanished as he headed across the room toward her.

"Uh-uh!" She shook her head and waggled her finger at him. "Shower first. Lesson second." She knew what had been on his mind earlier. But she'd make him forget about the bike, and quickly, too. They'd make long, slow love together, and he wouldn't even be able to think about a motorcycle. Besides, they both needed a good night's sleep. Tomorrow was going to be an awful day.

"I'll put Penny outside and I'll join you in a minute," she said, giving him a tiny push toward the bathroom.

He watched her through narrowed eyes, puzzled. She was up to something. He knew by now whenever she got that look in her eyes it meant she had something on her mind. He shrugged and headed for the shower, smiling. Whatever it was, it could wait. But this couldn't. Two days and three nights was a long, long time....

She heard the water running while she fed Penny and put her outside. She waited five minutes, brought Penny back in and headed for the shower.

The water was still running. She stood in the bathroom, watching Mike's form through the frosted glass doors while she removed the rest of her clothes. Then she slid the door open and slipped in behind him.

Water cascaded down over his shoulders and onto her as her breasts pressed against his back. She reached under his arms and took the soap from him and slowly rubbed it over his stomach, up and across his chest and around under his arms to his back. Then she reached around him again and took him into her hands, warm, slippery movements that made him groan out loud. He tried to turn around, but she kept him there for a minute, touching, teasing with the warm soap, loving the feel of his firm, bare body against hers.

He turned toward her and looked at her for a long minute. Then he took the soap from her and gently, so gently, his eyes never leaving hers, rubbed his hands over the bar of soap. Then he began moving his hands over her body, the slippery soap covering her skin and disappearing under the torrent of water.

The tips of her breasts were on fire from his touch; a fire that mere water could never begin to put out. Her inner thighs and the secret core inside ached with desire; desire to have him closer, overwhelming need to have him moving inside her in rhythm with her rapid heartbeat.

His fingers slid between her legs, moving slowly, touching nerves she'd never, before him, known were there. "Ah...yes..." she whispered, barely able to

speak against the raging flood threatening to burst at
his next touch. "Now," she whispered. "Now."

He heard her. Not her words; the fire that was consuming her was consuming him, too, relentless forces
sweeping through them both. There were no words
needed now. Only the touch of this woman's body so
close to his. Only the absolute rightness of this moment in time. Only the desire that had been rushing
through him for days and was now ready to pour out,
making her, finally and irrevocably, part of his life
forever.

He drew a deep, ragged breath. He couldn't wait
any longer. He *couldn't*. Murmuring soft words, warm
water still pouring over them, he entered her.

Their movements were slow and lovely at first. They
had all the time in the world; neither wanted to rush
toward the culmination of this feeling, this ultimate
trust in each other. Then the flood rushed toward
them, inside and through them, and they both gasped
at the same time, murmuring each other's names
through the bursting of the dam and through the slow,
throbbing stream that followed in its wake.

MOONLIGHT STREAMED between the slats in Joellyn's
vertical blinds, making a striped path across the bedroom floor and up over the bed, covering the lovers.

Mike gave a long, contented sigh, and Joellyn
laughed softly, stroking his cheek. "I thought you said
you weren't tired," she teased.

"I'm not. Well, maybe a little," he admitted.

"I knew it!" she boasted, pleased with herself.

He propped himself on his elbow. "Is that what you
were up to? Ah, you willful, wicked woman with your

wanton, winning ways! Isn't that what they say in those steamy historical romances?"

She curled her fingers through the hair on his chest. "Who cares what they say? Did you enjoy your lesson?"

He laughed. "Sure did." He rolled over and checked the bedside clock. "Now it's time for yours. What say we jump out of bed, get in my car and go get my bike? Aw, Jo, it's only nine o'clock," he protested when he saw the look on her face. "Don't tell me you're still worried about a little bike ride? Come on now. It's perfectly safe. I promise you."

"It is not safe!" she insisted. "Those things fall over all the time!"

He sighed. "I suppose you think you're safer, barreling down the road eighty-five miles an hour in that Porsche?"

"Seventy-five, and yes I do."

"Jo, how many nights like this are we going to have this time of year? It's beautiful out! Come on," he pleaded. "You'll love it. I know you will. It'll do us both good. Clear the cobwebs out."

So! She simmered inside. He hadn't forgotten about the bike ride, only postponed it.

"You amaze me," she said. "You really do! With all we have on our minds how could you even *think* of jumping on a motorcycle to go tooling across the country right now?"

"What's wrong with right now?" he protested. "It's relaxing. And may I remind you, it's *only* nine o'clock!"

She checked the clock. "Nine-fifteen," she pointed out. "And it's Sunday night. We have to go to work tomorrow. What on earth are you thinking of?"

She stared at him in irritation. Was this the way he was going to be? Totally irresponsible? If it was, she wasn't so sure she wanted this to go any farther. Correction. It had already gone too far.

"Look," she said, "you may think this is a great idea, but tomorrow I want to have my wits about me."

"*Why* are *you* worrying about tomorrow?" he asked. He sat up and snapped on the light. "You don't have to worry about it. I'll talk to Brice and Doug and take care of everything."

She shot straight up. "I *beg* your pardon! What did you say?"

"I said I'll take care of everything. I don't want you involved. What's the problem?" He stared at her, baffled.

"May I ask who gave you the right to arbitrarily decide *you* should take care of everything? This is my problem, too. I *am* involved! Why are you suddenly trying to coddle me? Hasn't anyone told you this is the nineties, not the fifties?"

"You career women!" he exploded. "I suppose you're planning on barreling into Marilyn's office with your—" he spotted the paper on the dresser and pointed "—'evidence,' demanding an explanation!" He scooped his socks up and yanked them on. "Or were you going to arrest her right then and there? A citizen's arrest—is that what you were going to do?"

"You...you..." Her face was flaming red. "You unmitigated, card-carrying, male chauvinist—how *dare* you!" She jumped from the bed, ran out of the room and slammed the door behind her as hard as she could.

He threw on his slacks and shirt, cursing under his breath. What was the matter with the woman? He was only trying to protect her, for heaven's sake! He stalked across the bedroom floor and jerked the door open. He stomped through the living room, grabbed his jacket and turned to glare at her, completely oblivious to the fact that she was standing by the sliding door, stony-eyed, her arms folded tightly across her chest, and she didn't have a stitch on.

"All I wanted—" he began.

"All you want," she interrupted, "is to make me into something I'm not. You want me to get on a damn motorcycle and I won't. You want me to be a quiet little thing with no brains and no opinions, and I'm not. And now you want me to keep my mouth shut and pretend I don't know a thing about what's going on with that tubing. Well, I refuse to do that!"

"You *have* to do that!" he shouted. "It's *not your problem!*"

"It *is* my problem!"

He could feel his forehead throbbing. "Listen to me," he said. "Please. Keep out of that shipping office tomorrow. Let me handle it. Don't go near Doug or Brice or Marilyn or anybody else. Don't answer any questions or ask any. Just go about your business until we know what the story is. Otherwise, *you may get hurt!*"

She shook her head stubbornly.

"Joellyn," he said quietly, "I'm telling you, keep out of this! You don't know who's involved and neither do I. I don't want anything to happen to you!"

"Thank you so much for your concern," she said. "Since you're taking over completely, and you don't seem to want me around, I promise you I won't be anywhere near you and your precious shipping office. Now if you'll excuse me, I have to go to bed. I need my sleep.''

She stalked past him without looking at him, went into the bedroom and closed the door firmly behind her. He heard the quiet, definite click of a lock turning. Then he pulled on his jacket and headed out the door, boiling inside.

JOELLYN LAY AWAKE, staring at the shadows on the ceiling. Lee had done the same thing. He'd tried to change her, make her more adventurous, tried to get her to travel all over the earth with him and had never understood that it just wasn't in her to do things like that.

She was a quiet person. She had been all her life. Maybe it was the way she'd been raised. Growing up in a family where the father was a professor of philosophy and the mother was a grade-school teacher wasn't exactly a background likely to produce a child who could tear around the country on a motorcycle or anything else without a lot of forethought.

But look at your mother now.

There it was again, that tiny inner voice, arguing against everything she believed in and felt comfortable with. That was the whole thing. She just wasn't adventurous by nature. The most adventurous thing she'd ever done had been the day she'd whipped around into that parking lot and bought the Porsche.

Felt good, didn't it? And look how fast you drive it.

She did drive it fast, she had to admit that. Maybe there was something inside trying to get out. As for her mother, she hadn't done anything all that earthshaking.

Are you sure? She had her hair frosted her first week in Florida. And what about the cha-cha lessons?

No, she wasn't sure. And it didn't matter. What did matter was, every time she met someone she could care about, they started trying to change her.

Is that really what this is about? Think about it. Is it?

She thought about it for a long while. David. Well, what about David? Was he the problem, or was it confusion over her own feelings? Could she love him on a permanent basis, as if he were her own? How did one go about giving another woman's child the same love and attention she'd certainly give to her own children? She had to admit, David had certainly come around. He'd come to her and given her a big hug right before bedtime Saturday night—was it only last night? She couldn't believe it. It seemed so long ago....

Could she possibly have been wrong? Could Mike really have only been trying to keep her from being hurt, or was he just trying to hog all the credit? They were forever pulling that on her at work, and she was *so* sick of it!

Maybe she was wrong, flying off the handle like that, but she didn't like the way he went about it, assuming she needed protecting.

On the other hand, someone had to be in on the theft with Marilyn. But who? She had no idea. Maybe Mike did. Maybe that was why he was so adamant. But, damn it, did he have to be so officious about it? Couldn't he at least have let her be a part of the decision? Wasn't that part of commitment?

Well, it didn't really matter now. There was no commitment. He was gone, and she wasn't sure they could ever patch things up again, after the way he stormed out. She wasn't even sure she wanted to.

And to think she'd believed all along that it was her Uncle John and David keeping them apart.

It wasn't Uncle John *or* David. It was herself.

And Mike.

MIKE GRITTED his teeth and twisted the Harley's left handle forward, then reached forward with his right hand, turned the ignition switch to the start position and kicked the starter.

She had to be the most bullheaded woman he'd ever seen! He couldn't understand her at all. Insisting on joining him when he and the FBI men questioned Marilyn tomorrow—as conservative as she'd fooled herself into thinking she was, the woman really had a wild streak in her. Except when it came to *his* motor-cycle.

So angry he couldn't think, he turned both handles all the way back toward himself and shifted his body, bringing his full weight down on the kick starter, then watched in openmouthed astonishment as it kicked back and cracked his ankle. Swearing loudly, he turned both handles forward and kicked again, trying to ignore his throbbing leg.

She wasn't mad about the bike. She couldn't be. She was scared, scared of commitment, and so was he.

The engine sputtered and roared. He kicked the starter again in frustration, bounced on the seat and spun off, leaving a streak of black on the gray asphalt as he headed out into the street.

This was more like it—yeah, who needed a woman messing up his life, telling him what to do and when to get sleepy and refusing to cooperate in even the smallest thing? Not him!

He careered around a corner and headed north. All he wanted to do was take care of her. Was that so bad? Was that against some unspoken rule he'd never heard of? He couldn't understand her, not at all. If that was the way she was going to be, it was a good thing he found out now. He was better off without her, that was for sure.

He reached his apartment, circled once around the block and pulled into his driveway. Who needed this? The aggravation, all this worry... What started that fight, anyhow? The motorcycle?

Nah, it wasn't the motorcycle. It had nothing to do with the invoice they'd found with Marilyn's handwriting. It was something a whole lot more important than that.

Maybe he'd rushed her about David, but that had seemed to be working out. Maybe he'd read all the signs wrong. Maybe she didn't want a relationship with a man who had a ready-made family. Although she really seemed to love children. After all, there were the kids at the home. But maybe Wednesday night kids were all she needed.

And maybe he shouldn't have been so hard on her, telling her to keep out of the way tomorrow, but, damn it, this was police business. There was no reason for her to be involved. Well, it didn't matter now.

He rolled the bike into the garage and locked it, then headed back into his apartment.

It was over. She'd walked into that bedroom without a backward glance and locked the door.

She only had to lock it once.

"THAT'S HARD TO BELIEVE," Doug Macy said the next morning. "If it's true, it's one of the most ingenious thefts I've ever come across."

"And the boldest," Brice Woodfield added. "My God, imagine how long this could have been going on."

"Yes," Mike agreed. "They probably started out with a little, just to see if it could be done. Then a little more, and a little more."

"Until they got greedy," Brice said.

Mike nodded silently. How many months, how many years, how much money had escaped, undetected, from United only to be written off at the end of the year as inventory shrinkage?

How simple. How terribly easy. And who would ever know?

More to the point, who were 'they'?

"The logistics of it fascinates me," Brice said. "Mike, was Joellyn sure this is Marilyn's handwriting?"

"Yes," he said. "She said Marilyn's left-handed, and her letters always slant in that funny way. And she always circles the dots on her *i*'s like that." He pointed at the paper.

"Well, that can always be verified by handwriting experts," Brice said.

"I'm anxious to find out who the other one is. Or others," Mike said.

"Yep," Doug agreed. "There have to be two here at least. Two could do it. And one at the receiving company."

"And someone in the freight company," Mike added. He breathed a sigh of relief. John Terrell might be the smartest shipping manager in the world, but this could have been going on right under his nose, and there was no way he could have known.

"You have to admire the mind that thought this up," Brice said. "Look how long it's been going on with detectives right here."

"Yep," Doug agreed. "Smart all right. But not smart enough. This is interstate. The freight company's records can be subpoenaed. And Marilyn will crack and tell us who the others are eventually. I'm betting she does it today."

"I don't know," Mike said. "It depends on who it is."

"Nope," Doug said. "She'll tell us."

"How can you be so sure?"

Brice patted his shoulder holster as he stood. "She'll tell us."

JOELLYN WAS SITTING at her desk, trying to concentrate when they came to get Marilyn. She heard their voices all the way down the hall.

"I don't know what you're talking about!" she heard Marilyn say. "Take your hands *off* me!"

She heard the low murmur of the men's voices and watched them escorting Marilyn toward the back of the plant, leaving her department in utter chaos.

"What the hell?" Randy said, sticking his head out of his doorway. "Joellyn, go see what's going on down there. Whatever it is, make 'em stop. I've got a splitting headache!" He disappeared back into his office, holding his head.

She spent the next hour and a half in the billing department, trying to calm the women. Then Randy showed up. "Are you still in here?" he asked, looking around. "Where's Marilyn?"

She bent her head down. "I don't know."

"Two men came in here and took her away," one of the women said. "I heard them say they wanted to ask her about some invoices."

Randy stood still. "Joellyn, are you sure you don't know what's going on? Where'd they take her?"

"I don't know, Randy," she said truthfully.

"Out back somewhere," the same woman said. "They said something about Mike Walker's office."

Randy looked at Joellyn. "Why didn't you call me?" he demanded. "What the hell's wrong with you?"

Her throat constricted. "I thought Mike would call you."

"Well, he hasn't, and I don't know anything!" he complained. "I've been sitting in my office for two hours trying to get rid of this headache. I come out here and find my billing supervisor gone and you playing nursemaid to a bunch of hysterical women. Why the hell should I know what's happening? Nobody tells me anything!" He stalked out of the office and headed for the factory.

MIKE SAT BEHIND his desk, chewing lemon drops. Brice lounged in a brown leather chair, watching intently as Doug questioned Marilyn.

"Is this your handwriting?"

"No."

"We think it is."

"Well, I can write void if I want to, can't I? What is your problem?"

"The problem seems to be yours, ma'am."

"It's going to be yours if you don't let me out of here. How dare you drag me down here to ask about a silly piece of paper? You could've asked me in my office and saved us all a lot of time!''

"No, ma'am. We couldn't. And I'm sure you know why."

"No, I don't, and I'm leaving!" She stood and headed for the door.

Brice jumped up and blocked the door.

"Marilyn, sit back down," Mike said in a commanding tone of voice. "You're not going anywhere."

"Oh, yes, I am," she insisted. She tried to push past Brice. "Would you *please* move out of my way!"

"Marilyn, *sit down!*" Mike said. "I'm not going to tell you again."

She stared at him for a few seconds, then walked back to her chair, her composure returning. "Well, gentlemen," she said coolly, crossing her legs, "in that case, let's get this over with. What's on your collective minds?"

"That's better, ma'am," Doug said. "Now let's begin again. *Is* this your handwriting?"

She glanced at the invoice. "No."

"You'd better take another look, ma'am," Doug insisted.

She glanced at it again. "No. If you think differently, then prove it."

"We'll do just that, ma'am," Doug said. "Who told you to do this?"

"I just told you, I didn't do it."

"Ma'am, this is going to go a lot easier on you if you just tell us who told you to void this invoice."

"Nobody told me to void it." Her eyes glinted. "I didn't void it."

Doug frowned. "Ma'am, we know what you did, and how it works. There's no question about it. We know about the void invoices. We know about the bogus shipments. We know you're involved."

She raised her eyebrows. "You *think* I'm involved."

"Ma'am, this little piece of paper is going to send you to prison. Do you want to go alone? Are you really willing to take the fall for this? We're going to find out eventually. Why not make it easy on yourself? Cooperate with us now and tell us who else is involved here. If you do, something can be worked out."

She snorted. "Are you offering me immunity? Come on, that went out with Watergate."

"No, it didn't. And we can't offer you immunity. We can only try to lighten your sentence, if you cooperate. You're going to do hard time for this, ma'am. No doubt about it. *Do you want to do it alone?*"

She laughed. "I'm not going to prison. No way, gentlemen." She looked him straight in the eye. "I haven't done anything wrong. If you think I did, prove it. Until then, leave me alone." She stood again.

Doug drew a deep breath as he stood. "I'm sorry, ma'am. You'll have to come with us."

Her face slowly turned red. She narrowed her eyes and stared at him. "What are you talking about?"

"You're under arrest, ma'am."

She gave a shaky laugh. "You can't arrest me. Who do you think you are, anyway?"

Doug pulled his wallet out of his pocket and held it in front of her face, the badge clearly visible. "Doug Macy. Federal Bureau of Investigation. And this is my partner, Brice Woodfield." He turned to Brice. "Read her her rights. And then let's go."

JOELLYN HUNG UP the phone and turned the pages of her report, trying to assimilate the information on its pages but failing dismally. She hadn't heard one word from Mike. Not that she'd expected to, but he *could* have called.

She checked her watch. Five o'clock. It had been a long day. Another half hour or so and she'd leave. She didn't have any reason to rush right home now, anyhow. She tried to quell the empty feeling inside. Eventually she'd find out what happened; somebody would have to tell her. But right now she'd better do some work while it was quiet.

Thank goodness it was as late in the day as it was. The women in billing were on their way home to recover from the morning's trauma. At least she wouldn't have to endure their searching looks until tomorrow. And she had to start thinking about covering Marilyn's position....

She sighed. She was probably going to learn all about the billing process now until they could hire somebody else. But she'd have to wait for Randy's okay on that.

Where was he, anyway? She hadn't seen him since he'd left for the factory that morning, and now his door was closed, which meant he didn't want to be disturbed for any reason. She lifted the phone and called him, but his phone rang several times and finally she hung up.

She shuffled through her papers. Funny about that invoice...Marilyn's handwriting. Someone else had to be helping her. Had to be. Or was it the other way around—she was helping someone else?

Who?

She sat straight up in her chair, suddenly remembering the last time she'd been upstairs in the storage room. There were more voids up there in one of the boxes.

She frowned, trying to remember which one. She wasn't sure. She just remembered getting a quick glimpse the day she'd gone up there with Mike.

Mike...

She looked at her watch again. Five-fifteen. She had plenty of time to go up into the storage room and look. No reason to hurry.

She pulled herself up out of her chair and headed for the stairs. She'd only stay long enough to take a quick look, then she'd go on home.

She climbed the stairs slowly, searching on her key ring for the right key. Ah... this was the one. She inserted it into the lock and swung the wire door open, wincing at the sound of the unoiled hinges warring with years of dust.

She pulled the door open and walked in. Which box? She knew they were here somewhere. Maybe these, the stack in front. Her foot kicked against something on the floor. What was that? She got down on her knees to look.

It was Lanagan's lighter. His old chrome Zippo, his favorite, the one he'd had ever since he was in the navy so many years ago....

Lanagan's lighter. She felt the hair rise on the back of her neck. It hadn't been here the last time she was up here; she would have seen it.

But what was Lanagan doing up here? He *never* came up to the storage room. She doubted he ever knew what it looked like; Lanagan never bothered with things like storing records.

Never.

She knelt on the floor with the lighter in her hand, staring at it. Then she heard a voice behind her, and the sound of it chilled her blood.

He spoke in a low whisper. "What are you looking for, Joellyn?"

CHAPTER FOURTEEN

RANDY'S VOICE.

Randy, who had told her to stop bothering Marilyn.

Randy, who was forever taking Lanagan's lighters.

Randy, who had tried to keep her from searching through the invoices, who had laughed at her for trying to find something wrong with them.

Of course he'd laughed.

There wasn't anything wrong with them. He knew that.

He'd known it all along.

She forced herself to turn around slowly and face him. Her heart hammered, adrenaline rushed through her veins and a drumming sound echoed in her ears, reverberating through the dim stillness of the attic.

"You," she said with sudden dead-on certainty "You're the other one."

He stood in the doorway, wearing his coat, his unlit pipe clenched between his teeth. He removed it from his mouth and stuck it in his pocket, never taking his eyes from her. "I'm the other what?" he mimicked his voice harsh.

She tried to struggle to a standing position, but he pushed her back down and stood over her. "I'm the other what?" he demanded, his voice low and icy.

"You...and Marilyn." Sickened, she shook her head. "Why didn't I see it before?"

He smirked, a cocky grin that stretched his mouth but didn't get as far as his slitted eyes. "I didn't want you to see it before. This isn't very smart of you, Joellyn. I told you to leave it alone. I told you to let them take care of it. Now look where you are."

"What do you mean?" she asked, terrified by the look in his eyes. She'd never seen them looking as they did now—gray-black and distant, glinting with cruelty.

"I mean, here you are." He gave an exaggerated sigh. "Staying late again as usual. Nobody else is here, Joellyn. They've all gone home."

He leaned against the doorway. "There are only three people in the building tonight, Joellyn. Just you and the guard and me."

"What about the second shift?" she whispered.

"Not working tonight. Don't you read the bulletin board?"

She hadn't. She hadn't realized she was alone. It had never entered her mind.

"The guard'll be here any minute," she stammered.

"Joellyn..." He shook his head. "The guard never comes up here. You know that."

She couldn't believe his casual tone of voice. If she lived to be two hundred years old, she would never forget his eyes and his face and his voice at this moment.

"What are you going to do?" she whispered.

He gave a short laugh. "I wasn't going to *do* anything except get some cash I had in the safe until I saw you heading up these stairs. I'm not totally stupid, after all. I know what you're looking for."

He laughed again, a low, pleased laugh. "You're looking for the voids, aren't you? Sure you are. But you're not going to have them, and neither is anyone else. Your FBI friends have one copy, only one." He laughed out loud. "And Marilyn's handwriting is all over it. Let her talk her way out of that, if she can. They don't have a damn thing on me."

He shook his head. "Joellyn, Joellyn. If you'd left things alone, I'd be on my way right now." He stared over her head. "But now... now things are a little different. Now I'll have to do something about you. It's a shame. I always liked you...."

She tried to pull herself up again, but he knocked her back against the metal filing cabinet.

Her eyes widened with shock. "Randy... don't be a fool," she gasped. "You'll never get away with this."

"Too late, Joellyn. I've already been a fool. I should have left a month ago."

She rubbed her aching shoulder where it had hit the edge of the cabinet. "Why didn't you?"

He grinned. "That'll be clear soon enough. But by the time Marilyn talks I'll be out of the country, someplace where nobody can find me."

She stared at him in dismay. "Randy... why?"

"Why? Don't be an ass. Three-quarters of a million dollars is why."

"But you had *plenty* of money, Randy."

"Correction," he said. "My wife had plenty of money. Notice I said had." He laughed. "Now it's mine...all mine..." His eyes took on a dreamy look.

She glanced past him at the open wire door. She had to get out of here. If only she could distract him long enough to get past him, she could get down the stairs and scream. The guard would hear her. He'd have to hear her....

Randy's eyes narrowed. "Don't get any funny ideas, Joellyn. You might as well forget it. You're not going anywhere for a while." He moved toward her. "Not until tomorrow. *If* they find you then . . ."

She tried to dodge his fist, but he knocked her arm out of his way and grabbed her wrist, and before she could stop him he aimed at her neck with the side of his open palm. She heard a loud crack and felt a white-hot flash of light, and then the room went gray and she was falling . . . falling . . .

MIKE REACHED his apartment and flopped down on the sofa, too physically and emotionally wrung out to move a muscle. He moved his hand slowly across his chest and began to unbutton his shirt, but he gave up after the third button. He was too tired to care.

What *else* could go wrong? First that insane argument with Joellyn last night for no reason at all that he could figure out now, and then the session today with Marilyn. She was a cool one, all right. Brice had been wrong. She hadn't said a word, had just sat for hours under the lights at the station and refused to budge.

Whoever it was, she was doing a good job of protecting him . . . or her. But Brice seemed to think she'd talk soon. She sure hadn't looked like it when he'd left the station, though. Still cool, still confident . . . still denying everything.

He'd been too hard on Joellyn last night. He should have thought twice about trying to get her to go out after—but that wasn't it, not really. It was his cursed bluntness again, making him say things he didn't mean. She probably had a right to be angry. More than a right. He should have listened to what she was really saying. Even if he was trying to keep her out of trouble, he didn't have to say it the way he had. No wonder she was mad . . .

He sighed and pulled himself up. Okay. Yeah. He'd call and apologize. Take her out for dinner.

He reached for the phone and dialed. Yeah, he'd show her he wasn't as overbearing as he'd sounded last night. They'd weathered some pretty big problems and come through them okay. And this wasn't even that big a problem. He wasn't even sure anymore what they'd thought the problem was.

The phone rang on the other end. He let it ring ten times and then hung up. He'd try again in a few minutes. She was bound to be home soon. Nobody was working at the plant, and tonight wasn't her night at the home. She'd be back soon, and then he'd make it all up to her. Sure, everything would be okay.

As soon as she answered the phone and he heard her voice again.

JOELLYN FORCED her eyes open, gagging from acid bile that rose in her throat, threatening to drown her if she didn't move her head. She tried to wipe her mouth, but she couldn't move her arms or her legs. She was tied up with something—what? She wiggled her fingers and felt the silky smoothness of her panty hose; Randy had torn them from her and tied her wrists and her ankles behind her back so tight that the blood was screaming to get through.

She couldn't move.

And Randy was gone.

But she *had* to move. She had to get to a phone. He was on his way out of the country now. He'd said so right before... She winced, remembering...if he wasn't already gone. What time was it? She couldn't tell; it was always dim in the storage room. It could be any time. Good Lord, why hadn't she listened to Mike? Why hadn't she left it alone? She could have called Mike or the detectives, anything but this. But it was too late to worry about that now.

But wait—the lighter! If she could scoot over and get it with her fingers, she could burn through the nylon that was binding her arms and legs and causing such excruciating pain that she wasn't sure how long she could endure it.

She forced herself to roll over to where she'd last seen the lighter. No, she'd been holding it when he came up behind her. Where was it now?

Where was it?

Inch by inch she moved through the narrow passageway. She slid over the board that squeaked. Every movement made a noise that sounded like shrieking in her ears...or was that her own voice? No, she couldn't make a sound. Her mouth was bound. Randy's handkerchief was stuffed inside the nylon binding.

Tears welled out of her eyes and down the side of her face and dropped onto the floor, dark wet spots on the unfinished wood. She had to find the lighter. Had to...

Her shoulder brushed against something. She turned her face and saw the lighter. Then she twisted around and tried to grab it with the tips of her fingers, but she heard it slide and then stop. She rolled back and looked to see where it had gone, but it had disappeared between the cartons.

MIKE HUNG UP the phone again. She'd stayed late at the office again; he was sure of it. He'd tried her apartment four times now. She should have been home an hour ago.

He shook his head and dialed the office. She was probably sitting at her desk right now, staring at the invoices again, but there was no point in that. Marilyn was bound to crack soon, then this nightmare would be over.

The phone echoed in his ears, an empty sound. He hung up and dialed again. He let the phone ring, frowning as something began to nag at him. A feeling that something was wrong. It just didn't feel right— *she should have been home by now.*

Unless...she was with someone else...or...unless she was in some sort of trouble. The hair prickled on the back of his neck, and he bolted upright. Something was wrong. He should have known it sooner. Good Lord, what if...?

He grabbed his jacket and headed out the door. If she was only staying after work, that was one thing, but if she was in trouble, he was going to be with her no matter *how* independent she was!

JOELLYN SLID closer to the boxes. Ah, there it was, stuck far back between the files.

She turned her back to the boxes and inched over, fingers stretching, reaching...

She whimpered with fear and frustration. It was too far in; she couldn't reach it with her fingers. But maybe...maybe she could reach it with her bare toes.

She slid again, ignoring the splinters that pierced and tore at her arms. She moved her foot slowly. If she moved too fast, she'd push the lighter back and she'd never get it out.

Carefully she inched it out from between the boxes with her toes, willing it to move toward her. Then she rolled over again and backed up to it. Her fingertips touched the cold, slick surface of the lighter and curled around it, and she gasped with relief.

She had it!

Her fingers were so numb that she could barely make them move, but she forced it to flick. She felt the flame, but it couldn't be helped—she had to get out!

She flicked it again and heard the sharp sizzle of burning nylon and felt a searing pain as her wrists snapped free of their bonds.

She was free!

She rubbed at her wrists, wincing with pain as she peeled off the rest of the melted nylon and tore the handkerchief from her mouth. Then she struggled with the bindings on her ankles, sobbing and yanking at knots that refused to come undone.

She'd have to burn them off. She picked up the lighter and flicked it one more time, moaning with pain as the flame seared her ankle. She felt the blood rush from her calves through her ankles and her toes, and she shivered with relief. Then she pulled herself up and looked at her watch.

Six-thirty. She'd been tied up for over an hour! It only took an hour and a half to get to the airport if that was where Randy was going.

She ran out of the storage room, past the wire door, down the stairs and toward her office, leaving her shoes behind. She grabbed the phone and dialed Mike's number, but the impotent ring on the other side told her he wasn't there.

Brice—no, she didn't know his number.

"Jo, are you in here?" She almost fainted with relief when she heard Mike's voice directly outside her office. He rushed around the partition. "I called your apartment, then I called here but didn't get any answer, so I thought I'd better ch—" His shocked gaze swept over her. "My God!" he exclaimed. He moved toward her and pulled her close. "What happened to you? What's been going on here? Who did this to you?"

"Randy Wagner," she whispered.

"Randy?" His jaw dropped. "*Randy* did this?"

"Yes," she said. "He's the one, Mike. You have to find Doug or Brice right away. Randy's on his way out of the country. He admitted the whole thing. I don't know where he was all afternoon. I thought he was with you, but he came back to get money out of the safe. He always keeps money here, and that's when he saw me go upstairs—" She paused and shivered. "Oh, forget that part. We've got to stop him!"

Mike grabbed the phone and punched rapidly on the numbers. "Brice," he said, "get someone to O'Hare and everywhere else you can think of. Have them pick Randy Wagner up." He listened for a minute. "Yes, Randy. He just attacked Joellyn—" he looked at her "—did you say *upstairs?*"

She nodded.

He shook his head. "In the storage room. He tied her up with—" he looked at her ankles with the stockings still dangling "—her own stockings." He listened for a minute. "Right. She says he admitted the thefts. Yes. Probably the airport. Right. Talk to you later."

He hung up the phone. "Jo, let's see those ankles." He knelt and lifted her foot, scrutinizing it closely. "Wow," he murmured. "I think we'd better get you to a hospital." He looked up at her, his eyes darkening. "Did he do anything else?" he demanded.

"Oh," she said, "nothing much. He knocked me out with a karate chop to my neck, that's all." She rubbed her neck. "I'm going to have an awful bruise, but other than that, and the burns, and the splinters in my arms, I'm fine, I think. I just hope they catch him before he gets away."

His eyes flashed. "So do I," he said grimly. "So do I. I'd like to get my hands on him myself."

She laid her hands on his arm and shook her head. "No, Mike. Please. Just let them handle it now."

Mike looked at her and snorted. "I remember saying the same thing to you yesterday." He wrapped his arms around her and held her close, rubbing her back to calm her shivering.

"We're going to get you to the hospital," he murmured. "Come on, let's go." He reached for her coat and slipped it around her shoulders. "And there's one more thing I want you to know."

She looked straight at him. "Yes?"

"Yes," he said. "I want you to know I love you."

A WEEK LATER they sat in Lanagan's office.

"Can you believe that guy?" Lanagan leaned back in his chair and stared out the window, shaking his head. "They nabbed the crooked son of a gun running down the ramp at O'Hare International just seconds before he could board the plane for South America. Mike, we have you and Joellyn to thank for your quick action. Doubly so, Joellyn, because of the personal danger you faced."

Joellyn turned pink with embarrassment. "Well, that's kind of you, Mr. Lanagan, but I'm fine now. The real thanks goes to Doug for getting his associates to the airport so quickly."

Doug smiled. "We were just lucky he came back here. That was the last thing anybody would've expected him to do."

"He wouldn't have if he wasn't so sneaky," she said. "He almost never carried money, but he always kept cash here in the safe. He said it was just in case he had to take a quick business trip sometime, but I always wondered if he wasn't hiding it from his wife."

"Evidently you were right," Mike said. He turned toward Lanagan. "He must not have had the big bucks on him."

"Oh, hell, no," Lanagan said. "That's all deposited in his own little slush fund in a South American bank."

Joellyn leaned forward, fascinated. "How much does he have?"

Lanagan looked her way and raised his eyebrows. "Oh, as close as we can figure, about seven or eight hundred thousand, counting last month's haul, although they probably haven't had time to sell that yet. Plus what he stole from his wife."

Joellyn nodded. "That's what he told me. About three-quarters of a million."

"Some slush fund," Mike murmured.

"Yeah. And the way things are politically in South America, I doubt we'll get it back very fast, if at all," Lanagan said.

"Do you know how much Marilyn got?" Joellyn asked.

"Huh! That's the good part," Lanagan answered. "She didn't get a dime of it. Dumb br—excuse me, Joellyn. She gave it all to Randy to deposit in the South American account. She thought they were going to leave together and live happily ever after." He laughed. "She had no idea he was leaving the country without her. At least that's the story she's telling now."

Joellyn's eyes widened. "Are you trying to say—"

"Yep." He nodded. "I sure am. Apparently she and Randy have been having a quiet little affair for over a year now."

"Randy and Marilyn," Joellyn mused, shaking her head. She turned to Mike. "And she had the nerve to spread that rumor about me!"

"You knew about that?" Lanagan asked. "Yeah, I heard it, too."

Joellyn's eyebrows shot up. "And may I ask when you heard this?"

Lanagan reached down under his desk and pulled at his sock, carefully avoiding Mike's eyes. "Oh, a while back," he answered noncommittally. "I hear a lot of things. It's nothing to get excited about."

Joellyn laughed silently. She knew that look and that tone of voice. The old buzzard knew all about her and Mike. She'd bet a year's salary on it.

She turned to Doug. "When did she finally tell you about Randy?"

Doug smiled. "We told her Randy had taken off, and she had a fit! Couldn't talk fast enough. Names, dates, the whole thing." He laughed. "She's one angry woman! If I were Randy Wagner, I wouldn't ever want to get out of jail."

Joellyn turned to Brice. "Will she stay in jail?"

"Well, she's trying to raise bail right now, but I don't think she's going to manage. It's set pretty high. And Randy's in there to stay. He's made one stab at getting out of the country already. They're not going to let him try that again."

"Can you believe," Mike said, "she would slip up like that at the last minute? Starting to write the whole invoice through the top copy, then ripping it off and voiding it with part of the order still visible? And then, as if that wasn't enough, leaving it in her desk? Honest to Pete, five more minutes. If she'd taken just *five more minutes,* destroyed the whole thing and started all over with a fresh one, we'd still be looking and Wagner would've gotten away with the whole thing."

"Yep," Doug agreed. "Pretty careless, especially after the meticulous planning he did to set it up."

Lanagan opened his desk drawer and reached for the candy jar. "Well, he didn't plan it all by himself." He peeled the aluminum foil from a chocolate kiss and popped it into his mouth. "Joellyn, do you remember a guy named Thatcher? Jack Thatcher?"

"Didn't he work for us a year or so ago?" She frowned, trying to remember. "He was one of our sales reps, wasn't he?"

"Uh-huh," Lanagan agreed. "He sure was, and a good one, too. Only problem was, we caught him stealing from us and fired him. Did you know he and Randy were good friends?"

Joellyn shook her head. "No, but I always wondered what happened to him. What does he have to do with this?"

"According to Marilyn," Brice said, "he went into business for himself after he left United. Bought an aluminum tubing and fencing distributing company in Ohio, small place. The stolen tubing was shipped collect to him. He sold it and split the profits with Randy and Marilyn. That stuff's gone to companies all over the country. It's spread around everywhere. We'll probably never get that back, either. A lot will depend on how well he kept his records."

"Well, in that case you can scratch the tubing," Lanagan said. "I saw his expense reports when he worked here. That guy had more ways of covering up money than the CIA ever thought of."

Mike turned to Doug. "What about the freight company?"

Doug laughed. "Give us time, Mike. From what Marilyn tells us it's been the same one every time. We've had their records subpoenaed. I'm sure the evidence we need will be there."

Lanagan looked uncomfortable. "Joellyn, I regret what you and your uncle have gone through over this. John's a fine man. I'm proud to have him working for me. Always have been. As soon as he gets back from Florida, his job's waiting for him."

"He's recovering pretty quickly now," Mike said, smiling. "But he may not want to come back. He's got a heck of a nice little sideline with those antique cars." He looked sideways at Joellyn. "I might buy one of them myself one of these days, if he does any more."

"He might not have the time to do any more," she said. "Last time I walked back into the factory one of the women asked about him. She said something about bringing him homemade cookies when he gets back." She laughed. "It looks as if she's got big plans for him."

Lanagan shook his head and smiled. "Good Lord! This place is turning into a romance factory—all these love affairs going on right under my nose! I'm beginning to think there must be something in the air. Doesn't anybody do any work around here?"

A slow blush crept up the side of Joellyn's neck. She turned to Mike. He stared out the window, trying not to grin. She glanced back at Lanagan just in time to see his mouth twitch as he reached for another piece of candy.

She laughed under her breath. Ah, yes. She was right. He knew.

Lanagan leaned back in his chair and smiled, looking every bit like an elf at Christmas time. "Is there something else you'd like to tell me, Joellyn?"

She wanted to laugh out loud. The sneak! He probably had their entire honeymoon itinerary memorized, and they'd only planned it last night.

"Well," she said, "I'm going to need a couple of weeks soon. And so is Mike. We both are...."

Lanagan smiled. "At the same time, I take it?"

She shifted in her chair, her face deep red. "Well, yes," she agreed. "We'd sort of like to take our honeymoon together."

"Joellyn, Joellyn." Lanagan shook his head in mock dismay. "I thought you were never going to get around to telling me."

"But we just—how did you—? Mr. Lanagan, we only decided to get married last night," she said.

He chuckled. "I could have told you that before. You just think I sit up here in this office and play miniature golf, or whatever you people downstairs think I do. I know what goes on around here. But sure," he added, "you take all the time you want." He rocked back in his chair and regarded Joellyn. "Answer me one small question first, though. How the devil did you figure out about the voided invoices?"

Joellyn gave Mike a slow, secret smile, reached for his hand and moved with him toward the door. Then she grinned back over her shoulder at her boss. "It happened when we were playing a game, Mr. Lanagan. Just an ordinary office game."

SUMMER DROPPED in on Chicago as it always did and always would—quickly, with almost no warning. All of a sudden everything was green and the air was heady and overpowering with the warm smell of lilacs and apple blossoms bursting open, scattering their perfume into the night.

Joellyn and Mike sat on the front steps of his apartment and stared at the huge bike parked in the driveway.

The 1947 Harley-Davidson. The genuine antique. Mike's pride and joy. The last obstacle.

"Mike," she said.

He took her hand and brought it to his lips as he'd done the night they'd first made love. "Yes?"

"I know you weren't putting me down the night you told me to keep out of the confrontation with Marilyn. I felt terrible about it after you left."

He looked embarrassed. "Well, it was my fault. I shouldn't have said it quite the way I did. And my timing could definitely have used some help."

"But I didn't have to fly off the handle the way I did," she said. "I guess things were moving so fast I sort of panicked. After all those years of living alone, I *was* afraid of change . . . and then there was David."

"There *is* David," he reminded her. He wiggled his eyebrows and leered at her. "We have exactly two more days alone before he gets here. Any ideas?"

She grinned. "Some you haven't even heard of yet." She shook her head. "I can't imagine why I was so afraid of him. I think I was just afraid to love him."

"He was afraid to love you, too, Jo."

She snuggled closer to him. "Well, he's wonderful, and I *do* love him. I hope all of ours are just like him."

"All six of them," he promised. He held up his hand. "Scout's honor."

She thought for a minute, then went on. "You know, I don't mind Monday night football too much. If you don't mind if I read while you watch."

He chuckled. "If you can read through all the noise I make when the Bears play, more power to you."

She thought for a minute. "And about your jogging every morning..."

He smiled. "Yes?"

"Well, we'll see. I might go along some morning just to see how it feels."

He was grinning now. "You might like it."

She nodded. "I might."

He waited.

She drew a deep breath. "As for the bike..."

He brushed her hair away from her face with the back of his hand. "You don't have to say anything, Jo," he murmured. "I love you too much to let a motorcycle come between us. I'll get rid of it."

She raised her eyebrows and laughed out loud, a joyful explosion that echoed and turned the night sounds into a song.

"Are you kidding?" she exclaimed. "I'm not afraid of that old thing!" She grabbed his hand and pulled him toward the bike.

He hesitated. "Are you serious? You're going to—"

"Ride on that bike?" she finished for him. "You bet I am!"

He was astonished. "But those burns on your ankles aren't healed yet," he protested.

"What burns?" she retorted. "Who cares about a few little burns?" She tossed her hair back and swung her leg over the Harley's seat. "Come on, climb on this thing and kick it out!"

It was like flying, with the wind in her face and whipping through her hair and leaving a part of her behind that she never wanted to see again. This was a new life, a new beginning and, oh, what a glorious feeling to be beginning it with a man like him!

She held his waist tightly, leaning into the corners with him as he headed toward home, moving as he moved and turning as he turned, laughing and free.

He took her over the peaks and into the valleys, every movement bringing her closer, closer, speeding and then slowing down...down...and finally...

Home.

Harlequin Superromance®
Family ties . . .

SEVENTH HEAVEN
In the introduction to the Osborne family trilogy,
Kate Osborne finds her destiny with Police
Commissioner Donovan Cade.

Available in December

ON CLOUD NINE
Juliet Osborne's old-fashioned values are tested when
she meets jazz musician Ross Stafford, the object of
her younger sister's affections. Can Juliet only achieve
her heart's desire at the cost of her integrity?

Available in January

SWINGING ON A STAR
Meridee is Kate's oldest daughter, but very much her
own person. Determined to climb the corporate
ladder, she has never had time for love. But her life is
turned upside down when Zeb Farrell storms into
town determined to eliminate jobs in her company—
her sister's among them! Meridee is prepared to do
battle, but for once she's met her match.

Available in February

my VALENTINE 1992

Celebrate the most romantic day of the year with
MY VALENTINE 1992—a sexy new collection of four
romantic stories written by our famous Temptation
authors:

GINA WILKINS
KRISTINE ROLOFSON
JOANN ROSS
VICKI LEWIS THOMPSON

My Valentine 1992—an exquisite escape into a romantic
and sensuous world.

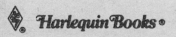

Harlequin Books ®

VAL-9